Over Your Dead Body

By

David L.

David L.

Over Your Dead Body by David L.

All rights reserved. No part of this book may be reproduced or reprinted without the written permission from the publisher, except for the use of brief quotations in a review.

All Total Package Publications, LLC titles are available at special quantity discounts for bulk purchases for sales promotions, premiums, fundraisers, educational and/or institutional use. Check website totalpackagepublications.com for ordering information.

Any resemblances of people, places, or events are unintentional and truly coincidental.

Copyright © 2007 David L.
All rights reserved
Printed in United States

Published by Total Package Publications, LLC
Edit and layout by Carla Dean
Printed by United Graphics, Inc. Mattoon, IL
Cover Design by Deneen G. Robinson
Photography by Leroy Evans

ISBN 0-9789276-0-5 (10 digit)
ISBN 978-0-9789276-0-8 (13 digit)

Sales inquiries should be forwarded to:
Total Package Publications, LLC
P.O. Box 3237
Mount Vernon, NY 10553

Over Your Dead Body

DEDICATION

I dedicate this book to all of my readers in the universe who at one point in their lives, picked up my book – or at the very least told someone about it! Without you, there is no Total Package Publications, and more importantly, no way for me to "**Tell the World My Name!**"

Also, to deceased family members that continue to look down on me in their spiritual form, cheering me on to excel – both in the literary world and in life.

David L.

Over Your Dead Body

INTRO

"You made me do this to you, Janelle!" I yell out loud, looking over at the lifeless corpse of my once loving wife. "Did you really think I was going to let you get away with keeping me from my children? Did you really think I was going to let you ruin my life and not do anything about it?" I look at her aimlessly – almost as if I am waiting for her to respond.

I know I can't run forever, and eventually, the law will catch up to me. I would be foolish to think I can run forever. From this moment on, I am a man on the run and will be forced to sleep with one eye open. With revenge finally out of the way, I should be content...but I am not. After all is said and done, Janelle was once my wife and the loving mother of my two children. Now Destiny and DeShaun are left motherless. They may not have a father for long, either, if I don't get out of here soon.

All of this because I wanted to be in my children's life, but not have to deal with a vengeful broad who was out to destroy my life. The funny thing is...she *did* destroy my life! My dreams. My career. Everything! All I wanted to do was awaken every morning to the sound of laughing, playful voices getting ready for school.

Moments earlier, my hands were clenched around Janelle's throat, slowly draining the life from

David L.

her diminutive body. Now, there is no more remorse in my heart...only the satisfaction of knowing my murder plan has been completed. My heartbeat continues to pulsate ferociously as I contemplate what to do with the body. The lake is frozen from the cold spell we have been having for the last several days, so throwing her body in is not an option. Besides, I wouldn't want to take the chance of her body resurfacing and being identified by some passing jogger. That would surely alert the authorities that I am now in Connecticut, and my current plans to continue heading north would be put in serious jeopardy. As it stands now, I still have unfinished business with Janelle's mother. She is the only one standing in my way of reclaiming my children and beginning a new life somewhere far away from my almost year-long murder spree. She is easy to find and the Mount Vernon homicide squad knows it.

"If I only had a shovel, I could bury Janelle's body right here!"

Exiting the car I stole from an unsuspecting, elderly couple back in November, I walk over to the passenger side and open the door. A faint smile appears on my face as I imagine a new life one day with my son and daughter. A new life free from unwarranted attacks on my personal property and psyche, outrageously expensive child support payments, angry phone calls from my crazy ex-wife, and an equally crazy ex-mother-in-law. I was optimistic that Janelle would be the last casualty in my never-ending desire to be with my children, but this is hardly the end. Her mother will have to be dealt with, as well! Then, and only then, will I be free from this madness that has consumed me.

Over Your Dead Body

Positioning myself against the car door, I lift the limp body from the passenger seat and open the trunk. Underestimating the weight of Janelle's dead frame, I almost land face first onto the pavement with the dead weight of my ex-wife to cushion my fall. Regaining my balance, I stuff the corpse into the trunk and quickly close it. Looking around suspiciously, I remind myself that I am all alone out here – on the outskirts of Candlestick Lake in Connecticut where Janelle and I first became engaged a little over ten years ago. I remember vividly the engagement ring I gave her and how much overtime I put in at the office to pay for that cursed ring! Why was she still wearing it anyway? Realizing I could get at least a grand for it, I pull it from off her lifeless finger. Or maybe I can one day give it to Maritza for an engagement present and eventually make her my wife. After all, none of this would have been possible without her by my side.

    I never imagined even for a moment coming back to this same spot. How ironic I think to myself: the ending of one relationship and the possible beginning of another. A relationship not built around lies or deceit. A relationship where I have the support of a woman who would do anything for me without hesitation. Maritza has shown her undying support for me by handing me the winning game ticket that, according to the numbers written in bold face, is worth approximately $20,000! The same amount of money that was offered as reward money to whoever found me and notified their local authorities!

    I want to go back and bring Maritza with me, but I cannot be selfish. She has her life, and unfortunately, I now have mine. Who am I to include

David L.

her in a life filled with running from the law and not knowing where your next meal is going to come from? Everything important in her life is in New York...her daughter, her career, and more importantly, her innocence. Her place is in New York. She has shown me what true love really is by not giving me up to the police. Tomorrow, when I am safely over the Canadian border or wherever I end up, I will mail her back the winning game ticket so she can enjoy life to the fullest. This way, she won't have to return to stripping and can use the prize money for a new lease on life. It never used to be this way.

    Getting back into the car and shifting it into drive, I look around one last time. My hands are still shaking from feeling Janelle's life force slowly drain from her body. Even after all of the senseless killings, I am still not a free man. That is something I can never be. Physically, I may be free, but spiritually, I am still a modern-day slave to my vengeful emotions. My thoughts are still preoccupied with revenge and my soul has lost its ability to feel pity for another. Janelle and I were once a close, loving family. We were once husband and wife with two beautiful children born from our love for each other. Damn! I still can't believe it was just one year ago...

Over Your Dead Body

CHAPTER ONE

New Years Eve, 2003

"Honey, did you put the baby to sleep yet?"

The voice belongs to Janelle. Despite her small stature, her voice emanates throughout the entire house. Meanwhile, I am upstairs getting ready for tonight's New Year's Eve party. I've got friends and family on their way over and have to look my best for the celebration.

"Preston, did you hear me?!"

"Shhh, you're going to wake the baby. I finally got him to fall asleep!"

Janelle adds more salt and pepper to her "famous" home-style green beans and places the lid on the pot in order for them to finish marinating in its buttery juices.

"Try some of this for me!" she yells upstairs, requesting that I stop what I'm doing to sample her culinary masterpiece.

"One minute," I respond, dropping my belt onto the bed. "Damn, girl, you really hooked it up this time. It tastes perfect!" I conclude, and then rush back up the steps to finish getting dressed.

After adding a few more various seasonings and spices to her green beans, Janelle moves on to prepare her chicken casserole and her mother's

9

David L.

buttermilk biscuits – just like her mother taught her when she was a little girl.

Upstairs, I turn the television channel to Sportscenter to view my favorite college team's bowl game. Walking into the bedroom, my pretentious five-year-old Destiny startles me.

"Gotcha, Daddy!" she announces, placing her little hands over my eyes.

"You got me. I give up!" I mockingly announce, picking her up and placing her onto my lap.

"What is you watching, Daddy?"

"I'm watching a college football game. It is very important that we cheer for the team with the blue helmets on. You want to watch it with me?"

"Sure, Daddy, but afterwards, you have to promise you will play with me and all of my doll friends. You promise?"

"Yeah…sure. I promise."

With halftime ending, the game resumes and ninety minutes later, the team with the "blue helmets" wins. Stopping myself from jumping up and waking the baby, I look over at my sleeping six-month-old son and Destiny, who has fallen asleep on my lap.

"I swear on my life I will always be here for you," I whisper while looking back and forth between the both of them. "Nothing and nobody will ever keep us apart. I would sooner die first."

Friends and family slowly enter our modest four-bedroom home. The first person to arrive is my mother-in-law Pearl Davis, affectionately known as "Mama Pearl." She is followed shortly afterwards by my best friend, William "Skip" Willis. Janelle's best

Over Your Dead Body

friend, Shontell, walks in bearing an assortment of liquor in her hands.

"Where's my favorite son-in-law?" Mama Pearl asks.

"Oh, he's in his "man's room" playing that stupid video game of his," Janelle responds.

"I have to wonder about a grown man playing with dem little children games!"

"He just does that usually to unwind after a hard day at the office, or if the baby kept him up for half the night," Janelle rationalizes.

"What up, girl!" Shontell shouts as she enters the kitchen with a bottle of liquor in her hand. Surprised by Mama Pearl's presence, she quickly places the bottle of Moet on the kitchen counter and hugs her affectionately.

"What up, Mama Pearl!"

"You ain't change at all! You been running wild and crazy ever since you and Janelle stopped wearin' dem training bras!"

All three women laugh at Mama Pearl's remark and proceed to set the table for the New Year's party, which will begin as soon as the casserole comes out of the oven.

In another room near the back of the house, I yell with excitement because I just ran seventy yards with my fantasy football team on my X-box system in a pivotal overtime game that will send me to the playoffs.

"How long you been playin' this?" Skip questions.

11

David L.

"About three months. I got it a little bit after it came out."
"You play this game a lot, don't you?"
"Yeah, I guess I do. It relaxes me after a long day at work"
"You need to turn this stupid game off and hook me up wit' Janelle's homegirl."
"C'mon, man. You just got out of a messed up marriage! You really want to hook up with another woman already?"
"What! Are you crazy? I'm just trying to hit it – that's all!"
"Nah, man, you ain't gonna dog one of Janelle's girls out like that. You dis her and then I got to hear about it from not only Shontell, but Janelle, too! Sorry, man, you gonna have to be by yourself on this one!"

"Dinner is ready, everyone!" Janelle yells out, trying her best to get everyone's attention.
The dining room table is covered with all sorts of food items and desserts: sweet potato pie, potato salad, rice and peas, apple pie, turkey wings, baked macaroni and cheese, and of course, Janelle's signature chicken casserole.
"Everyone, sit down and eat!" she commands. I hear the sound of my doorbell, and after getting up to answer it, I let out a big smile at the person at the door.
"What up, Uncle Cliff!"
There is an "Uncle Cliff" in everyone's family who is the life of the party. The guy most likely to get drunk, place a lampshade on his head, and dance around the room for laughs.

Over Your Dead Body

"What up, youngsta!" he responds in his signature raspy voice while giving me, his only nephew, a big, hearty hug.

"Where the food at? I could eat a horse! You're not serving horse tonight, are you?"

"Let me get your coat, Uncle Cliff. Everyone is in the dining room. Go on ahead and make yourself at home."

Seating himself next to Mama Pearl, Uncle Cliff does as instructed.

"Pass dem green beans over this way, sweetheart!" Uncle Cliff says, motioning for the bowl of green beans in the center of the dining room table.

Within moments, the room is devoid of sound, with the exception of forks and knives hitting everyone's plate.

"Pass that bottle over this way," Uncle Cliff shouts, referring to the bottle of Moet that Shontell walked in with earlier.

"That's for midnight, you old drunk!" Mama Pearl blurts out. "You can get yourself one of them beers in the bottom of the fridge!"

As the company disperses into various parts of the house, Skip seizes his opportunity to make a play at Shontell.

"So what have you been up to?" he asks, trying his best not to focus on the gravy stain planted firmly on the collar of her shirt.

"Oh, I've been chillin'. What about you?"

Small talk is passed back and forth between them before they are interrupted by Janelle's mother.

"Help me bring these dirty dishes into the kitchen."

13

David L.

Displeased with the interruption, Skip waltzes back over to me and DeShaun, who just woke up from a two-hour nap. Others look on in awe as the center of attention yawns, showing a newly developed set of bottom teeth for everyone to marvel at.

"Man, I'm glad I ain't have no children wit that crazy bitch!" Skip blurts out.

"You ain't lyin'. You dodged a bullet on that one!"

"You and Janelle ever gonna have any more children?"

"I don't know. She doesn't want anymore, but I wouldn't mind at least one more."

"You want a boy or girl?"

"A boy, of course! DeShaun looks like he's going to be a football player. The next one could play basketball or something...or maybe baseball."

"Just as long as they both hook their Uncle Skip up with some front row tickets after they go to the pros!"

"You know it, baby!"

All the males scurry down into the basement to watch the Dallas Cowboys take on the Philadelphia Eagles. Meanwhile upstairs, the women clear off the remaining items of food from the dining room table and wonder aloud about what crazy antics Uncle Cliff is going to involve himself in during tonight's New Year's Eve celebration.

It is minutes before the ball drops, and everyone looks on in anticipation at the television screen. Janelle and I hold hands as I rock the baby to sleep in my arms. Destiny is valiantly fighting sleep, and eventually loses minutes before the beginning of the New Year. Skip looks aimlessly around the room, wondering if he could get himself a celebratory kiss from Shontell when all this is over. Mama Pearl opens up her pocket Bible and says a silent prayer. Uncle Cliff, who is surprisingly still conscious after downing almost an entire bottle of champagne, grabs another champagne glass from off the mantle and prepares to toast in 2004.

"This is it, everyone!" Janelle candidly points out.

Everyone shouts out in unison: "10! 9! 8! 7! 6! 5! 4! 3! 2! 1! HAPPY NEW YEAR!"

The party begins to wind down, but not before Skip works up just enough nerve to get a hug from Shontell to bring in the New Year. Even Uncle Cliff got a friendly peck on the cheek from Mama Pearl. Meanwhile, Janelle and I sneak off to another room to get in a long, passionate kiss.

"Even after ten years of marriage, you're still the romantic dog," Janelle confesses.

"You know how I do! Mess around and we may make ourselves another baby tonight."

"I don't know about all of that. If you're good, I might give you a little of this, though."

The guests slowly begin to grab their coats and head home.

"Do you want to spend the night in the guest room, Uncle Cliff? You've been drinkin' all night," Janelle points out.

David L.

"Let me tell you something, sweetheart," Uncle Cliff affectionately responds. "I been drinkin' since you been stinkin'!"
Janelle tries her best to persuade Uncle Cliff to hang around and spend the night, but he's not trying to hear none of it. Even though he smells like he just fell into a pool of liquor, Uncle Cliff is a professional drinker. He'll be alright to drive home. And just like that, Uncle Cliff locates his car keys, stumbles into his mini-van, and drives off into the early morning.
"What about you, Mama Pearl?" I question.
"No, no, no, baby. I haven't drank the "Devil's nectar" in over thirty years, and I don't need to be stayin' around here getting in y'all way anyways. I'm gonna leave you two be so that you can make me 'nother one of dem granchil'ren!"
Mama Pearl quickly exits, gets into her car, and drives off. Janelle and I, wondering where Skip and Shontell could be, look on in unison as Shontell gets into Skip's ride about fifty feet down the block. Knowing Skip like I do, I'm gonna wake up tomorrow morning with a voice message on my cell phone and have to endure a long-winded message about how he "hit it like no other!"
"Damn, baby, they didn't even say bye," Janelle points out.
"Didn't say bye? Do you really think either one of them got us on their minds right about now? You know what's about to go down!"
"Shontell's just using him for a ride home. That boy ain't gettin' none tonight from her!"
"Whatever. Hey, everyone is gone. Let's go make ourselves 'nother one of dem granchil'ren!"

Over Your Dead Body

* * *

"Honey, what did you do with the baby's car seat?" Janelle yells out of her car window. "Hurry up! I'm already late for work!"

"It should be in the trunk of your car," I respond from the front door.

"Daddy, you didn't kiss me goodbye," Destiny pleads.

Running down the steps in my robe and slippers, I open the back door of Janelle's car and plant a kiss on Destiny's cheek.

"Don't forget to kiss Mommy goodbye, too, Daddy!"

Doing as instructed, I plant another kiss onto the lips of my wife.

"So what are you going to do on your day off?"

"I talked to Skip last night, and he may come through and get his ass cracked in a few football games."

"Yeah, well, since you got so much free time, you can paint the baby's room like you promised to do over a month ago."

A frown appears on my face, showing my displeasure at Janelle's remark.

"I mean it, Preston! Don't spend the day doin' nothing with that fool Skip! I swear, every time you two get together, nothing ever gets done."

"I heard you the first time. I'm going to take care of it. I promise."

I consume two bowls of Frosted Flakes and a slice of leftover apple pie before beginning my

David L.

painting project. The ring of the doorbell alerts me to Skip's arrival.

"What up, son!"

"And what you so happy about?"

"You know I hit that the other night, right?"

"Hit who? Shontell? I saw the two of you drive off. So you finally came correct, huh?"

"No doubt, baby! You know how I do!"

"Yeah, well, remember what I said. If you dog her out, I'm the one who has to hear her mouth. And Janelle's mouth, too."

"Don't even worry 'bout it. I'm not gonna dog her out...not yet anyways!"

Surprisingly, I am able to convince Skip to help me paint DeShaun's room, and after about three hours of on and off breaks to watch some ESPN classic on the television, we complete our mission and celebrate with an early afternoon six-pack.

"Yo, man, I never told you this, but I'm kind of proud of you."

"What the hell are you talkin' about now?"

"I mean, you busted your ass to get this house, and I know it couldn't have been easy with you all the way out here in Westchester County."

"Yeah, it was crazy with all the extra hours I put in and all just to come up with the down payment, but you can do it, too, Skip."

"I don't know 'bout all that, man. I have to pay that worthless bitch of an ex-wife alimony, and they take that shit right out of my check! I don't even get a chance to see the money. You know what I'm sayin'?"

"Alimony? You ain't even got a job!"

Over Your Dead Body

"That's exactly my point! If I were working, they would make me pay! I ain't paying nobody shit! When it comes to my money, it's mine and mine only! You feel me on that one?"

"I feel you, man. I'm lucky I got a wife I can grow old with and who loves me unconditionally. I wouldn't trade that for the world."

Sensing Skip's growing despair, I wisely opt to change the subject.

"Yo, let's get out and do something. I finally got the day off...the children don't need to be picked up for like another five hours, and I might not see another day off like this for months."

"Well, you can treat since I ain't got no job and you just got that big ass promotion."

"Whatever. What do you have in mind?"

Taking a moment to gather his thoughts, Skip sits up from off the couch to emphasize his response.

"Let's go over to the Nasty Kitty!"

"The Nasty Kitty? Man, it's like twelve o'clock in the afternoon. We gonna look like perverts up in there. Only old, lonely men go there this time of the day to spend their Social Security checks!"

Nonetheless, we head out to the Nasty Kitty, but before stepping into the South Bronx establishment, we stop at a nearby bank in order to make change so that we can tip the dancers.

"GODDAMN, she is thick!" Skip candidly points out, passing a dollar bill off to the first dancer that approaches him.

"Let me get a straight Hennessey, please," I instruct to the barely dressed bartender.

David L.

"Order me a Jack Daniels – no ice! Yo, you need to check out dat Spanish bitch right over there in the corner!"

Looking over, I motion for her and eventually get her attention. Walking over seductively, the brown-skinned enchantress sits demurely onto my lap.

"Let me get an Alizé Blue, please, Wendy," she requests.

After she quickly downs her drink, she motions for me to walk with her into the back room.

"Don't tip her too much, man, or else they will all be clownin' you as soon as we bounce from out of here!" Skip warns.

Doing as instructed, I enter the back of the establishment, and within seconds, my companion for the next several minutes mounts me like a wild stallion. I avoid eye contact at the beginning, mostly because I don't know if I should initiate conversation or just enjoy my limited time with her in silence.

"What's your name?" she asks.

Unable to take my eyes off her C-cup breasts, I avoid responding.

"I'm Maritza...but in here, you can call me Mocha."

Eyes now wandering over to the bouncer seated strategically to the left of me, I contemplate whether or not I can grab her "twin pack."

"Hey, baby, you can touch me. Don't worry 'bout Clyde over there. He's a pussycat."

I grab onto both of her breasts, eventually moving my fingertips to her nipple rings. I slowly gather my confidence and bob my head to the

Over Your Dead Body

background music blaring out of the speakers located in each corner of the room.

"These don't hurt?" I ask in reference to her nipple rings.

"Only when someone pulls on them too hard."

I pay for another lap dance, and Mocha does just that...grinding her inner thighs against mine. I close my eyes to enhance the experience. With the song finally ending, so does my extended dance, and I graciously thank Mocha with another five-dollar bill to add to her collection of twenties.

Back over at the bar, Skip realizes he only has a couple of dollar bills left and places them into the g-string of a dark-skin honey with an enormous backside.

"Let's be out of here!" I say.

"Yeah, it's 'bout that time. I ran out of them singles you gave me earlier anyways."

Walking out of the Nasty Kitty establishment, my progress is temporarily halted by Mocha.

"You leaving me so soon, baby?"

"Yeah, my man here has to go pick up his car. I have to come back here, though. Maybe I'll come back through this weekend."

"That is too bad. I was hoping to get another song with you."

Mocha reaches up in her high heel shoes and places a kiss on my cheek.

"I'm going to look for you when you come back."

"Not if I find you first," I respond.

Skip and I take one last look at the assortment of almost butt-naked honeys inside the Nasty Kitty and sigh. I desperately want to re-enter, but I know today is

21

David L.

my day to pick up Destiny and DeShaun from the daycare in a couple of hours.

"So what did you end up doing today, baby?" Janelle questions. She is busy spraying Bath and Body Works mist onto her petite figure. Still dripping with water from my scalding hot shower minutes earlier, I am oblivious to her questioning and ask Janelle to repeat herself.

"I said what did you do today?"

"Me and Skip mostly hung around the house. You should have seen the way I beat his ass in Madden football!"

"I should hope so. You play that silly game every chance you get."

I chuckle slightly, mostly because I know she is right.

"You didn't compliment me on my painting masterpiece."

"Well, you missed a couple of spots, but I guess it looks alright."

Before Janelle gets the opportunity to lotion her hands and feet, I unexpectedly grab her from behind and place her across the bed, shutting the bedroom door with the back of my foot.

"What are you doin'?"

Saying nothing, I quickly unbutton her pajama shirt and caress her erect nipples. Placing one hand onto her pajama bottoms, I begin to slide them off.

"We can't do this now. Destiny is still up and she may hear us."

Over Your Dead Body

"Don't worry about it, baby. It won't take long."

"Yeah, well, as exciting as that may sound, I don't want to take any chances with her in the next room. Besides, we got the rest of the night."

"The rest of the night? You'll be asleep in an hour...tops."

"Well then, tomorrow night...I promise."

"Tomorrow night? You buggin', Janelle! You haven't given me none since 2003! You fell asleep as soon as you hit the bed after the New Year's party, remember?"

Removing myself as fast as I got on top of her, and in disappointment, I quickly exit the bedroom to see if DeShaun is up yet.

"What up, little man," I say in a low voice.

DeShaun has just awakened and his little baby eyes are fixed on his daddy's proud grin.

"I can't wait until you can walk. You and I are going to do everything together."

I watch intensely as my prized baby boy turns himself onto his stomach and lifts his head up in response to my familiar voice. Watching from the door with a doll in her hand, Destiny walks over and wraps her little arms around her daddy.

"Do you love me still, Daddy?"

Lifting her onto my broad shoulders, I respond as diplomatically as only I can. "I love you more and more every day. I could have ten more babies and that still would never change. Don't you ever forget that."

Content with my answer, Destiny hops down from my shoulders and happily runs back into her room.

23

David L.

The hungry cries of DeShaun startle me. For the last several seconds, I have been daydreaming about my earlier encounter with Mocha. Running into the kitchen to grab a bottle from out of the fridge, I quickly place it into my son's waiting mouth, temporarily silencing him. The scent of paint alerts me that the baby will have to sleep with his sister tonight as I tiptoe with him into her room. By now, Destiny is fast asleep, and I break into a slight grin – hopeful for some last minute sex from the wife.

Walking softly to avoid DeShaun awakening, I enter my bedroom, and to my dismay, Janelle is already snoring, thus canceling my bedtime sexcapade. With the remote control in my hand and a slowly diminishing hard-on under the covers, I catch the last few minutes of Nick at Nite and gradually fall asleep.

* * *

"How are sales looking this week, Bernadette?" I ask my secretary.

"You mean that new act you signed a few weeks ago? It's looking real good. The last time I checked, he was about twenty thousand units from going gold."

"Good…good! My R&B group Fantasy is going to get me that VP gig over at Columbia in no time. You just watch and see."

"You better not let Stan hear you talk like that. He'll probably hang himself if his main A&R man broke out and went over to the competition."

I am dressed in my best business suit, ready for a three o'clock late lunch with an up-and-coming artist

Over Your Dead Body

that I am strongly courting. Hearing Bernadette call me Stan's number one A&R man has got me feeling a little extra cocky today.

"Hey, Bernadette, have you seen Dani today? She was supposed to meet me at a studio session earlier this morning."

"She called about an hour ago. She is stuck in traffic over by the Westside highway. She is going to have to meet you another time."

Grabbing my jacket to catch the elevator, I am halted by my boss and president of Downtown Records.

"You ever follow up with that underground artist you've been eyeing? What's his name...Joe Blow? Joe Buttocks?"

Laughing at his sarcasm, I correct the man that signs my paycheck every week.

"His name is Joe Banger...and you are going to thank me big time when his album blows up on Soundscan. I guarantee he is going to be the next big thing."

"He better be all that. I still haven't forgiven you for passing up on that country grammar clown that mailed us his demo a few years ago. Now he's like fifty million times platinum!"

Entering the number five train to 14th street, I place my headphones onto my ears to escape the misery of the lost souls around me. To my left, a homeless woman talks to herself and her body stench is unbearable. Although it is the first week of January and snowing slightly, she is wearing a shredded spring jacket and a pair of ripped up K-Swiss sneakers.

25

David L.

Directly across from me, what looks to be a mentally ill man plays the harmonica, trying to get some spare change from those around him. Almost missing my stop, I exit the train, but not before handing the homeless woman a dollar bill from out of my pocket. Walking at an accelerated pace, I try to make up for lost time from the ten-minute train delay. I've got about six blocks to walk and I barely make it to the restaurant without being late. After browsing the menu, I look down at my watch to notice that my afternoon appointment is late.

"Would you like to order now, sir? Or are you still waiting for your other party?" an eager, young waitress questions.

"I'll take a glass of white wine."

At about three-thirty, a familiar face enters the restaurant. Looking directly into a heavily-polished spoon, I make sure I don't have any crumbs around my mouth from the bread I was snacking on.

"Preston, sorry I'm late, man! I got caught up in traffic over on the east side."

"That's cool. I just got here myself a little while ago."

After placing his order, Joe Banger, the aspiring rapper, and I get to politicking.

"I don't want to overwhelm you with numbers so soon or anything, but are you being represented by anyone right now?"

"Nah, man. That's just another person to pay at the end of the day."

"Well, nothing is official yet, but I think I could get like two or three videos at a modest budget. I usually don't advance anyone more than fifty

Over Your Dead Body

thousand, 'cause at the end of the day that's money you got to pay back to the record company anyways."

"True. True. But what about my points and publishing royalties? I get to keep that, right?"

"You got to understand something, Joe. You probably will not see much overhead for your first album. Most artists don't start seeing royalty checks until their third and fourth albums."

"But do I keep my publishing?"

I display a devilish smirk. I've been in this business for almost twelve years, if you count the year and a half I spent interning. I've paid my dues. That means I get to play the "game" with others trying to get in the business. After all, it's the American way!

"We'll talk about that sometime later. Come by the office in a week and we'll review the paperwork. My advice to you: go and get yourself a lawyer."

Back at the office, I immediately walk into chaos. Five aspiring rappers are trying to get a minute of my time; over twenty voice messages are lighting up my phone; and an irritable receptionist who hasn't had a lunch break yet is eyeing me like she wants to stick a fork through my eyelids.

"Stan wants to see you in his office – NOW!"

"I'll get with him later," I respond as I begin checking my phone messages.

"Dani is on line three!"

"Tell her to hold for me, please, Bernadette."

With my back toward the door, I am oblivious to the arrival of my boss, who is standing directly behind me.

David L.

"Didn't Bernadette tell you I wanted to see you in my office as soon as you returned?"
"Yes, sir, uhh – Stan. I'm about to come see you right now."
Picking up line three, I alert Dani to my meeting with Stan and promise to call her back later.
"Hey, Preston, good luck in there," Bernadette says. "Stan's been walking around here all day in a pissed off mood."
Entering Stan's office with caution, I am caught off guard by another familiar presence.
"You remember Mr. Byron Townsend, right? He is here today because he is concerned about this new group you signed – Fantasy."
Taking over the conversation, Mr. Townsend rises from his chair to emphasize his point.
"We at your parent label, Pacific Records, are concerned because although these girls are doing relatively respectable numbers for a first album, they retain one hundred percent of their publishing. They're getting twelve points per record, and they can opt out of their contract after their next release."
"I know, sir, but…"
"And to top it off, you got a clause in the contract that reads: option to retain twenty-five percent of catalog upon entering fifth album! What were you thinking?"
Rarely ever speechless, I look over at Stan for some assistance and get none. My once cocky mood from earlier is replaced with humility. It is an emotion I don't ever want to feel again.
"This conversation is over as of now, Preston. You and I will discuss this further before the end of the

Over Your Dead Body

day. That will be all!" Stan sternly warns, motioning for me to exit his office.

"Hey, Preston, is everything alright?" Bernadette questions. "Dani wrote something that she wanted you to read as soon as you got a chance. I put it on your desk."

Still worried about the tongue lashing from Byron Townsend and Stan, I enter my office to finish playing my messages. Outside in the lobby, eager and aspiring rappers, some of them with their managers, continue to wait patiently for me to show them some attention.

"Bernadette, can you tell everyone that I'm not seeing anyone today!" I yell into the speakerphone.

"Will do!"

Moving a stack of envelopes over to the side, I notice the memo Bernadette left for me earlier: *Preston, call me after work! I got an idea to make us rich!!*

Grabbing my coat and making a beeline for the elevator, I shrug off Bernadette's reminder to see the boss at the end of the day.

One block away from meeting up with my co-worker Dani, I call Janelle to inform her that I am going to be late for dinner.

"Can you get Destiny and DeShaun for me? I need to meet up with this new artist of mine," I ask, talking softly into my cell phone.

Hanging up, I enter a popular after-work sports bar to find out what Dani's note is all about.

"'Bout time!" she responds, reprimanding me for being five minutes late. "If Stan found out you

29

David L.

were late for a meeting with someone, he would chew your ass out."

"Man, fuck a Stan!" I angrily respond. "Dude blew me up today in front of that Townsend clown 'cause of the contract I worked out with Fantasy!"

"What about Fantasy?"

"They actin' all crazy about the contract I had them sign a while back, that's all. I don't really want to talk about it right now."

Shaking her head in apparent disbelief, Dani gives me the obligatory "I told you so" speech and switches the course of the conversation.

"That's why I called you down here today. We make people like Stan and Townsend millions in revenue every year, and what do we have to show for it? Not a GODDAMN thing!"

Becoming more and more curious at where Dani is going with her tirade, I listen attentively to her every word.

"Furthermore, we rape these artists every day and feed them slave wages, but as soon as they blow up, what happens? They end up switching labels, and then Stan and them look at us like we can't keep our artists happy!"

"So what are you getting at?"

There are over a hundred people inside the after-work bar on this particular workday. However, Dani and I are unmindful to anything else right now. Moving her chair closer to mine, Dani makes direct eye contact with me.

"Bernadette is best friends with the secretary that works over at Sheisty Records. She is the one that types up the final draft contracts for their artists. She has agreed to have a courier bring us copies of the contracts to look at."

"What good would that do us?" I interrupt. "If they are already going to sign to Sheisty Records, they ain't worth nothing to us."

"Think about it, Preston. We make a pitch at those same artists before they sign, and we wouldn't have to worry about overpaying for their services. Plus, we would have more access to the free agent pool out in the streets."

Contemplating what was just told to me, I think it over, and after about thirty seconds of silence, I lift up my glass of beer to toast the new partnership.

David L.

CHAPTER TWO

January 19, 2004

"Yo, Skip, I'll talk to you later. Janelle just walked into the house."

"Be easy on her, man. I can't be bailing you out of jail tonight," Skip jokingly responds, referring to Janelle's M.I.A. status for the last couple of hours.

"I thought you were picking the children up for me, Janelle?" I question. "I got home tonight and there were like three frantic messages from the people at the daycare!"

"I asked my mother to pick them up for me. She got to the daycare late, that's all."

I direct Destiny upstairs and place DeShaun in his walker. He's got a perplexed look on his face, as if he somehow knew we were getting ready to get into an argument.

"And besides," Janelle adds, "you hang out all the time and have fun after work. Why can't I hang out with my girls every now and then?"

"What I do is not fun, Janelle! It's business! You might want to learn the difference!"

"Yeah, well, I can smell your business all on your breath! You've been drinking, haven't you?"

"I had one drink after work. What's the big deal with that?"

"The big deal is you should have handled your responsibilities!"

"I handle my responsibilities! How else are we able to live up in this house? Own brand new cars? Or eat out three and four times a week? Tell me, Janelle!"

"You think all that fancy stuff means anything to me? All I ever asked was for you to spend more time with your family, that's all!"

Our back and forth bickering is eventually halted by errant cries from the baby, and Janelle and I mutually decide to resume our argument after the children go to sleep. Later that evening, Janelle gets wrapped up into her phone conversation with Shontell.

"So how was he?"

"Girrrl, you know I don't kiss and tell, but I will tell you this…I could've swallowed his thing like I do when I eat tic tacs!"

Laughing even harder, Janelle turns the T.V. volume down with the remote control.

"Damn! It was that small?"

"I've seen razor bumps bigger than that," Shontell responds.

Reaching over to Janelle's side of the bed, I increase the volume on the television to where it was at previously. Responding immediately, Janelle places the T.V. volume on mute, obviously to piss me off.

"So are you going to give him some again?"

"Yeah, I'm going to give him one mo' chance to hit this right. But if he don't…"

"Are you going to cackle on the phone with her all night?" I question.

David L.

The only response I get is Janelle rolling her eyes at me, grabbing the covers from off of me, and placing them around her body.
"Oh, so it's like that, huh?"
Angered by the apparent lack of attention, I grab a pillow and remove myself from the bedroom to go sleep downstairs on the living room couch.

* * *

"Destiny, can you go back inside and keep an eye on your brother for me until Triple A arrives, please?"
Twenty minutes earlier, a phone call was made to Triple A in response to my dead car battery. An hour and a half later, they finally arrive.
"The woman on the phone told me you would be here in thirty minutes," I inform the driver.
He is looking at me like he could care less. After all, I'm sure he gets paid whether he arrives on time or not. Not allowing a dead battery in my brand new midnight blue Yukon Denali to dictate the course of my upcoming day, I wait patiently while my SUV is jumpstarted.
Taking back roads to avoid the heavy morning traffic, I enjoy the rare opportunity to bond with my two young children.
"So what are you learning in school this week?" I question.
"We're learning adding and subtracting," Destiny responds.
"Well, I need to file my taxes in a couple of weeks, so maybe you can help Daddy."

Over Your Dead Body

Destiny does not respond, mainly because she has become fixated on getting a knot out of one of her doll's ponytails. A loud car horn quickly gets my attention. I barely avoid a head-on collision with another car because I am preoccupied with making funny faces at DeShaun, who is sitting in the back seat sucking on his pacifier.

"Good morning, Mr. Price," one of the daycare staff says exuberantly. "You had us worried yesterday," she adds, referring to DeShaun's late pick up.

I reluctantly explain myself and promise her it will not happen again.

"Bye-bye, little brother," Destiny says, waving her hand.

For the first time since DeShaun has been attending daycare, he begins to cry uncontrollably, as if he was never going to see his daddy again. Guilty about leaving DeShaun behind, but at the same time running late, I quickly drop Destiny off at her school and head to work.

"Look who decided to show up for work today!" Bernadette heckles. "Damn, Preston, you got dirt all over your fingernails. What you been doing? Sleeping in the woods or something?"

"Not today, Bernadette," I respond. "I got a whole bunch of phone calls to return and I have to hurry up and choose what the next single for Fantasy is going to be."

Before entering my office to check messages, I'm halted by Bernadette's verbal warning. "Before

David L.

you do anything, you better go see Stan. He's been asking for you all morning."

Expecting the worst, I comply and enter the boss' office. Also inside, my co-worker Dani looks over at him sheepishly. Usually outspoken, she is eager to speak her mind, but chooses wisely to keep quiet.

"I asked for the two of you to come in here today because fourth quarter sales were way down and salaries may be cut. To top it off, I'm going to have to let go of a few of my top grossing employees."

Almost in tears, Dani contemplates walking out prematurely, but decides to wait it out.

"Furthermore," Stan continues, "promotion and marketing will also be negatively affected due to the lack of fourth quarter sales."

Finally mustering up the courage, I decide to speak my mind. "What is going to happen to us, Stan? We are your two top-selling A&R people, and we have been your top employees for two years straight. I got urban music on lock, and Dani has your alternative and contemporary division in a stranglehold."

"And that is why I called you both in here today. All of your interns have to be let go, as well as your junior A&R staff. I'm holding on to you two because you're too important for me to let go."

Dani and I both take a deep breath and silently thank GOD for saving our asses momentarily.

"But I got to tell you this, and listen to me carefully," Stan adds. "One screw up and I will replace you two with someone that I can pay half the salary to!"

As Dani and I walk out of Stan's office, Bernadette hits us with a concerned look and we each

Over Your Dead Body

give her the tell-all wink of the eye. Gracious that we've made it at least this far, we both decide it's time to get out for a late day drink to calm our nerves.

"You call your wife to tell her you're going to be home late again tonight?" Dani questions while sipping on her Cosmopolitan.

"Yeah, but I am going to have to leave soon. I have to get my ass home."

"We'll just have one drink. Stop actin' like such a square all the time! Live a little!"

"Who the hell still says words like 'square'? And why are we here at this bar again anyway?"

"How could you say that after what went down earlier today? I don't know about you, but I ain't tryin' to go back to living check to check. I like my six figure income!"

Downing a shot of Absolut vodka, I envision my encounter earlier with Stan. Hell! Dani has a point! I've come too far to go back to working your average nine-to-five job like the rest of the people I know. How would life be without the fancy corporate credit cards and company perks, like six week vacations and company limousine whenever I'm traveling to a business meeting out of the state?

"I hear what you're sayin'. I sure ain't trying to go back to living with my mother-in-law...that's for damn sure!"

"So then, now that we're on the same page, let's get down to business!" Dani concludes.

* * *

37

David L.

"Yo, man, I overheard Shontell talking to Janelle last night. You in the doghouse or something?" Skip questions.

Not really wanting to get into it, I respond nonetheless.

"Something like that. We ain't really on good speakin' terms 'cause I've been doing some side business with one of my co-workers for the past few weeks."

"Is your co-worker a he or a she?"

"What?"

"You heard me! Is your co-worker a he or a she?"

"My co-worker is a she. So what? What difference does that make?"

Nodding his head in disbelief, Skip fills me in on the finer aspects of a woman's ego and why Janelle is so mad at me. Although Skip is a known womanizer around town and somewhat "hard around the edges", he is insightful and talks from his heart. On top of that, Skip has five sisters, so he definitely has some knowledge on the opposite sex.

"Well, does she look good?" Skip asks.

"She looks alright. Okay, I'm lying. She looks good!"

Nodding his head vigorously, Skip warns me about the temptations of the flesh.

"I know you ain't talking," I jokingly respond. "Your ex used to catch you out there all the time."

"Not all the time – just twice!"

Promising Skip to ease back on the extra hours after work, I hear the familiar sounds of Janelle's house keys.

38

"I'll get up with you sometime this weekend," Skip announces as he greets Janelle while passing by her to exit out the front door.

I'm again greeted with Janelle's "cold shoulder" and she proceeds straight to the bedroom. Without acknowledging my presence, I enter my only personal room in the house and occupy myself with a quick, relaxing game of Madden football.

Upstairs, Janelle receives a disturbing phone call from Shontell, who informs her of my alleged activity the night before.

"Yeah, girl, I seen his ass all hugged up and close with some ho at a sports bar out in the Village around seven last night!"

"Oh really? His ass was supposed to be working on a video shoot. That's why he's been coming home late," Janelle responds.

"Yeah, well, there wasn't no film crew when I seen his ass, and the ho I seen him with ain't look like no film director."

Becoming more and more enraged by her friend's testimony, Janelle listens on and begins thinking the worst.

"So what are you going to do?" Shontell asks.

"I don't know yet. It's too early to jump to conclusions. I'm going to give him the benefit of the doubt…for now."

Hanging up the phone, Janelle allows her mind to wander, and she wonders to herself if my recent extra-long hours at the job have anything to do with my possible infidelity.

David L.

Prematurely awakened by another sexless, silent night, I rub my eyes in bewilderment as Janelle stands over me with her hand behind her back.

"Are you cheatin' on me?" Raising her voice, Janelle repeats her question. "Preston, open your eyes! I asked you a question. ARE YOU CHEATIN' ON ME?"

"What the hell are you talking about?"

Throwing an envelope down onto the bed, Janelle continues her interrogation.

"What the hell are these hotel receipts doing hidden in your briefcase?"

"Do you really think I'm stupid enough to keep hotel receipts in the house if I was messin' around behind your back?"

Momentarily silenced by my response, Janelle waits for further clarification. I can tell whenever she is furious. Her left brow is raised and her complexion has become reddened with anger.

"I booked a hotel at the Marriott for a rapper out of Cali I'm tryin' to hook up with."

"So where was this so-called rapper from Cali last night around seven o'clock?"

"What do you mean by that?"

"What I mean is Shontell saw you out last night all hugged up on some bitch! Now what do you have to say about that?"

Gathering my thoughts so as to not look guilty, I respond with intense emotion. "First of all, fuck Shontell! She ain't nuttin' but a troublemaker who would like nuttin' better than to see us fight! That's why her ass ain't got no man now!"

Over Your Dead Body

Unable to silence Janelle by shifting the topic to Shontell, I hear it from her and she is only silenced by the awakened cries of DeShaun rolling around in his crib. Quickly getting both children dressed for another day of school and daycare, I exit the house, but not before Janelle's promise to finish our argument after work.

* * *

"Let me get a closer look at that contract on top of the pile there," I suggest as Dani hands me the requested piece of information. "This dude out of Brooklyn is hot in the streets right now. His name is Black Trash, and I seen him do his thing at an Apollo taping one night."

"So then call him!" Dani responds, biting into a glazed Dunkin Donut. "What cha waiting for?"

"Nah, not tonight. I can't. I'm already on the wife's shit list because for some crazy reason, she thinks you and I are messin' around."

"And what in the world would make her think that?"

"'Cause her stupid, trouble-making friend saw us having dinner two nights ago at that sports bar over on Fourth and Broadway."

Gathering my items, I begin heading for the door, but not before Dani speaks her mind.

"You know, a marriage ain't a marriage without trust. Think about that tonight on your way home."

David L.

Contemplating her remarks, I stop momentarily in my tracks to respond to my opinionated co-worker.

"That's true, but trust shouldn't ever be an issue if the only thing I'm guilty of is trying to put some extra money on the table for my family. Besides, it ain't like you and I are doing anything anyway."

"Well, that's your fault! Maybe if you stepped your game up..."

Catching herself in time, Dani silences herself – albeit, a little too late. Not wanting to add to the already uncomfortable topic of discussion, I smile discreetly while reaching for my cell phone.

"The children and I are staying at my mother's house tonight. I will take them to school in the morning," Janelle says over the phone.

"Alright then, I'll probably hook up with Skip over by his place."

With no reason to exit, I return to my seat and grab another pile of envelopes to review with Dani. Racing thoughts of where Janelle is *really* going tonight begin to manifest. Not like she could go far with Deshaun and Destiny with her anyways. Besides, am I justified to become as paranoid as she already is? I can't go out like that!

"I didn't see you at all in the office today," Dani says, smiling gleefully because the Caesar salad she ordered twenty minutes ago has just arrived. "You're not cheatin' on me, too, are you?"

"Oh no! Not you, too! Are all you women so damn jealous?"

Not responding to my reply, Dani also grabs an envelope and reviews the contents.

Over Your Dead Body

"Hmmm, this is dated two weeks ago. It must be a mistake. It says here your group Fantasy was offered a contract by Sheisty Records with clauses similar to what you signed them for."

"That's some bullshit!" I angrily exclaim. "I signed them one year ago. Eleven months ago to be exact!"

There is an awkward silence lasting approximately a minute before Dani breaks the silence.

"That means your little girl group is trying to split from Downtown Records! They have a buyout clause, so if they follow through, you're going to lose your marquee clients in exactly one month."

Becoming more and more nervous, I try to reach the lead singer, Simone, on her cell phone, but with no success.

"I will deal with them in the morning," I promise myself. "But for now, pass me another pile of them envelopes. You and I are going to be here for a while."

Outstretched arms flail in the air, signifying collective exhaustion from working through half the night.

"I can't believe we've been sitting in this here diner for almost eight hours," Dani confirms, looking at the clock on the wall.

I let out a mighty yawn, also signifying Dani's claim to being overworked and exhausted.

"We got to be at the office in seven hours. I am going to be a mess."

Absorbing my comment like a sponge, Dani responds with a well-aimed comment of her own. "If

David L.

we had overnight bags and some spare clothes, we could split a room at a hotel."

I think about the idea of "shacking up" for a few hours with my co-worker and wonder if anything would transpire. Skip's sentiments echo in my head as I think about what Janelle must be thinking with me spending so much time with a good-looking co-worker of the opposite sex. Like it's my fault Dani looks good and has a perfectly-sculpted body! Maybe if Dani was married or had a man I would be in the clear. Or maybe Janelle wouldn't be acting so paranoid if one day, I invited Dani over to meet her. Then she wouldn't be so enraged over my long working hours…yeah right!

"I am going to head home and catch a few hours of sleep. I'll see you at work."

Parting ways, I barely make it onto the number five train. Taking the opportunity to catch a few minutes of sleep on the almost deserted train, I speculate the notion of one day giving in to Dani's outright flirting.

* * *

Finally! Saturday morning. The only day I get to sleep in late and get some much-needed rest. WRONG!

"So are you sleeping with that bitch or what?" Janelle angrily questions, referring to my almost all-nighter forty-eight hours ago.

"What are you talking about now?" I sheepishly respond.

Over Your Dead Body

"Don't play with me, Preston! Are you sleeping with that bitch or what?"

Preferring to respond in silence, I roll over and place the covers over my head, symbolizing my reluctance to add fuel to the already burning fire in Janelle's remarks. Becoming further enraged by my disregard toward her questioning, Janelle does the unthinkable. Lifting the covers from off of me in a fury, she unleashes a mighty blow to the back of my head with an open hand.

"GODDAMN!! What the hell you do that for?"

Writhing in pain, I quickly get out of the bed to avoid a repeat hit. Janelle's arms are raised once again to strike me. Her eyes are bloodshot red and the veins just above her forehead are moments from bursting out from under her skin.

"I swear I hate your cheatin' Black ass!" she screams.

This is the first time I was ever hit by the opposite sex, let alone my wife. The shock is still apparent on my face.

"I never ever hit you, Janelle. NEVER! What if I hit you back right now? You would probably call the cops on me!" I defiantly conclude.

"You wouldn't hit me, 'cause if you did…"

"What? What's gonna happen? You gonna sic your mama on me? She ain't ever like me anyways!"

With DeShaun and Destiny spending the night at Mama Pearl's house, there are no interruptions to save me from Janelle's tongue lashing this time.

"I gave your trifling ass ten of the best years of my life, and this is how you repay me?"

45

David L.

"You got it all wrong, Janelle! I'm not doin' anything with my co-worker. We're just working on a project, that's all. I swear!"

"And I'm supposed to believe that? Shontell saw you all hugged up with her at the bar the other night! What cha gotta say about that?"

With the back and forth arguing escalating to epic proportions, I eventually dress and head out through the front door. Alone in the house, Janelle is still enraged and lifts the receiver from the phone to place a call.

"Hello. Is Dr. Rogers in? I'd like to make an appointment for me and my husband, please."

In a basement studio apartment nestled discreetly in the Castle Hill section of the Bronx, I give Skip the play-by-play of the events which transpired earlier between Janelle and me.

"Yo, she is really buggin' out, dog!"

"She came after you like that?" Skip responds.

"Yeah, man! She is wildin' out for real! I bet you anything she's calling that Dr. Rogers clown right now as we speak."

"Who is Dr. Rogers?"

"He's this quack that Mama Pearl put her onto when we first got married and we were arguing all the time about whether to have children or not."

"You still hittin' that co-worker of yours?"

"Don't play with me like that! I told you her and I ain't doing nuttin' but working some side deals for extra money."

"Side deals, huh? That's what they're callin' it now."

Over Your Dead Body

Not amused by Skip's humor, I offer to treat for lunch after a routine stop at the bank to deposit my earnings for the past couple of weeks.

"So, Preston, explain to me how you make this alleged 'side money' of yours."

Giving into Skip's sarcastic inquiry, I offer a simplistic overview on my "get rich" formula.

"It goes like this," I begin. "I get contracts from a rival record label hand-delivered to me. From there, I contact those same artists who may be unhappy with their deal or trying to switch labels. Whenever I get someone to sign and my boss' label gets out of the red, I receive a side royalty based on how well the single or the overall album sells."

The look on Skip's face signifies his ignorance to the aforementioned details of my business dealings, and uncharacteristically, he declines my offer to lunch in order to meet up with Shontell over at her place.

"Leave that troublemaking girl alone, Skip. She's bad news."

"That's a good piece of ass, and she can cook! I ain't leavin' nothing alone!"

"Well, she's the reason I'm in my predicament now."

"Shontell may have lit the fire, but you're holding the gasoline."

"What do you mean by that?"

"All these long nights and hanging out at the bar. It's time to ask yourself, Preston, is all of this really worth risking your marriage?"

Walking off in separate directions, I reflect on Skip's comments about my predicament with Janelle and what to do with the rest of my empty day.

David L.

* * *

As the weekend draws to its inevitable conclusion, I methodically prepare for my first day back in the office. While in the basement ironing my "power suit" in preparation for probably the most important meeting of my life, I take the opportunity to reflect on my marriage and the recent non-speaking terms between Janelle and I. Upstairs, Janelle fixes a bottle for little DeShaun, and in another room, Destiny watches her favorite SpongeBob cartoon on DVD.

"I have been working a lot of hours and spending crazy time with Dani," I say out loud. "I need to make it up to Janelle."

As I think out loud, I pause momentarily from ironing the stubborn wrinkles lodged in my suit jacket to set forth my plan for normalcy of my marriage.

"I know! I'll order her some flowers to be delivered to her job tomorrow."

Walking upstairs to locate the phone, I stop in my tracks to overhear Janelle's conversation in the next room with Mama Pearl. I feel real warm inside all of a sudden. The kind of feeling one has when something is about to go wrong. The kind of feeling one has when "shit is about to hit the fan!"

"I can't take this no more!" Janelle says over the phone. "Shontell told me the other day that she caught him all up on some girl out in the street!"

Inching closer to the door, Janelle is unaware of my eavesdropping and continues to berate my being to her mother.

Over Your Dead Body

"The only time we speak is when we argue," she adds.

Fuming, I have no recourse but to continue listening so as to not give myself away – furious that I cannot barge in to save my innocent name.

"The children and I will be coming over to stay with you for a few days," Janelle says, ending her conversation with her mother.

I can feel my heart drop and my knees are shaking. This is how it all started with Skip and his ex-wife. They both swore they were going to work it out, but they never did. Now, they hate each other! I refuse to allow that to happen to Janelle and me...or to our kids. Entering my bedroom as she hangs up the receiver, I embrace Janelle and hold her affectionately. She is resistant to my touch and immediately removes herself from off of the bed.

"Where are you going now, Janelle?"

"Over to my mother's house. There is no reason for me to stay here. Besides, I'm sure that would give you more opportunity to do whatever it is you do when I'm not around!"

"It's not even like that, Janelle. You have to learn to stop being so paranoid over everything."

"Well, I'm going over my mother's house, and I'm taking the kids with me."

"Why would you want to disturb them while they're sleep? They got nothing to do with this!"

"Sleep? You're worried about them sleeping all of a sudden? Where was that concern all the times you disappeared and left me to care for them? You can pick them up in the morning from my mother!"

49

David L.

There is an uncomfortable aura in the air the following morning as I knock on Mama Pearl's door to retrieve DeShaun and Destiny to take them to daycare and school respectively. Entering her house, the look on Mama Pearl's face describes her current feelings towards me.

"So, Preston, how's that record job of yours going?" she asks, looking me up and down indiscriminately.

"My job? It's alright, I guess. It's very stressful at times, but at least it pays the bills."

"I sure bet it does!" she sarcastically responds, finishing up on the ponytails she placed in Destiny's hair. "You ever get tempted by any of those big-butt girls I be seeing up in dem videos?"

"That's not what I do, Mama Pearl. I'm more behind-the-scenes. I'm the guy that makes it possible for the artists to be seen like that. That stuff is only to sell records anyways," I rationalize.

Making the interaction even more awkward, Destiny grabs me in a mini bear hug, thanking me for picking her up on time and commenting on not seeing me as much anymore. The ride to daycare to drop off DeShaun is uneventful as I quickly arrive to avoid being late – again.

"Daddy, what's 'dultery?" Destiny questions.

"What?"

"'Dultery. I heard Mommy say it talking to Aunt Shontell yesterday."

Thinking for a moment, I wonder what my daughter could have overheard on the telephone...and then it hits me.

"Adultery? Is that what you heard?"

Over Your Dead Body

"Yeah! Adultery! And then she said a bad word, but I can't repeat it."

"You can tell me. What did Mommy say to your aunt Shontell?"

Leaning over from the back seat of the car to whisper in my ear, Destiny responds, "She said that payback is a bitch."

* * *

"Keep the change," I say, handing the cab driver a ten-dollar bill.

Placing a Final Call newspaper I purchased from a Muslim brother into my briefcase, I barely manage to make it onto the crowded elevator and up to my office at Downtown Records.

"Good morning, Preston," Bernadette says, handing over my schedule for the day. "Stan wants to know your status with that Joe Banger rapper guy you've been tryin' to sign. He told me to tell you that you better sign him soon or else."

"Or else what?" I respond with slight cockiness in my voice.

Unaware that Stan is simultaneously walking in on our conversation, my face cannot hide my surprise.

"Or else you're going to be packing groceries at your neighborhood grocery store!" Stan confirms with his most serious tone of voice.

"I'm just kidding, sir. I saw you from the corner of my eye. Didn't I, Bernadette?"

She doesn't respond. Instead, Bernadette picks up the telephone receiver and simulates making a phone call to avoid the obvious uncomfortable

51

David L.

encounter between Stan and me. Motioned into Stan's office, I am reminded of my recent salary increase and my responsibility to find the best possible talent for the company that signs my paycheck. Forty minutes later, I exit Stan's office and slam the door behind me, retreating to the seclusion of my own personal office to contemplate my future at Downtown Records. Breaking the monotony of looking aimlessly at the four walls surrounding me, I am interrupted momentarily by a phone call from Dani.

"Grab ya coat and meet me at our diner in midtown."

"What's going on now?"

"Just do as I say! I'll meet you there in exactly half an hour. And don't be late!"

Doing as instructed, I inform Bernadette that I will be out for the rest of the day, and to page me in the event of an emergency.

"You know she's feeling you, right?" Bernadette blurts out with a devilish smile.

"What are you talking about now, Bernadette? Who is feeling me?" I respond, already knowing the answer to my question.

"The person you're going to see, that's who! She's been feelin' you for a long time now, so stop frontin' like you don't know."

"I'm a married man, Bernadette. You know that."

"You're married…not dead, Preston. There is a difference."

I do my best to ignore Bernadette's comments about Dani liking me. After all, she has been playing the role of matchmaker for years, and I don't have the heart to tell her it's never going to go down like that between the two of us. My mind is on other things right now, and hooking up with my overzealous co-worker is not one of them. Besides, I don't mix business with pleasure!

Getting over to the diner five minutes early, I order a chocolate milkshake while I wait for Dani to arrive.

"This has got to be the first time you have ever been early for anything," Dani says, walking into the diner. "If I did not know better, I would think you rushed here 'cause you missed me or something."

I don't say anything; instead, I take a deep sip from my milkshake. I clutch my chest as a result of swallowing too fast and almost fall out of my chair. Dani laughs hysterically as a result of my comic relief. The look on her face quickly turns serious as she pulls a chair out to take a seat.

"You and I have some problems, Preston…big problems!"

"What's the matter now?"

Now I have a look of seriousness on my face. Dani is often a very calm, calculating individual who doesn't let anything or anyone get in her way of accomplishing things.

"Bernadette's friend over at Sheisty Records was fired Friday afternoon for what they are saying was improper practices related to fraud."

"What the hell does all that mean?"

"What do you think it means? If they decide to investigate the situation further and question her, she may start talking. You and I are both in on this!"

"Damn, Dani! When did you find all this out?"

David L.

"I found out earlier this morning. I was going to call you, but wanted to make sure I was positive with my information."

"Do you have the contract offer for that rapper Black Trash at least?" I question, getting off of the undesirable subject, if only for a moment.

Handing over the offer, Dani warns me about being too enthusiastic about pursuing the unproven rap artist.

"Have you heard from anyone from Fantasy yet?"

"Nah, they haven't returned any of my phone calls. That's not like them."

"That's probably because they are tryin' to dodge you. They are tryin' to sign elsewhere, you know."

"Yeah, well, they can run, but they can't hide."

"How's everything going with the wife? Y'all make up yet?"

"I don't want to talk about it."

"Damn! That bad, huh? Tell you what...before you get home tonight, pick up some flowers or something. Women love flowers! Don't be a cheap ass, though. Don't do the dozen roses for ten bucks at the gas station trick. She will see right through that. Get her a bouquet from a recognized flower shop. The more the better...trust me on this one."

Penn Station terminal is uncharacteristically empty tonight. I look up at the clock on the wall in front of me, which reads half past nine o'clock. I want to hurry and get home so I can give Janelle the dozen roses I just purchased for her for Valentine's Day from

Over Your Dead Body

some foreign dude on the corner. Instinctively, I know I should've taken Dani's advice, but I just didn't have the time or patience to seek out a flower shop still open at this time of night.

I am standing patiently waiting for my courted rapper Black Trash to arrive to offer him a contract deal. My hands are sweating slightly over the possibility of signing who is probably the hottest rapper out of New York at the present time. Ten more minutes go by, and I surmise that he is a no-show.

Barely managing to get inside the closing subway door, I seat myself on the seemingly deserted subway car. Grabbing the sports section of a newspaper conveniently left behind for my enjoyment, I am unaware that I have company entering from the far side of the subway car. Dressed in all black, with the exception of a bright red Arizona Cardinal baseball cap turned backwards, the mysterious looking figure walks ominously over to me and stares in my direction. Looking to the left and to the right of me, there is no one in the immediate area. Keeping my head down would make me look like a potential victim waiting to get jacked. On the other hand, making eye contact with the dude could be seen as an invitation for a confrontation.

"Run yo wallet!" the man says with his left hand placed strategically inside his jacket pocket. "I'm gonna need that coat and briefcase, too!"

Weighing my options, I look around aimlessly throughout the subway car, as if to say *Someone Help Me!* Hardly an imposing figure, I wonder if it's worth my life to put up a fight. After all, my wallet's contents consist of last week's paycheck stub, a couple of

55

David L.

maxed-out credit cards, my driver's license, an ATM card, and about forty dollars in cash. My winter coat was a Christmas present from my mother-in-law. My briefcase, however, is another story. It's got important documents and some other information that, in my opinion, is priceless. Running out of patience, my unwelcome visitor repeats his command – this time with some fire in his voice.

"I said, run yo wallet and that briefcase! Or you rather try to be a hero?"

Doing as instructed, I reach slowly into my back pocket and hand over my coveted wallet. Looking over at my very important briefcase, I am not as receptive to parting ways with it.

"Let me open it up for you. There's nothing in here that you want."

Growing even more agitated, my adversary slowly reveals a knife wrapped in a handkerchief. I quickly change my mind about negotiating for my briefcase. Halfway to its next scheduled stop, the train goes through a tunnel, causing pitch-black darkness in the process. Just my luck, I picked a subway car with no one else in it. What the hell am I thinking? I'm in New York City! I could be on a crowded bus and nobody would help me. That's how it is in the city. Taking advantage of the opportunity to reclaim my goods, I immediately retaliate, striking the knife-wielding man to the side of his temple with a well placed punch.

"Muthafucka!" he screams, momentarily falling backwards against the train door.

Swinging wildly, the man eventually lands a blow of his own to the side of my chin. With his other

Over Your Dead Body

hand still holding the knife, he again swings wildly – this time making direct contact with my torso.

"AAAGGH!!" I shriek while holding my side in obvious pain.

My body is overcome with numbness and I drop to one knee. Although where he struck me with the knife feels warm, the rest of my body feels cold. I reach out aimlessly to throw a blow, unsuccessfully swinging at nothing but air. Blood droplets materialize on the subway car's floor, almost causing me to pass out. I've never been one to like the sight of my own blood, especially if I'm not in the doctor's office having blood drawn by a beautiful big-breasted nurse.

As the train exits the tunnel, I am hunched over in agony and watch helplessly as my assailant scurries into the next subway car – and to eventual freedom.

Getting off at the next stop and searching for loose change in my pants pockets, I grimace from the bitter cold. Still hunched over in obvious pain, the sight of my own blood almost causes me to pass out from what is probably shock.

"Just my luck," I say out loud. "I'm out here with a dead cell phone and no coat on one of the coldest days of the year!" Even the roses I purchased for Janelle were left on the subway for some other lucky fool to claim his love interest of the moment.

There are only four people I can call collect that will come pick me up in a minute's notice: Janelle, Skip, Uncle Cliff, or Dani. Calling Janelle will only get me into more hot water. She is so paranoid now that she would probably blame me for getting jacked. She'll probably say it was karma for sleeping with

David L.

Dani, and that it was her boyfriend that jacked me on the train. Skip probably won't even answer his phone. Knowing him, he's knocking boots with Shontell and could care less about me right about now. At this time of night, Uncle Cliff is probably already on his second bottle somewhere with his poker-playing buddies. Choosing the latter, I wait patiently inside a corner grocery store after my phone call to Dani. Enthusiastic about the impromptu phone call, Dani arrives quickly to pick me up.
  "Where's your coat, Preston? It's freezin' out here!"
  "It's a long story. I'll tell you about it in the car. You do have heat, right?"
  Grimacing in pain, I grab my side and look down at my hands. My hands and fingers are bright red with blood. While I'm leaning up against the side of her car, more blood has shown itself.
  "Oh my GOD! What happened? You're bleeding!" Dani gasps out about the obvious.
  Helping me into her car, Dani's excitement escalates, causing me to panic even more.
  "I got to get you to a hospital right now!"
  "NO! Don't take me to no hospital! It's just a flesh wound. Just get me somewhere where I can lay down for a few minutes."
  Dani's sudden U-turn in the middle of the road almost causes me to go flying out of her car; however, she manages to get me back to her place in one piece. Her apartment is immaculate and all of the walls are painted an off-white color, except for her kitchen which is decked out in a light shade of green. I can tell from my "playa" days that she set up her apartment

58

Over Your Dead Body

right after she got off the phone with me. The candles burning on her mantle are recently lit, the disc changer on her surround sound stereo system is only on track five and playing an old Barry White song, and she is wearing a Victoria Secret tank top under the coat she just threw onto the living room couch.

"Take your shirt off so I can put this on," Dani instructs.

She is holding heavy gauze in one hand, and in the other, a cup half filled with a clear liquid, which looks to be peroxide.

"Now, Preston, this is going to hurt just a little."

Just as the words are uttered from Dani's mouth, I let out a loud yell in response to the stinging sensation.

"Damn, girl! Did you have to put so much on?"

"You rather get an infection instead? Now suck it up and sit still! We really should get you to the hospital. You look like you could use stitches. Your wound is pretty deep."

The threat of infection quickly enters my mind, and I graciously thank my consoling co-worker for the speedy recovery.

"You never did tell me how this happened," Dani reminds me. "And, Preston, for once, tell me the truth."

"I got stuck up on the train. Five dudes with guns rolled up on me while I was sitting there minding my business and reading my Final Call paper."

"Oh my GOD! You're lucky to be alive!"

David L.

"That's not the worst part of it. I had all the contracts and notes in my briefcase. I lost EVERYTHING!"

Furthering her attempts to console me with a meaningful hug, I unapologetically allow myself to be embraced in Dani's arms.

"How ironic is this?" Dani questions.

"What do you mean by that?"

"I mean, you could have called anyone tonight, but yet, you called me...and of all days!"

After several awkward moments of silence, I receive permission to use Dani's phone to call a taxi, but she oddly grabs the phone from my possession. With a renewed sense of courage, Dani unexpectedly lunges forward and plants a big, wet kiss upon my lips. The look on my face indicates total surprise; however, I say nothing, waiting to see what happens next. Inching closer, Dani thrusts me onto her sofa and again kisses me, this time with even more passion.

Former feelings of awkwardness are replaced with a shared sense of intimacy and comfort level only two close friends could experience. Although I've thought about it in the past, I never imagined it becoming a reality, and her unexpected attempts to seduce me have caught me totally off guard.

Every one of my male friends I've known from my college years straight through to my adult life has cheated on their girl at one point or another. Hell, I can't even count the number of times Skip cheated on his ex-wife! But I'm an oddity. I've never cheated on ANY girl. Not my third grade girlfriend...not my prom date...and sure as hell not Janelle! I mean, I've fantasized about other women and flirted with some of

Over Your Dead Body

them during my work in the record business, but I've never cheated. Even during the exotic trips for video shoots to the Bahamas and the Dominican Republic...never cheated! This is definitely a new experience for me. An experience I don't ever want to experience again.

"Let me up, Dani! I got to get home to my wife and children!"

After pausing momentarily, just in case I came to my senses and wanted to finish what she started, Dani does as obliged and removes herself from off of me. I can tell from the look on her face that Dani is feeling slightly embarrassed. She is a thing of beauty, that's for sure. Women like Dani aren't used to getting turned down by anyone, especially when they are the ones to initiate the first move.

"You sure you don't want to stay a little longer?"

"Yeah, I'm sure. I got to get home to my family."

"Well, I guess you have to do what you have to do. Too bad, though. I was going to give you something I've always wanted to give you ever since I started over at the record company."

"I can't get down like that. My conscience wouldn't let me."

"I'll say one thing about you, Preston Price; you are a one-of-a-kind type of man!"

Irritated, but seemingly understanding to my ethical dilemma, Dani graciously plants an innocent peck on my cheek, reminding herself that I am truly one of the last of a dying breed.

"You understand, right?" I ask apologetically.

David L.

"You don't have to explain, Preston. I shouldn't have thrown myself on you no way."

"I wouldn't say you threw yourself at me, Dani. Sometimes things just happen, that's all. What happened tonight won't change anything about our friendship, right?"

"Of course not, Preston…whatever you say."

Taken by surprise at my own humility and sense of respect for the opposite sex, I feel the inclination to further explain my decision to forego "doin it" with my co-worker.

"Don't get me wrong. Given the right set of circumstances, I would wear dat ass out!"

Shaking her head in approval, Dani reluctantly watches as I exit her apartment in response to the cabbie outside her apartment waiting to take me home.

CHAPTER THREE

Valentine's Evening, 2004

    Nearing my Mount Vernon home five minutes before midnight, I grudgingly walk up the steps of my front porch and open the door, expecting another all-out fight with Janelle. The muffled sounds of her crying can be heard as I head straight for my bedroom.

    "What's wrong? Are the children alright?" I ask.

    "You ungrateful bastard! I HATE YOU!" Janelle yells.

    Mama Pearl and Shontell are beside Janelle, restraining her from going after me. An open vial lies on the counter. Reaching over to view its contents, I conclude Janelle consumed what appear to be prescription sleeping pills. Her heavily sweated brow and lethargic demeanor further confirms my suspicion.

    "What the hell are you talking about now, Janelle? Why did you take sleeping pills?"

    "Forget him, baby. We got to get you to the emergency room," Mama Pearl says, ignoring my presence completely.

    "I'll go start the car up," Shontell declares.

    Shooting me the meanest of looks, Shontell and Mama Pearl walk right by me as if I don't even exist, supporting Janelle at the same time.

David L.

"Janelle, where are Destiny and DeShaun?" I ask, worried more for my children's safety.

Gathering all of her depleted strength, Janelle reaches back, and with all the force she can muster, slaps me hard across my face.

"I WISH YOU WERE DEAD!" she screams.

"GODDAMN! What the hell kind of bullshit is Shontell feeding you this time?" I ask her angrily.

"Shontell didn't have to tell her anything, Preston," Mama Pearl responds. "We can smell the guilt all over you from whatever bitch you were sleeping around with!"

"I hope the sex was worth it, Preston! I really do!" Janelle blurts out. "And as far as the children are concerned, don't you worry yourself 'bout where they are 'cause you are not ever going to see them again...NOT OVER MY DEAD BODY!"

"First of all, don't play with me, Janelle!" I spit back. "Those kids have nothing to do with what is going on here, so leave them out of this!"

Before Janelle has a chance to respond, she is whisked away by Mama Pearl and assisted into the back seat of her car. I have an empty feeling in my gut, and I can't help but think she has finally gone over the deep end. Anyone who would take sleeping pills just to prove a point can't be right in the mind! Nah! But something else is going on around here. It's more than just Janelle acting jealous and trying to get some attention from me. And doesn't she know there is nothing she can do to keep me away from my most precious gifts? I may not understand what is going through her demented head, but I do know I'd better make things right...and soon!

Over Your Dead Body

An hour later, I am downing my third shot of Absolut Vodka while looking up at the clock on the barroom wall. I'm silently wondering where the hell Skip could be, and impatiently awaiting his arrival.

"Have you seen my uncle tonight?" I ask a bartender, referring to my uncle Cliff, who owns the bar where I am currently drowning my sorrows.

"Yeah, he was in here earlier. He left out a little over an hour ago. All he said was he would be right back."

Dropping a five-dollar bill on the counter, I order a beer on tap to wash down the aftertaste of the Absolut. In the reflection on the glass ceiling above me, I can see the imprint of Janelle's hand on the side of my face. A familiar-sounding voice momentarily startles me.

"It's about time, fool!"

Entering my uncle Cliff's Bar–n-Grill, Skip gives me a "pound" and asks me to explain my frantic message for him to meet me as soon as possible.

"My marriage is over, man," I sadly confirm. "Janelle left me tonight 'cause she thinks I'm messin' around behind her back."

"Man, I told you to leave that girl at work alone!"

"I don't need to hear your 'I Told You' comments right now, Skip! I need you to help me fix this crazy shit!"

"I got it!" Skip blurts out. "This might sound crazy, but if what you say is true and you and this girl ain't messin' around, then you need to have Janelle meet this co-worker of yours. If this woman talks to

David L.

Janelle and assures her of your innocence, you got about a fifty-fifty chance of keeping your marriage intact."

"I thought of that, and I don't think it would work. Janelle is so mad right about now that if I introduce the two of them, she may straight try to strangle her."

"Yeah, well, right about now, you got nothin' to lose."

Thinking it over, I offer my own rebuttal. "Yeah, but if it doesn't work, I'm gonna have two crazy women mad at my ass!"

I shuffle slowly out of my uncle's bar, and after convincing Skip that I'm alright to drive the three miles it takes to get home, he leaves to hook up with his current girl of the moment, Shontell. Just as I am getting ready to enter my ride, my uncle pulls up in his car.

"What up, Uncle Cliff?"

He gives me a hearty hug and handshake, and asks me what brings me to his side of town. Making sure not to slur my speech, I inform Uncle Cliff of all the dramatic events.

"...And I think she's at the emergency room right now as we speak, 'cause when I got home earlier, there was an empty bottle of sleeping pills on the counter."

"So then, what the hell you doin' here drinkin' at my bar? You need to head over to the hospital and be with your wife!"

"Easier said than done, Uncle Cliff. If I show up at that hospital, she may attack my Black ass all over again. You know that crazy woman told me that I wouldn't be able to see the kids again?!"

"Boy, don't you know all women say that when they are angry? Trust me, the last thing she wants right now is to lose you AND her weekends of you watching dem kids!"

"You funny, Uncle Cliff! Good lookin' out. I feel better already."

"You are getting more and more like your old man every day, boy…no damn patience at all."

"I ain't got no damn father, Uncle Cliff! Don't even mention his name to me! That fool took off on me right after my mama died!"

"I'm not sticking up for him, boy, but you don't know all the facts. He fell on hard times, and before he knew it, he lost everything. Next thing you know, he began drinking and just stopped caring. He loved your mama that much!"

"You ever hear from him again?"

"Now you want to be curious, huh? Last I heard he was out walking the streets in the Bronx somewhere. After all this time, I wouldn't be surprised if he's dead. All he did was drink after your mama passed away, just like you are beginning to do!"

Uncle Cliff pulls his wool cap over his forehead to combat the night's bitter cold air. Then, he pulls out a flask of liquor and downs a shot for the sake of it. This is the same man who just finished telling me that I drink too much!

"Let me give you some advice I wished I used when I was a young man. If you let Janelle's anger grow like one of dem cancer cells your dear old mama

David L.

died from, you are never going to be able to contain it and you will lose her forever."

Digesting Uncle Cliff's advice, I shift my car into drive and pull out in the direction of the hospital. I'm unaware that I'm being followed, and moments later, a cop pulls up behind me in his unmarked car, turns on his lights, and orders me to pull over to the side of the road.

Seated nervously in my car, I turn my radio down and place my hands on my steering wheel. Seconds feel like hours as the cop calls in my plate number over his radio. Looking around for a breath mint, it is clearly evident this cop saw me leaving my uncle's bar. *I can't get a DWI! Not tonight!* Scattered thoughts and the possibility of being arrested cause sweat beads to form on my forehead. *Let's get this over with!* A uniformed presence walks over to my car and instructs me to step out of the vehicle slowly.

"Officer, I..."

The officer interrupts me before I have a chance to complete my sentence.

"I would recommend that you don't say anything. I need you to breathe into this, please."

Following the officer's directives, I blow into the long tube, and knowing my blood alcohol level has to be over the legal limit, I expect the worst – and get it. I have a brief flashback to my senior year in college. Thoughts of having my body pushed into the back of a cop car with my hands cuffed from behind remind me that I'm glad I am married with children and no longer hanging with the same crowd from back in the day. It's a five-minute ride to the Mount Vernon police station, but with every pothole, the handcuffs constricting my wrists grow tighter and tighter.

"Officer, do we really have to go through this? My wife is in the emergency room, and I have to go and make sure she is alright."

"You won't be seeing your wife…not tonight anyway!"

His partner seated next to him lets out a slight chuckle as he bites into what looks to be a jelly doughnut. I wonder how much more trouble I could get into if I suddenly regurgitate all over their car seat. Inside the precinct, I cover my head in shame with my right hand, while my left hand is handcuffed to the desk. Sitting directly across from me is a prostitute and her pimp, talking quietly amongst each other. Seated in the same hallway, a couple of teenage boys are also handcuffed. I overheard one of the arresting officers say they were being detained for joyriding through the neighborhood in a stolen car. One of them looks real familiar as it takes me several moments to recall where I know his face from. He is one of the boys that attend my church every Sunday morning. He comes in every Sunday all decked out in a pinstripe suit, and his father is this loud, obnoxious character who is usually seen wearing some type of loud suit to make himself stand out that much more.

I again cover my face to avoid detection. The stained ink from the fingerprinting pad is a dismal reminder that I have been detained for driving while intoxicated. Remembering Skip's ordeal with his DUI experience several years ago, I shake my head in frustration, wondering how I allowed this unfortunate mess to happen to me.

David L.

* * *

There are over fifteen messages I need to check on the answering machine before I leave for work. One message that stands out is from Dr. Rogers calling for Janelle, which says, *Just calling to see if you changed your mind about canceling tomorrow's appointment. I hope you don't do anything you will regret.*

Shaking my head, I continue to listen to the next several messages. Doing an overnight stint behind bars for the last twenty-four hours, I got a weird feeling, as if something isn't right.

"Where the hell are all my CD's?" I say out loud while looking.

Running upstairs to the bedroom, a look of disbelief develops on my face. All of my clothes are scattered across the bed. They are drenched in what looks to be spray paint. On the large dresser mirror, another message is written in spray paint: U WILL PAY!!!

Face red with anger, I dismantle my entire bedroom searching for my .380 handgun I've had for over five years...a gun I purchased and had registered because of an attempted break-in when Janelle and I first purchased our home...a gun I keep unloaded above the ceiling tile in my bedroom, but which is now missing! The only other person who knew where I stashed it was – JANELLE! I can't believe she would take this so damn far.

"Uh-oh, I better check the rest of the house out!"

Over Your Dead Body

My search is methodical. All of my favorite clothing items have either vanished or has been completely destroyed. All of my NBA jerseys have been destroyed: Lakers, Celtics, Knicks, Clippers, EVERYONE! I notice garden scissors left on top of the pile as a mockery to Janelle's unwarranted destruction.

"GODDAMN!" I blurt out upon discovering the destruction of my favorite food items.

Several of my favorite cereals are ripped open from their packages and scattered across the kitchen floor. The strong aroma of warm beer is present in the kitchen area. After further exploration, I discover why. Janelle has poured all of my Miller High Life into the hanging plants that line the kitchen window frames. I can do nothing but sigh meagerly at the message written in ketchup on the dining room table that reads: LYING BASTARD!

"She went too damn far this time!" I reason to myself.

Reaching for my car keys in order to drive somewhere to clear my thoughts, the realization hits me. I have no car to drive because it was towed away last night as a result of my getting pulled over.

Janelle has gone from model wife to psycho queen in a matter of weeks, and I don't know what to do about it!

"Good lookin' out picking me up."

Moments earlier, I called Skip to come over to the crib and pick me up. It took some convincing, but ultimately, I won in the end.

David L.

"No doubt, man. But I got to know, are you gonna press charges on your crazy ass wife or what?"

"Man, I don't know. She's going through some problems and all. I mean, she tried to take herself out with sleeping pills. How many people you know would do that to prove a point?"

"Yeah, well the last thing you want to do is mess with a crazy woman. I'd sooner fight Mike Tyson when he's not on his meds."

"That's what I'm talking about! That's why I have to calm her down, because she's not in her right state of mind right now."

Skip has that signature smirk on his face. The same look he always gets when he wants to crack a joke at my expense.

"You can laugh all you want, man, but I'm the one who's got to deal with this stupid nonsense!"

"So tell me about your DWI charge."

This time, he lets out a hearty laugh that causes him to almost kneel over. Real funny for a guy who got his first DWI not even twenty-four hours after returning home from his honeymoon!

"Man, it was like straight out of a movie or something! I spent the whole night behind bars like I was a stone-cold killer or something. No shower. Nothing! And all I had to eat was a dry ass salami sandwich and some fruit juice that tasted like soapy water."

"I bet your ass won't drink and drive again."

"Whatever! I know you ain't talking! You were busted for drinking while driving a couple of times!"

Somewhere during our reminiscing, I got a sudden inclination to get over to the bank as soon as possible. The ride there is uncharacteristically long. There is a car overturned on the opposite side of the Sprain Brook Parkway, and all the "rubberneckers" are further slowing up traffic.

"That shit must've just happened," I say to Skip. "The ambulance isn't even on the scene yet."

Skip appears grumpy. Knowing his horny ass, he is probably trying to quickly get me to the bank so he can get back over to Shontelle's place.

"Make this left right here," I instruct.

A couple of blocks on Central Avenue and we are at our destination. Thoughts of Janelle's recent escapades must be taking a toll on me, 'cause that same eerie feeling from before is back.

"Good afternoon, Mr. Price," a cheerful teller greets. Something about the way she says my name always makes me think she wants me. "I could have sworn I saw your wife over at one of the other tellers about a half hour ago."

Now I know what that eerie feeling was all about. If the teller saw my jaw drop, she didn't let on. I nervously wait as I hand the teller my withdrawal slip.

"Uuhh – I'm sorry, sir, but you don't have sufficient funds for this transaction."

"Well then," I respond, "how much money do I have in my account?"

"Approximately one dollar."

"That's impossible! Can you check again?"

Doing as requested, the teller checks my account…and checks again. A supervisor, who has been quietly watching, walks over and reiterates what I already know.

David L.

I grit my teeth and clench my fists, but I cannot show my anger. I will not show my anger! My first instinct is to call Janelle and curse her out for this bullshit game she is playing with me. And for no reason! But if I do call her and start cursing her out on the phone, she will win, and I cannot – I will not allow that to happen!

Outside in the parking lot, Skip is oblivious to my dilemma. I decline to tell him what just transpired in the bank a few moments ago because I know he would snap on me all the way home. As expected, Skip is preoccupied listening to 50 Cent and humming his lyrics word for word.
"Can you turn that shit down before you make me go deaf up in here?"
"Do I tell you who you can or can't listen to when you're in your ride?"
Point well taken. I'm down to my last three hundred dollars, and I succumb to my better judgment and inform Skip of my problem at the bank.
"You idiot! You mean to tell me you kept all your money in one account? You ain't got nuttin' stashed away somewhere? I taught you better than that! Why don't you just get a cash advance from one of your credit cards or somethin'?"
The blank look on my face says it all. I've known Janelle since we were college freshmen, and I have never had a reason to distrust her, especially when it came to my money. Before I started at Downtown Records, she was the major breadwinner of the family. And now that I make over double what she comes home with, my appreciation has always been

intact. Up until today, I've never had a reason to think otherwise.

"I know you got to have credit cards, don't you?"

My silence again answers Skip's question. Momentarily reflecting on everything Skip said, I know in my heart he is right. It's just unfortunate it took what happened at the bank for me to realize how stupid and trusting I have been all these years.

"Ain't that a bitch! You make well over six figures a year, and you ain't even got a major credit card to your name!"

"That's because all the credit cards are in Janelle's name. I haven't charged anything on a credit card in years."

Although Skip's proposal to go drink away my sorrows at the Nasty Kitty sounds enticing, it is only a temporary solution. I got enough sense to know my problem isn't going to fix itself with some lap dances and some damn fake titties in my face. Besides, getting too drunk has gotten me in enough trouble.

"Yo, Skip, I need you to drop me off at the train station."

"What the hell for?"

"Remember that advice you gave me over at Uncle Cliff's bar the other night? The night when I got pulled over by the cops?"

"What advice are you talkin' about? I give people lots of advice. I'm the Answer Man! Don't you know that by now?"

"Yeah, whatever! You told me to catch up wit' my co-worker and have her meet Janelle. Well, I am desperate enough to see if your plan is going to work."

David L.

* * *

As I gaze into my full-length mirror wondering what has happened to my life in the past few days, I suddenly realize – I'm the victim here! Janelle has cast me out of her life and Mama Pearl's phone just keeps ringing, neither of them returning any of my phone calls. Even Dani hasn't returned any of my calls. My attempts to see her last night were unsuccessful.

I'm fully adorned in my "lucky suit": a burgundy Armani suit, black Kenneth Cole shoes, cream pinstripe Versace tie, and the gold cufflinks my grandfather gave me before he passed away a little over three years ago. I don't know if it's from a lack of sleep, but I'm getting that same "queasy" feeling I got yesterday at the bank. A closer look in the mirror reveals slightly bloodshot eyes courtesy of hours of rolling around in a lonely bed. How many more nights will I have to sleep in that damn bed alone without Janelle's warm body next to mine?

Looking at my cell phone, I realize it hasn't rung in a while. It seems like an eternity since I've seen either of my precious children. DeShaun is so damn young…will he remember my smiling face? Recognize my voice? And what about Destiny? She is used to me tucking her in every night. I hope she doesn't act out in school over my absence.

But I can't worry about that right now. If I don't hurry up and catch that eight o'clock train, I'm going to be late for work.

Over Your Dead Body

"Look who decided to show up for work today!" Bernadette heckles.

Giving her my "I'm not in the mood for your nonsense" look, I head towards my office.

"Oh, so you're so large now that you changed your number and couldn't tell me!" Dani says, opening her office door.

"My phone hasn't rang in like two days," I explain. "What do you mean change my number? I've had the same cell phone number for almost a year."

Reaching for my office phone, I call my cell phone number, already expecting the worst. I don't let on to Dani my shame when I hear an automated message telling me the number I have called has been temporarily disconnected. It doesn't take a rocket scientist to figure out that Janelle is behind this, I conclude. After all, my cell phone was purchased with Janelle's credit card last summer, and she knows my access code.

"I need a favor," I blurt out.

I hesitate to continue because my mind tells me not to listen to Skip's advice, but my heart tells me it is probably my best shot to get back in good with Janelle.

"What do you need now?"

"I need you to call Janelle for me and straighten out the mess I'm in."

"What mess? What kind of trouble have you gotten yourself into this time?"

Listening closely to my every word, Dani eyes me attentively.

"Her jealous ass thinks I'm messin' around on her. If you tell her that she's got nothing to worry about, that will probably save my marriage."

77

David L.

"I don't believe you! We share a GODDAMN kiss the other night – Valentine's night of all nights, and you want me to call your jealous ass wife? Fuck you and fuck her! I hope you both go to hell, Preston!"

Dani's intense ramblings reach a feverish level, almost to the point where her eyes begin to water. As office co-workers begin to inch closer to see what all the commotion is about, I immediately motion everyone to return to their posts and mind their business.

"Dani, you act like I led you on or something! I'm the one who stopped us from going any further because I didn't want to hurt you and end up being mad at my ass!"

"You conceited idiot! You think you are all that, Preston? I felt sorry for your Black ass, that's all! Nothing more…nothing less!"

Dani storms out of the office without looking back. I'm almost sorry I listened to Skip's advice in the first place.

"Did anyone from Fantasy call for me, Bernadette?"

"You mean you didn't get the message I left for you?"

"What message? This is my first day back to work. You know that."

Checking my phone messages on the office phone, I skip through at least twenty messages before cueing in on an all-too familiar voice. Bingo!

"Preston, this Is Sandy. Sorry you had to get the news like this, but we signed a contract with

Sheisty Records yesterday. Thank you for giving us our big break."

I feel my jaw drop as I slam the receiver down.

"Where is the loyalty?" I yell.

I wonder if Stan knows about this. Impossible. He would've tracked me down by now.

"They left me, Bernadette! Sandy and the other girls sold me out for another label!"

The look on her face reveals she already has gotten the news of Fantasy's departure from Downtown Records.

"Forget about them!" Bernadette responds. "You need to get in there and work out your little beef with Dani," she adds while pointing over to Dani's office.

"I can't worry about that right now. Dani will get over it eventually."

"Are you stupid? Don't you know anything about a woman? We don't forget nothing!"

"Yeah, well, I have to figure out what I'm going to do next. When Stan finds out about this, I'm a dead man."

Both Bernadette and I are oblivious to Dani exiting her office. What happens next is still a blur. Bending down and slipping a yellow envelope under Stan's office door, Dani exits the office through the side door and barely gets onto the elevator, vanishing for the rest of the day.

"I'm expecting two important calls today, Bernadette – one from a rapper named Black Trash and the other who goes by the name of Joe Banger."

David L.

"You still tryin' to sign those guys? I saw them both leavin' Stan's office yesterday afternoon. They looked pretty excited, too."

"You saw them leaving his office? Why the hell wasn't I contacted? Something strange is going on around here, and I'm going to find out what it is!"

After a last minute telephone message telling Stan I won't be in for the rest of the day, I travel over to DeShaun's daycare to check on him. I haven't seen him in days and it's driving me crazy. I think about all those deadbeat dads you hear about on the news, the radio, and on the lips of disgruntled Black women, and I privately swear I would never become one of them.

The train ride brings back memories of the other day when I was jacked for my personal belongings. If I ever see that clown again, I will kill him. Well, maybe not kill him – but I will bust his ass for sure! Feelings of revenge are replaced with curiosity. Why were my future artists walking out of Stan's office? What is he concocting? I know he's not trying to steal my artists to avoid paying me a finder's fee bonus!

"Well, Mr. Price, we didn't expect you here today." The voice belongs to DeShaun's daycare counselor, Tiffany.

"I had the day off, so I figured I'd stop by to check my little man out," I respond.

"What a coincidence. Your wife called about an hour ago and said she was picking DeShaun up early today."

DeShaun's eyes light up as he immediately recognizes my smiling face. Just as I go to lift him out of his walker, Janelle enters.

"What are you doing here?"

My response is immediate. "What am I doin' here? Last I checked he was my son, too!"

Fearing a heated argument in front of the other children, Tiffany instructs us to go outside.

"I don't want your lying, cheating ass around my children!"

"You need to check yourself, Janelle! They are my children, too, and I haven't seen either of them since you left the house!"

"Left the house? In case you forgot, I was admitted to the hospital. I almost died and you don't even care! That's why I could care less what happens to you! It's over between the two of us!"

"I don't care? I didn't tell you to swallow a whole bottle of sleeping pills!"

"What kind of man stays out all hours of the night knowing he's got a nine-month-old son and a little girl who waits in her bed for her sorry-ass father to come home and tuck her in?"

"What kind of woman destroys a man's house, destroys all of his personal belongings, steals all of his money from his account, and has his cell phone turned off?"

"That should be the least of your worries. This ain't over…NOT BY A LONG SHOT!"

Janelle places DeShaun into his car seat and quickly drives off. Just as I'm sure she had planned, she had the last word.

David L.

* * *

I've been going to Mr. Willy's barbershop since I was about eleven or twelve years old and allowed to walk there by myself.
"What up, young fella!" Mr. Willy announces. "I haven't seen you in here in a minute. Don't tell me you went and found yourself another barber."
"C'mon now, Mr. Willy. You know I would never sell you out like that."
"I was the first one to put one of dem parts up in yo' big head when you were a youngsta. How's the record business doing?"
"I'm still doin' my thing, but working my behind off at the job."
"I saw your buddy with the funny looking walk pass by here a few times."
"Who? Skip? I'm 'bout to see him in a few hours. He hooked up with one of my wife's friends, so I don't see him as much as I used to."
The walk to Mr. Willy's was worth the mile it took for me to get there. Not only did it help me clear my head, I forgot the tranquility it provides when your life is in disarray. Besides, with my driver's license currently suspended because of my DUI a few days ago, I'll be doing a lot more walking.
An hour and half goes by, and I'm finally called upon for my much-needed shape-up. Looking over at the seat I occupied seconds ago, a hyperactive toddler claims it as his father sits down next to him. It's only been a few days that I've been unable to put my children to sleep, but it feels like an eternity. I wonder if I will one day walk into Mr. Willy's

barbershop with DeShaun to watch him get his first haircut.

"Let me get about a quarter inch off the back, Mr. Willy."

Doing as instructed, Mr. Willy grabs his clippers and gets to work on my emerging 'fro. The vibrating sounds of the clippers lulls me into a semi-state of sleep. Awakening to the sounds of children laughing, I envision my own children running around the house. I hand my last twenty-dollar bill to Mr. Willy and exit his chair.

"What up, man!" an old workout acquaintance says to me. "I haven't seen you over at the gym in a minute."

"I've been busy. man. I'm gonna start going back soon, though." Although I know I'm not going back to the gym anytime soon, it seemed like the right thing to say.

With a new shape-up to be proud of, I strut out of Mr. Willy's barbershop to think about what to do next. Mount Vernon is only about four square miles, so anybody schemin' or up to no good is usually busted in a short amount of time.

"Well, look what we got here!" I say to myself.

Directly across the street, Shontell has one foot out of some dude's car door. As I zoom in on the happenings, she reaches over and plants a seductive kiss onto the mouth of some Jamaican-looking dude I ain't ever seen before. He looks like a real cornball, too. Does he really think he's profilin' driving around in what looks to be a 1994 Honda Accord with played out five-star rims? Not wanting Shontell to spot me, I casually re-enter the barbershop and wait for her to

David L.

make her next move. Like a chess master waiting for his opponent to counter-strike, I watch their every move. That triflin' bitch ran her mouth off to Janelle and she's the one trickin' out here in the streets? I don't know whether to feel good about myself or bad for Skip. Still, he has got to know!

"What are you up to?" my old workout partner from the gym questions.

"Nothing. Just playin' a game of chess," I respond.

The look on his face indicates he has no idea what the hell I'm talking about. Exiting the vehicle, Shontell drops a couple of quarters into a parking meter.

"I know where she's going."

Entering a hair salon a couple of stores down, I remember bringing Janelle to that same hair salon back in the day. What happens next proves to me beyond a shadow of a doubt that dude is every bit the cornball I pegged him for. Getting out of the driver's seat, dude enters the hair salon behind Shontell and seats himself to wait for her to get her hair done!

Skip lives about twenty blocks away, so I catch a cab over to his apartment, hoping he's home. As luck would have it, he is, and I get him to give me a ride back over to the barbershop.

"Fool! How you leave your wallet at the barbershop?" he questions.

"Man, I don't know. Just hurry up and get your coat on so you can get me back there before someone gets their hands on it!"

Over Your Dead Body

On the ride over, I keep smiling to myself. I'm finally going to get that troublemaking bitch back for all the mess she created! My allegiance will always be with my boy Skip, but I told his ass Shontell was no good from the get-go.

"What are you thinking about?" Skip calmly asks.

"You wouldn't understand, man. You're about to pass the barbershop. Pull over in that spot right there."

Doing as instructed, Skip parallel parks his ride and we both get out.

"Hold up!" I blurt out defiantly. "Damn! His car is gone!"

"What the hell are you talkin' about? Whose car is gone?"

I got a sour look on my face. My quest for redemption will not be denied. Entering the hair salon, I walk directly over to the chair that Shontell is occupying. She doesn't even see me at first because her fake-ass weave is under the hairdryer.

"You're livin' foul, Shontell! I saw you a little while ago kissing on some clown in a Honda Accord. Where did he go?"

With a straight poker face, Shontell does as expected. After all, who could blame her? I would probably do the same thing in her predicament.

"What guy are you talkin' about, Preston? Just because you got busted by Janelle, don't try to involve me in yo mess!"

Looking over at Skip for encouragement, he offers none, shaking his head in disbelief.

85

David L.

"That's a good one, Shontell! And don't try to bring Janelle and me into it. Don't deny I saw your ass getting out of some fool's car!"

"The only car you seen me get out of was a cab, you fool! Now get out of here! You're embarrassing yourself!"

She's right. I am embarrassing myself. Skip and I are the only guys in the hair salon, and we're outnumbered by at least ten women with sewed in horse hair. Every female in the establishment is looking over at me to see how I react. They probably think I'm going to hit her or something. I walk out disgruntled, but not before looking back over at Shontell and promising myself to get her back.

"What was that about?" Skip questions.

"Yo dog, she can say whatever she wants, but she's tryin' to play you!"

"She ain't playin' nobody, man. She do her thing and I do mine. You know the game. Stop tryin' to make it like that's my girl or something!"

"Yeah, I guess you're right, man. My bad."

"I mean, I know you're goin' through your own thing with Janelle and all, but you're letting it mess with your mind. Is that why you told me you left your wallet at the barbershop?"

I shake my head with approval over what Skip just said. I can't let my emotions get the best of me. I am letting Janelle and Shontell get inside my head. I have to step my game up!

* * *

Over Your Dead Body

"May I speak with Janelle, Mama Pearl?" With the help of Uncle Cliff's credit card and some smooth talking with a T-Mobile saleswoman, I was able to purchase a new cell phone without any additional money down.

Mama Pearl's feelings towards me are made very clear. "I'm Mrs. Pearl to you. And she's not home anyways."

"Gimme the phone, Ma. I'll talk to him," Janelle is overheard speaking in the background.

"What do you want, Preston?"

"You know what I want, Janelle. I want to see my children. I haven't seen either one of them in over a week."

"Whose fault is that? When you were runnin' around town with that bitch, supposedly working all those hours, you weren't worried 'bout seeing them then, were you?"

"What are you trying to prove, Janelle? I called out of work for three days straight to hang with DeShaun, and his daycare told me that you withdrew him. Why didn't you tell me you pulled him out of his daycare?"

"Why didn't I tell you? Who are you?"

"I'm their father, that's who the hell I am! I'm tryin' to have a civil conversation with you, Janelle, and you're attacking everything I say or do!"

"You should be happy I'm even talking to ya' ass! And as for DeShaun – yeah, I withdrew him because I don't trust you anymore! Destiny doesn't go to that school no more either, so don't waste your time trying to pick her up from there!"

David L.

As hard as I try to keep the conversation in control, Janelle continues to yell and scream. How could such a sweet, quiet woman turn into such a bitch? A slight smirk emerges on my face on account of something Uncle Cliff told me once: Be careful of a woman scorned. I try to satisfy Janelle's out-of-control ego one last time before giving up in despair.

"Janelle, for the last time, can I come by and see the children?"

Her response is callous and swift. "You want to see the children? See this…"

SLAM! And just like that, the deafening sound of the receiver hanging up can be heard in my unsuspecting ears.

"Janelle has got you trippin'!" Skip warns.

Moments earlier, Skip picked me up in his ride to bring me over to Mama Pearl's house.

"She ain't expecting you to come over tonight, is she?"

"Nah, not really. But if I call back over there, she ain't gonna pick up anyway."

"I must really got love for you 'cause I could be diggin' Shontell out right now."

"That's a little too much information for me, man."

"Don't hate on me 'cause you can't get none from your wife."

Unbeknownst to Skip, he has hit me with a low blow. I think the last time I got me some from Janelle was New Year's Eve after everyone left the party. Damn! It was that long ago?

The ten-minute ride to Mama Pearl's house is an especially important one. If I could just get Janelle to listen to me, things will work out – or so I hope.

"You ever think about taking her to court?"

"What do you mean by that?"

"Man, do I have to explain everything to your dumb ass? I mean, you missed the last few days of work, and for what? You out here lookin' like a damn fool! Go over to family court and get yourself visitation rights for your kids or something."

"I never even thought of that. I want to talk to her first and try to get her to see that I ain't messin' around."

"Whatever! If you ask me, you need to handle your business."

The late day rays of the sun try their best to hang around, but ultimately, lose out to the evening darkness.

"Pull up right over there," I instruct Skip, referring to an available parking spot in front of Mama Pearl's house.

"Is that the house?" Skip questions. "I see a light on."

"Yeah, that's it. Stay here in the car."

I can't front. I'm nervous and I don't know how Janelle will react, or Mama Pearl for that matter, when they see who is on their front porch.

"Who is it?" Mama Pearl questions after I ring the bell.

I open my mouth to speak, but strangely nothing comes out. Mama Pearl repeats her question, and after I finally respond, the front door is opened.

David L.

"Wait right here a minute!" Mama Pearl announces.

Five minutes elapse, and as I contemplate turning around and returning to Skip's car, Janelle appears. She is adorned in a burgundy silk pajama outfit with matching fluffy slippers. I forgot how good she looks. I want to desperately reach over and embrace her with a hug, but I decline my urges. I might not be the smartest person in the world, but I do know that timing is everything.

"Can I come in to talk to you?"

The thought of Skip waiting anxiously for me in his car doesn't even matter. Knowing my boy, he is probably using up his anytime minutes talking to that crab Shontell or blasting his stereo system, waking up Mama Pearl's neighbors. Seated with Janelle in the living room, I can sense Mama Pearl's nosy presence in the other room. Mama Pearl and I have always had a pretty good relationship, but I guess what they say is true: blood is thicker than water!

"So what do you want to talk about, Preston?"

"I know I've been neglecting you and spending a lot of time at work, but you've got to believe me. I'm not cheatin' on you. I never have and I never will."

Just as I plead my case, Destiny runs into the room. She must've heard my voice. She wraps her arms around me with anticipation and excitement.

"Hi, Daddy! I missed you!"

"I missed you, too."

"Let Mommy and Daddy finish talking, baby," Mama Pearl interrupts. "You can go and hug on your daddy after him and Mommy finishes their

Over Your Dead Body

conversation. Janelle, I hope for your sake you are taking your medication."

"Medication? What medication?" I question.

"Never mind that. It's not important."

Janelle shoots her mother a fierce look and subtly changes the conversation. Destiny is escorted out as I watch her tiny feet scurry quickly out of the living room.

"I just need some time to think and get my life in order," Janelle explains. "I need to start thinking about me for a change."

"Well, while you are taking the time you need, do you think I can begin spending some quality time with my children?"

"Stop by here tomorrow about this time and we'll work out a visiting schedule. But I promise you this," Janelle adds, "if you don't show up for whatever reason, you can forget about ever seeing the children again."

"Thank you, Janelle. You won't regret this. I'm gonna make things right. You'll see."

I open up my arms to engage Janelle in a hug; however, my efforts are futile. She walks off, and just like Mama Pearl promised, Destiny is returned and we both embrace with the same heartfelt hug that I had planned for my estranged wife. Taking in Janelle's threatening statement, I exit Mama Pearl's house and leave with Skip – without ever looking back.

David L.

CHAPTER FOUR

March 1, 2004

    It's nine o'clock Monday morning, and I haven't stepped foot in the office in almost a week. Instead, I've left a permanent indentation in my sofa bed watching morning talk shows and playing Madden football on my X-Box game system. I don't know what it is, but I've got an awkward feeling about today.

    "Well, look who decided to show up for work! Had yourself a little mini-vacation, huh?"

    "Good morning, Bernadette. Is Stan in his office?"

    "Yeah, he is. He wants you to go see him right away, too."

    "I'll see him when I'm ready."

    I ignore Bernadette's warning and head to my office.

    "What the hell!"

    Everything in my office has either been removed or replaced. There is a new rug on the floor and the top of my desk has been cleared of all my personal possessions.

    "Where's my picture of Jimmy Walker and Malcolm X?" I say to no one in particular. "And where is all of my Jet Magazine beauty's of the week?"

Over Your Dead Body

Anxiously going through my desk drawers, I quickly realize all of my personal belongings have been emptied out, as well. Even the password on the computer has been changed.

"Bernadette, what happened in here? What the hell happened to my office?"

Shaking her head in frustration, Bernadette responds as diplomatically as only she can. "I told you to go see Stan. I don't know what you did. I'm just the secretary, but I can tell you that he's in there right now with Mr. Townsend."

My heart feels like it has stopped as I take one last look at the empty remnants of my once beautifully furnished office and reluctantly head over to Stan's office. Reaching for the doorknob, I can hear them talking about something. Putting my ear closer to the door, my name is mentioned over and over again, but I have no idea what they're talking about. I feel as if the world has come to a standstill as I slowly turn the knob and enter my boss' office.

"You wanted to see me, Stan?"

My eyes are focused on the several gold and platinum plaques that line his office walls.

"Let me get right to the point, Preston. I've terminated you based on practices deemed unethical in the workplace. I need you to give security your I.D. badge on the way out."

"What are you talking about? What unethical practices?"

"He's talking about this right here," Mr. Townsend interrupts, handing me a large, yellow envelope.

David L.

It doesn't take long for me to connect the dots. The contents in the envelope contain documents showing my contract offers to potential Sheisty Record artists. To top it off, Dani's name is not on any of them!

"What were you thinking, Preston? You thought you could run around New York City and not eventually get caught?" Stan questions.

"Stan, don't do this! You got this all wrong..."

"The proof is in the envelope, Preston. Unless you can tell me there is another Preston Price running the streets of New York trying to tarnish your reputation, our conversation is over!"

"Yeah, but..."

"Good day, Mr. Price," Mr. Townsend interrupts.

I don't say another word. My silence is the burden I must now pay for my collaborative efforts with that turncoat Dani. And to think she sold me out because she has romantic feelings for me and I didn't reciprocate those same romantic feelings! Would she have preferred if I "hit it" and never acknowledged her again? That night in her apartment should never have happened. I blame myself because I could've called anyone that night to pick me up from the train station, but I decided to call her, a mistake I promise to never make again.

My departure from Downtown Records is swift and precise. Dropping my office keys on Bernadette's desk and grabbing my overcoat and newly-purchased briefcase, I exit – never to see the gold and platinum record-lined walls I helped create ever again.

Over Your Dead Body

* * *

"You must have a black cloud over your head," Skip snaps, referring to my getting fired.

"That ain't funny!" I respond. "At least I had a job!"

Skip obviously thinks it is, because he is laughing hysterically and almost crashes into an oncoming car from laughing so hard.

"I can't believe you let a woman set you up to get fired. And all because you wouldn't put out! That has got to be the most ironic thing in the world! That's almost like sexual harassment – in reverse!"

"I'm glad you're getting a kick out of my misery! How you know that bitch Dani set me up to get fired anyway?"

"'Cause Shontell told me all about it. She called me last night and told me what went down Monday morning."

"Shontell told you?"

Now I'm confused. If Shontell knows, that means Janelle knows, and I sure as hell would never tell her I got fired. So how the hell did the two of them find out?

"Where we goin' anyway?"

"Be patient. You'll find out in a minute."

I should have known we were coming here. The flashing Nasty Kitty sign is a dead giveaway and so is the silly grin on Skip's face. The Nasty Kitty is one of the most popular nudie bars in the area and has some of the baddest girls in New York. I remember passing by here one day in the middle of the day and it was packed to capacity as if it was a Friday night.

David L.

"Let's go have a good time inside the nudie bar. I got a pocket full of one dollar bills, and I'm ready to get my lap dance on!"

"I just lost the best job I've ever had in my entire life and you think I feel like rubbing up on some damn titties right about now?"

"My treat!"

My two favorite words. Downtown Records cut me a check as part of my termination package this morning, but hell, Skip does not have to know. As many times as I treated his non-working ass, it's the least he can do. I'm sitting on about three thousand cash, and I'll be damned if some trick-ass stripper is going to get into my pockets tonight. The most important thing about walking into a nudie bar is your presentation. If we walk in there acting like we are larger than we really are, they are going to try and "trick" on us. However, if we walk up in there looking like some regular dudes trying to pass some time, we won't get any play from anyone.

"You've been sitting there sipping on that same damn warm-ass beer for like ten minutes. What's up wit' you?" Skip questions.

"I'm just tryin' to figure out how Shontell and Janelle found out I lost my job, that's all."

"You sittin' here at the Nasty Kitty with ass all up in ya' face and all you can think about is how Shontell and Janelle found out about you losin' your job? How did you get fired anyway?"

"Trust me, it's a long story."

Besides, Skip is right. I got Black, White, and Spanish – hell, even a Chinese chick dancing up on the stage and walking around the bar practically butt naked, and here I am thinking about scandalous-ass Shontell. I order a double shot of Absolut to forget about my current problems.

"That's more like it!" Skip reassures. "Have some fun up in here! You're not going to let all this ass go to waste, are you?"

I'm kind of feeling it from the double Absolut shot, so I order another for extra measure. Hell, Skip is paying for it! Midnight comes and goes, and here I am on my third double shot of Absolut vodka. As usual, Skip is acting a fool with a bad-ass White girl on the other end of the bar. She's got dirty blond hair and an ass like a Black woman…just his type of woman!

"Care for another shot of Absolut?"

The bartender is a looker herself. She's got on a cut off tee shirt with Daisy Duke jean shorts. If she were to jump on stage, she would probably cash in on more dollar bills than the majority of women working the pole right now.

"Yeah, why not," I say. "Put it on his tab," I add while pointing over to Skip, who is on his way to the back of the club for a private lap dance.

"I got this one, Sheryl," a woman's voice standing behind me commands.

Turning around to thank the woman, I immediately recognize who is paying for my drink.

"Mocha, right?"

"In the flesh, baby! You came all the way back here to see me?"

Mocha and I make like two old friends playing catch up and find a cozy place in the back room to talk – among other things.

David L.

The DJ has played over five songs and I haven't reached into my pockets yet to pay Mocha. More importantly, I got the green light to feel up on her as much as I want because the bouncer is nowhere in sight.

"Where we at?" I question.

"We are in the VIP section. You can do anything you want here…well, almost anything."

My instincts tell me she's "runnin' game" on me just to fatten her pockets, but after several shots of Absolut, I'm not thinking straight anyway. What makes it even more tempting is the fat knot of bills I got in my back pocket.

"What do you mean ALMOST anything?"

Even in the darkened room, I can't help but notice Mocha's grin as she responds to my question.

"That means if you want intercourse, we are going to have to either go back to your place or get a telly somewhere close by."

"A telly?"

"Yeah, a motel, silly! You don't do this too often, do you?"

"I've never done this at all."

We sure as hell can't go back to my place. Wait a minute! Why can't we? Janelle broke out days ago, and it beats spending money for a motel. Better yet, I got the keys to Skip's place, and judging from his actions, he ain't tryin' to leave the Nasty Kitty no time soon.

"Let's take a ride."

Before Mocha has a chance to change her mind about leaving the Nasty Kitty with me, I somehow manage to get Skip's car keys from him, and he agrees to catch a cab back to his place in two or three hours. That's just enough time for me to handle my business.

"Just make sure you wear a jimmy," Skip says, handing me a Ruff Ryder condom from his back pocket. "You don't want to be another statistic."

"Good lookin' out, man," I respond as I motion for Mocha to meet me outside.

Mocha and I immediately head for Skip's bedroom as I turn on every light switch to avoid tripping over all the junk in his living room.

"So you're married, huh?" Mocha asks, looking directly at my wedding ring.

"Somethin' like that. Actually, we're separated for the moment, but I don't want to talk about that right now."

"That's alright. I get just as many married men as I do single guys."

Mocha is not the least bit shy as she quickly removes the jacket I let her wear during the ride over to Skip's place. What happens next is like straight out of any horny teenager's wet dream. Mocha grabs me around my waist, and in less time than I can blink, my pants are pulled down below my knees. A little wary about looking down at her getting ready to go to work, I go against my better judgment and look anyway. After all, Mocha is a professional, and I'm sure she doesn't mind me watching her perform. Her neck gyrates up and down as she pleases me beyond satisfaction. Saving the best for last, we move over to Skip's sofa bed and I reach for my pants pocket to pull out a Ruff Ryder.

"I like it from behind," Mocha announces.

David L.

She removes her bikini string underwear and stiletto high heels, and as requested, I enter her from behind. She is uncharacteristically tight. Either that or I am more blessed than I have ever imagined! All of the top shelf liquor I devoured earlier is beginning to take its toll on me. Standing up behind Mocha, the room is spinning faster and faster, and on a couple of occasions, the weight of my body almost causes me to fall forward. After sixty seconds of heavy pounding and thrusting inside of Mocha, I am depleted. Hell, it has been quite some time since I had sex with the wife!

"Come lay down next to me, baby. I want to feel your heart beating next to mine."

Thank GOD! I thought she was going to say she wanted to go another round. With my last bit of strength, I lay my body across Mocha's outstretched frame.

"Let me give you a massage. Damn, baby, what are you so stressed about? You feel so tense."

Mocha's long, manicured fingers run over my entire upper back and shoulders. Tonight could not have happened at a better time. I tell Mocha if she ever decides to retire from the stripper game, she could always open her own massage parlor the way she is moving her fingers up and down my spine.

"Right there," I groan as Mocha massages my lower back, eventually moving down to my left and right calf muscles.

"I went to school for massage therapy about three years ago."

Oh great! I hope she doesn't give me a depressing story about how she is only stripping so she can pay back her college loans or something. I don't

Over Your Dead Body

say anything. I want to enjoy every single moment of my full body massage. Within moments of Mocha's magic fingers all over my aching body, I curl up in the fetal position and fall into a deep sleep.

The sound of Skip's phone ringing awakens me from my self-imposed mini hibernation. I must have been asleep longer than I thought.

"I'm on my way home," Skip announces. "You better not have had that ho all laid up on my sofa bed."

"C'mon now, I wouldn't do you like that."

Hanging up the phone, I immediately look around to notice Mocha has left without saying goodbye. Hell, even if she did, I wouldn't remember from the way I was hammering down those Absoluts at the bar. It is quite odd that I got to hit it without coming out of my pockets. I mean, I know I got game, but damn! Not like this! I quickly reach for my shirt and pants. Looking over at Skip's caller I.D., he spent the night at Shontell's place and might come back with her. I'm not trying to give that treacherous skank any reason to go running back to Janelle with some more shit. I don't know what makes me dig into my pockets, but I do.

"NO FUCKING WAY!" I scream. "I'll KILL HER!"

The only items in my pockets are two leftover Ruff Ryder rubbers, my house keys, and my wallet, which is now empty.

"Three thousand dollars. THREE GODDAMN THOUSAND DOLLARS! I can't believe that bitch got me!"

David L.

My mind is blank. She played me like a damn musical instrument! There is no way I should have let her leave this house without checking my stuff! No job...no money...no wife. Nothing! It is suddenly beginning to occur to me that every woman in my life has either left me or played me at one point or another.

Before I jump to any more conclusions, I diligently search Skip's apartment in the unlikely event I accidentally misplaced my stash of money. No luck, just as I expected. Vacating Skip's apartment is now the last thing on my mind.

I begin to daydream about all the scandalous women in my life and how they betrayed me. My mother – Margaret Price. She died when I was three years old. I have faint memories of running around in the backyard as she kneeled down to plant seeds in her garden. My once-cherished wife – Janelle. She and I are not even on speaking terms. She hates my guts, and I'm beginning to hate hers! My mother-in-law – Mama Pearl. She once told me no matter what happens between me and her daughter, I would always family. Yeah right! Even Dani, my ex co-worker, backstabbed me and left me for dead with Stan and Mr. Townsend. I don't even know why she did what she did. And now this!

I should have known something was up when Mocha didn't ask for any money up front to take a ride with me. But how could she have known I was carrying such a large amount of cash? Thoughts of revenge race through my mind. I think about the destruction Janelle caused to the house days ago and I think about what I would do to Mocha, if only my gun wasn't missing!

Over Your Dead Body

The scent of old beer is still lingering in my kitchen as a result of Janelle's rampage days earlier.

"DAMN!" I forgot to stop by and see Janelle and the children.

I quickly reach for the phone and dial Mama Pearl's house. Just as I feared, no answer. I contemplate leaving a message, but it's not like Janelle is going to call me back anyway. I really screwed up this time! I might have to take Skip's advice and find a lawyer to get visitation rights, because Janelle is going to use this to her advantage.

Responding to a light, tapping sound at the front door, I notice a delivery service van parked outside. At the bottom of my steps, a uniformed individual is writing something on a pad.

"May I help you?" I question.

"I have a letter for you. Sign here, please."

Doing as instructed, I thank the driver and immediately open the envelope. My heart begins to race as I realize what the contents of the letter consists of.

"This bitch wants a divorce!"

It seems like just yesterday we shared a New Year's kiss in DeShaun's room and held each other in a meaningful embrace...and now this! Looking around at the destruction Janelle has caused, both physically and emotionally, I make myself a promise I swear I will never break: she can have her divorce, but no man will raise my children as long as I have breath in my body! With no job to go to and about thirty dollars in cash that I found next to my X-box console, I head out

103

David L.

the front door with only one thing on my mind: my children coming home with me!

"Come down here and talk to me, Janelle! I know you're up there!" I yell from Mama Pearl's backyard.

A moving silhouette on the top floor alerts me to what is probably Janelle's presence.

"I want to talk to you about this letter I got served with!"

A light is turned on and the upstairs window is opened halfway. Sticking her head out, Janelle finally responds.

"You are trespassing on my mother's property! Take yo' ass home, Preston! You might as well enjoy it while you can, because I'm going to get it in the divorce anyway!"

"Where in the hell are the children, Janelle? They are coming home with me!"

"You must be high or something, Preston! You are going to have to kill me before I let you take my children away from me!"

Picking up a large brick, I contemplate throwing it, but wisely reconsider.

"You want the children, Preston? Hold on one second!"

Not liking the way she said that, I back away from the window. I've known Janelle for over a decade, and when she is angry, she is capable of anything. Just as I expect, Janelle returns to the window with a bucket filled with water and empties it by tossing the water towards me. My college track skills come in handy, and I barely manage to avoid the downpour.

"What is going on out there?" Mama Pearl questions as she opens her front door and comes out onto the porch. "Preston, don't be coming here trying to start no trouble!"

"Mama Pearl, uh – Mrs. Pearl, it ain't even like that. Janelle won't let me bring Destiny or DeShaun over to the house. I don't mean no disrespect, but I'm not leavin' here without my son and daughter."

Standing outside of Mama Pearl's house for several minutes, it occurs to me that they are inside calling my bluff. If I don't do something drastic…anything – I won't be taken seriously ever again. Just as I reclaim the brick to use against the screen door in back of the house, Mama Pearl returns and opens the front door.

"Hi, Daddy!" Destiny cheerfully says.

"Hey, sweetheart!"

Mama Pearl is holding DeShaun in his favorite Barney blanket. He is wide awake and looking at me with his innocent eyes. He has no idea what is going on, which I am thankful for.

"What up, little man! You ain't walkin' yet, huh?"

"He's trying to walk. Mostly, he is just holding onto things and falling right back down on his fat butt! Janelle is upstairs fuming, but you're right. You have a right to see your children, too. Just don't do anything that will make me regret this!"

"Don't worry, I won't. You can count on that."

After thanking Mama Pearl repeatedly and promising her to return Deshaun and Destiny

David L.

tomorrow night, I enter a nearby cab and head home to spend all the time I got with my children.

* * *

The thought of endless nights of sleeping alone doesn't even enter my mind. With one hand on the alarm clock, I realize it will be hours before Destiny or DeShaun awaken. Getting out of my bed to get some iced tea from the fridge, I almost slip on one of Destiny's dolls. If I had money for one of them sleep disorder specialists, I would probably make an appointment.

"That's weird," I say under my breath. "I could've sworn I closed the hallway door before I went to bed."

As I reach for the pitcher, the light emanating from the refrigerator door unintentionally alerts me to an unwelcome visitor.

"What the hell!" I blurt out as a well-aimed fist connects with my chin.

Caught off guard, I fall quickly to the ground. Slowly getting up and still disoriented, I'm hit with a barrage of fists from many different directions. I quickly theorize that there is more than one person in my home. I can taste the blood in my mouth, and I am losing consciousness at an accelerated rate. With a desperate lunge at one of my attacker's legs, I am kicked in my head and drop hard to the ground – this time remaining motionless on my back.

"STAY DOWN, MUTHAFUCKA!" one of them shouts.

Over Your Dead Body

It's a familiar sounding voice. Then again, I'm not even sure where I am right about now. My eyes are beginning to close, but before I pass out from my unjustified beat down, the main attacker stands over me.

"Shoot his punk ass!" one guy says to the other.

The guy standing over me is holding a gun aimed directly at my face. A gun that looks a lot like my missing .380! The light from the open refrigerator door illuminates his lanky frame and allows me to connect the voice to the individual, who is the rapper I tried desperately to sign…JOE BANGER! No longer able to stay conscious, darkness overcomes me.

Racing up the steps to check on DeShaun and Destiny, I almost fall on my face. Entering each of their respective bedrooms, my worst fear comes to life to my dismay.

"WHY? WHY?"

I check every square inch of the house with the slight possibility that Destiny is playing a game of hide-n-seek with me. Playing a bad game of detective, I begin to look around the house for any subtle clues: a mysterious scent, forced entry of any kind, a ransom note – anything that could help me to reclaim my children. And then it hits me! There was no forced entry! They used a key to get inside the house!

"Why would Janelle do this to me? And what is her connection to Joe Banger?"

With no money in my pockets, I call Skip to come through. Within minutes, Skip arrives and we both sit down to devise a plan.

107

David L.

"You sure Janelle is behind this?" Skip candidly asks. "I mean, I know she's high strung and all, but DAMN!"

"I don't know for sure, but there is only one way to find out."

Waiting patiently for me to continue, Skip grabs a paper towel from a nearby table and hands it to me to wipe the blood from off my face.

"Let's go wait for Janelle about a block away from her mother's house. She has to get ready to leave soon, and she's not going to recognize your car."

"That's a stupid idea! What good is that gonna do?"

"Hear me out. Destiny has her swimming class every Saturday morning. If Destiny is with her, that means Janelle is the mastermind behind this whole kidnapping thing."

"You got me out here like Five-0!" Skip announces.

"Yeah, I know," I respond, opening a bag of chips.

"You're real calm for a man who just got knocked the hell out in his own house. You better make her pay."

"When have you ever known me not to handle mine? Janelle is not gonna get over on me. NO WAY!"

Skip's car windows are beginning to fog up, but we can't roll them down because it's starting to rain.

"How long are we going to wait out here? We've been out here for over twenty minutes, and we ain't seen nothing."

"Chill out, Skip. I look calm, but I'm stressed the fuck out! What if the children aren't with Janelle?"

"They got to be with her. You said it yourself, remember? There was no forced entry."

Hearing Skip repeat those words makes me feel ten times better. More importantly, nothing was stolen from the house, so I know it was a planned kidnapping set up by Janelle. Five more minutes pass, and I can tell Skip is becoming antsy.

"We can leave now, Skip. I don't see her coming out."

Doing as instructed, Skip puts the car into drive. As soon as he does, Janelle exits her mother's house. My eyes widen with anticipation. Walking right behind her, my little Destiny emerges from the doorway.

"JACKPOT! I told you that crazy bitch me set up, Skip!"

"Yeah, you did. And now that you know who set you up, what are you gonna do about it?"

"I don't know yet, but for now, follow her. Don't follow too closely. I don't want her to notice us."

Ending my undercover surveillance without any drama, Skip and I decide to make the most out of our Saturday afternoon by heading to Brooklyn so I pick up some Timberland boots. I own about ten pairs, but as one knows, you can never have enough. Afterwards, we catch a matinee movie.

* * *

David L.

I'm decked out in my favorite Kenneth Cole outfit and Skip is "slumming" in a hooded BOSS outfit with black Timberland boots. Skip has been "rough around the edges" since grade school and nothing is going to get him to change. Me, on the other hand, I have to stay fly and flossy. There is no other way!

"You sure you gonna be able to get up in there with those boots?" I question.

"I told you. I got this. My boy Cease is in charge of security."

The Wet Spot over on 133rd Street is jam packed tonight, and for once, Skip is right. I notice a slew of music industry folk profilin' like I used to when I was at Downtown Records. This is just the environment I need to be in to hopefully get my foot back in the music industry's door. A couple of old interns from my first job as head of promotions walk over in my direction.

"Hey there, Preston, uhh - I mean, Mr. Price," one says. "I haven't seen you in a minute. What have you been up to?"

"I started my own record label a couple of weeks ago, and I'm in here tonight lookin' for some new talent."

"Well, it was good seeing you again, Mr. Price," the other says. "We have to do lunch one day."

Hating to lie to save my image, but hating even more for them to know my true story makes me feel justified.

Skip has already taken off somewhere, probably looking for a chickenhead to take back home. Over in one of the far corners, I see a familiar face. It should be familiar; it's the bitch that cost me my job at

Downtown Records...Dani! She hasn't noticed me yet, and what's even better, her back is turned from my hate-induced line of vision.

Thirty minutes has gone by. Every beautiful woman in a tight fitting outfit that has walked by me remains oblivious to my one-track mind of executing revenge on Dani. The only problem I am faced with is how to get her back for what she has done. It is times like this I wish I ran the streets and hung with the kind of dudes who would make her disappear for the right price. Not like I got any money to pay someone off anyway! Walking back over towards me with two drinks in his hands – one I'm assuming is for me, Skip gives me his patented head nod.

"Ain't that one of the girls from Fantasy sitting at the bar, Pres? Yo, hook me up!"

"Yeah, that sure is Simone! Forget her, Skip. That turncoat bitch bounced on me and signed with some other label after everything I did for her."

"Man, are you crazy? Have you seen her video? That chick is hot! Introduce me to her."

"Skip, forget about her!"

Taking a closer look, I quickly realize Dani is sitting right next to her. I feel like I am in the old Geto Boy's video, "My Mind Is Playing Tricks On Me!" What is Janelle's connection with Joe Banger? Even my money getting taken by the stripper bitch, was that prearranged, too? And look at Dani profiling with my former act. Did Dani coerce her into parting ways with me?

It's four o'clock in the morning, and everyone is departing from the club. The gold diggers are casing the joint to see whose pockets they can get into, and the wannabe ballers are walking over to their rides parked outside, hoping to pull a last-minute score.

"Hey, Dani. Hey, Simone. The two of you enjoy yourselves tonight celebratin' my termination from Downtown Records?"

"Fool, ain't nobody tell you to take all those days off from work and allow your artists to jump ship!" Dani angrily responds. "You might want to learn how to separate your personal life from your work duties!"

"Yeah, and I guess you dropping off those contracts to Stan didn't help any, right? It's real convenient that your name wasn't on any of them!"

"What is he talkin' about, Dani? What contracts?" Simone questions.

"Girl, don't pay him no mind. He's just pissed off at everyone at the record label 'cause he got caught up thinking he was Mr. Untouchable or something! Preston, you're going to have to learn one thing in life. When you shit on the people that care about you, eventually they are going to shit on you right back!"

Dani has a crazy look on her grill like she wants to fight me or something. Either she had one too many drinks tonight, or she really thinks she can pull off a win against me. When she walks right up in my face, I position myself defensively in the event she does try to hit me.

"And just for the record," she whispers, "if you want to hold a grudge against someone, you should go have a talk with your loving wife. She's the one that orchestrated this whole thing."

Dani, denying me further clarification, walks off with one of my former flagship artists from my

Over Your Dead Body

glory days at Downtown Records. Fittingly, their backs are the last thing I see as they both walk away from my continued questioning over what was just said.

* * *

    With a little over four hours of sleep, I manage to get up for Sunday morning church service. Even more surprisingly, Skip called and said he would meet me in front of church and we could walk in together. Knowing Skip, he hasn't seen the inside of a church in years. Arriving at New Hope Baptist Church on the border of Mount Vernon and the Bronx, everyone is decked out in their best outfits. One clown even comes in wearing a purple jumpsuit, like he is a pimp or something!

"Good morning, Reverend Fletcher."

"All praises due to you, young man, on this beautiful Sunday morning," Reverend Fletcher gleefully responds.

    Despite alleged gambling sprees and adulterous activities in his younger years, Reverend Fletcher continues to be a ray of hope in the mostly urban community of Mount Vernon. A ray of hope for the lost souls that inhabit his Sunday morning church service once a week.

"It is good to see you here this bright morning on the Lord's day, although I've missed that winning smile of yours for the last several months."

"I know, Reverend, I know. I've been busy, but I'm back on track. I promise."

David L.

"And where is that beautiful bride of yours? The one I married in this same church not too long ago. It seems like it was just yesterday."

"We're having some minor problems right now, Rev, but we'll be alright. She might already be inside."

"It pains my heart to hear that, son. But don't you fret. GOD is merciful, and at the same time, he can be an enigma in itself. What he does sometimes can't be explained, but you must not give up your hope in him. Always believe, son!"

"I will do that, Reverend. I will see you inside. My buddy Skip just arrived and I told him I'd walk in with him."

The Rev's advice was well meaning, but the distrust and contempt in my heart is beginning to become unbearable. Once in a while, Janelle frequents New Hope Baptist with her mother and Shontell. The way I feel right now, I would probably slap her in the face while she was placing her money in the collection plate. The church bell begins to ring, announcing to all the latecomers that service has begun. Hoping for a shorter than average service so I can make it home in time for the first college basketball game of the day, Skip and I enter through the church doors.

We're both strategically in the back of the church, just in case Reverend Fletcher gets into one of his zones where he does not want to stop preaching the word. One overzealous fool in a middle aisle keeps sliding during his readings like he is on Soul Train. Some old lady seated in the very front is babbling some incoherent language like she got the Holy Ghost in her or something. Halfway through the service, the collection plate is passed around, and I look at Skip with shame to place a couple of dollars in the plate for me.

"Don't even worry about it, Pres. You will be back on your feet in no time," Skip whispers. "Then I can go back to bummin' off you like in the good ol' days."

As usual, Skip's unusual wit snaps me out of my "woe is me" mode, and I stand to sing the next selected hymn of the day along with the rest of the congregation.

"Yo, Pres, check out Janelle up at the front of the church wit' yo mother-in-law."

As those fateful words are spewed from Skip's mouth, I envision a new life, one that does not involve Janelle. After all, she is the one who filed the papers for divorce.

"Yo, Skip, I forgot to tell you. Janelle served me with divorce papers."

"Word? So she really ain't playin', huh?"

"That's what I've been tryin' to tell you. She is taking this whole thing to the next level."

Skip and I get looks from those around us, informing us that we're doing a little bit too much talking and not enough praising the word.

"You think there's another man in the picture?"

"I don't know what to think. All I know is she got me fired somehow, and now Dani is in on it. And let's not forget, she had me set up in my own house."

Even sitting in back of today's service cannot help me escape the well wishers and random

David L.

acquaintances probably wondering why I was not seated with Janelle and her mother.

"Hey there, Preston. I haven't thanked you enough for that sizable donation to the Boys and Girls Club a few months ago," one woman says. "You keep doing what you're doing and you're going to be our next mayor one day."

"That's alright, Mrs. Johnson. You know I'd do anything for the children in our community."

A lady standing over Mrs. Johnson asks the question I am sure at least a handful of others wanted to ask, but were afraid to.

"I saw your wife sitting up at the front. Is everything alright between you two?"

As luck would have it, I took my wedding band off for the first time to go out to the Wet Spot with Skip last night. I'm sure every woman in here will pick up on that minor detail.

"Uh, I don't really know what's going on, Mrs. Samuels."

"Well, I'll pray for you, baby. Don't you worry."

Waiting for me in the car, Skip wisely escapes the stares of being the guy hanging out with the "man separated from his wife."

"Hello, Preston. Good seeing you in church this morning," Mama Pearl says.

She is wearing some type of crazy-looking hat with a flower poking out from the side. Walking about twenty feet behind her, Janelle is attempting to walk out of the church with both DeShaun and Destiny. Destiny does not notice me because she is preoccupied

Over Your Dead Body

with one of her many dolls, and DeShaun is asleep in his stroller.

"Hello, Mrs. Pearl."

Either Mama Pearl does not know what recently went down between Janelle and I, or she is playing one helluva act.

"Hi, Daddy!" Destiny yells while running over and giving me the tightest bear hug she can muster.

"Hello, Preston," Janelle nonchalantly says.

She is now holding DeShaun in her arms and grabbing a hold of Destiny at the same time. If our interaction right now was a card game, Janelle would be holding both jokers, and she knows it! She knows instinctively that I would never purposely sabotage my impeccable reputation in the community by calling her out at this exact moment.

"Let's go, Mama. I got a friend meeting me at the house in about an hour."

And leave they do. I can almost hear Janelle laughing at me as they both drive off with my children. Outside the church, Skip is bobbing his head to whatever it is he is listening to at the moment.

"What did you say to her?" Skip questions as I enter his car to inform him of the brief interaction between Janelle and I.

We are not even five minutes out of the Lord's house and he is blasting that damn 50 Cent CD of his already.

"I didn't say anything. She smiled at me and said what's up, that's all."

"That's all? Your wife sets you up, causes you to lose your job, and you ain't slap the shit out of her?

117

David L.

Let's not forget she withdrew all your money from your bank account and left you for broke!"

"What was I gonna do in front of everybody, Skip? You wanted me to step to her and cause a scene right after church?"

"Yeah, I feel you, but you better think of something. Right now, her and your mother-in-law are probably laughing their asses off on the way home."

Thoughts of my soon-to-be ex-wife and her mother laughing at my expense continue to fuel my growing hatred towards them. Hell, the "friend" she has to see in an hour is probably that slime Joe Banger! My thoughts quickly shift from them laughing to Joe Banger with my daughter sitting on his lap watching one of her favorite cartoons, or DeShaun pointing to him and calling him Daddy! Then it finally hits me, like a sign from up above.

"Yo, Skip, you ever want to just kill someone?"

"Yeah, no doubt. I wanted to kill my ex-wife. Hell, I still want to sometimes, especially when I look at one of my old paychecks!"

"No, I'm dead serious. I mean really go out and kill someone?"

"Nah, I mean, I don't think so. I've wished for bad things to happen to certain people, but I've never seriously thought about killing someone. Why you ask? What are you thinking about? Killing Janelle? Well, leave me outta it! I'm still on probation!"

I can tell from his signature smirk that Skip is not taking me or what I have just said seriously. Hell, why should he? I'm probably the most passive, down-to-earth person he knows.

Over Your Dead Body

"You're laughing, Skip, but I'm dead serious. Matter of fact, I've never been more serious in my life. This bitch Janelle is trying to ruin my life! Hell, she already ruined my life! She destroyed our marriage; I lost my job because of her; and because of her, I got my ass beat down in my own house!"

"So what are you sayin', Pres? You thinking 'bout taking her out of her misery or something? You do something to that girl and the cops will be all over you. Don't you watch the movies?"

"Whatcha mean by that?"

"The broken-hearted husband is always the number one suspect!"

"You're making jokes, but Skip, you gonna find out soon just how serious I am!"

"You really serious, ain't you?"

My response is immediate, and the tone of my voice alerts Skip to just how serious I am.

"Yeah, I'm gonna kill her, Skip! HER DAYS ARE NUMBERED!"

David L.

CHAPTER FIVE

April 5, 2004

    It is the first Monday of the month and my first day of employment as the head of artist development over at Destiny Records. I feel right at home because Destiny Records used to be Downtown Record's main competition in the late nineties, and now I get to bring them back into the spotlight. How ironic that as I begin a new life at a new place of employment, I am reminded daily of my old life with a daughter by the same name, who I don't even get to see!

    I am walked around to various cubicles being introduced to everyone as if I'm going to remember their names. My new secretary is the epitome of "ghetto fabulous." She has burgundy hair, long-ass fingernails, six-inch high-heeled shoes, and an apparent chip on her shoulder.

    "So you're the new guy up in here, huh?" she says to me.

    She is loudly smacking her chewing gum and has this annoying facial tick.

    "Yeah, that would be me. I'm sorry, I forgot your name."

    "It's Sandy. I've been here for over six months and still ain't got no promotion yet. I guess you think you going to come up in here and take over, huh?"

Over Your Dead Body

"Good meeting you, Sandy."

I bury my head in a pile of CD samplers from aspiring musicians and get to work. I can't complain about the look of my new office. Although this company is much smaller and less prestigious than Downtown Records, I've got a flip-down television to watch all the music videos, a private fax machine and copier, and even my own view of the Brooklyn Bridge. Surfing through the one hundred plus channels at my disposal, I instinctively stop at a recent taping of 106 and Park.

"Just my luck, I missed the number ten video!"

Upon its return from its commercial break, I see a sight that almost causes me to jump through the window.

"That's that fool Joe Banger up there with Free and AJ! How the hell did he get booked on that show so fast? 106 and Park has to have at least a ninety day wait list for their musical guests!"

He is up on stage grinning like everything is sweet. A month ago, dude was up in my house kicking my ass all over the floor. Although the seeds of Janelle's death have already been germinated in my subconscious, I need to exact revenge on Joe Banger first. After all, it will be excellent practice for my grand finale!

At my new job over at Destiny Records, I have access to a parking garage for my Range Rover that I can finally drive again. It took several dozen hours of alcohol counseling and hundreds of dollars that I paid to the Department of Motor Vehicles courtesy of an advance-signing bonus, but I'm back on the road.

David L.

"I'm out of the office for the rest of the day, Sandy. I have to go to an Open Mic contest and scout some up and coming talent."

Sandy just rolls her eyes and buries her head into some book she is reading. It is probably some feminist trash that tells women all across America they don't need any man in their lives.

The Open Mic contest is an annual event held in downtown Brooklyn, so I call Skip to see if he wants to meet me down there. Knowing Skip, he is sitting around in his apartment in his boxer shorts blaming "whitey" for not being able to hold down a decent job. I would have given Skip a job years ago when I was over at Downtown Records, but he is just too damn lazy and unmotivated. He probably would have quit anyway after a couple of weeks.

After leaving a message on his cell phone, I brace myself for probable late day traffic on the FDR.

As expected, I am stuck on the FDR, barely moving more than five miles an hour. I block my cell phone number and call Janelle. I leave my tenth message of the day, asking her to call me so I can come by and visit with the children. Reaching into the glove compartment, I pull out a cigarette and take a few drags – something I haven't done in months. Arriving at the Open Mic contest fashionably late, I give a hug to the security guard and enter through the club's rear entrance.

"Are you one of the judges?" one eager MC questions.

Over Your Dead Body

He is standing extra close to my face, but I don't have the heart to tell him that his breath is about to make me pass out.

"Yes, I am. Are you getting on the mic tonight?"

"Oh yeah, no doubt. Look out for me, too. I say some ill stuff on the mic!"

It feels good to be back in the music game. With the exception of the politics and the two-faced phonies that are ever-present, it is an enjoyable way to make a living.

The Open Mic contest is down to three participants, two males and a female. Just as I figured, Skip is a no show. The two other judges, one a promoter from Queens and the other a VP at some Virginia radio station, are head over heels over the girl MC. She has on a mini-skirt with her cleavage showing in a semi see-through, so it is not hard to figure out why they are both so interested. She is obviously trying to play the Foxy Brown slash Lil' Kim role, and fortunately for her, she will probably get away with it.

"So who gets the grand prize?" I question the other two judges during intermission.

As expected, my vote doesn't count, and the Lil' Kim impersonator gets the Open Mic prize, which is a check for five hundred dollars and some free studio time at a popular recording studio located somewhere in the heart of Times Square.

"Hey man, you're Preston Price, right?"

123

David L.

The voice belongs to an artist that I was checking out at a convention one weekend back in my Downtown Record days.
"I just signed with your record company. You and I are going to be working together!"
"Nah, man, I'm not over there no more. I left out of there like a month ago."
Him and I trade small talk for a few moments until I realize I have to be up early tomorrow morning for an early breakfast meeting with a couple of production assistants who are trying to shop a few beat tapes.
"I'll see you around," I say to the MC whose name I don't remember.
In my attempt to head home for a good night's rest, more eager artists run over to me to get some pointers on how to get into the game. One overzealous MC has the nerve to think breaking out in a freestyle rhyme is going to make me sign him on the spot. After kindly informing the hopeful rapper that I have to be up early for another day of work, I jump onto the Jackie Robinson expressway to avoid the construction going on near the Brooklyn Bridge.

It is a little after two o'clock in the morning, and I am wide awake looking up at the ceiling tiles above my bed. Although my body feels tired, my mind is not listening, and I have a sudden burst of energy to do something. But what? Recollecting the day's events, I realize I left at least a dozen messages on Janelle's answering machine.
"So she wants to play hardball, huh?"

Over Your Dead Body

I am now sitting in my SUV in the driveway contemplating whether or not I should head over to her mother's house at this time of night. Turning on the ignition, my mind is made up, and I drive off towards my destination. Thoughts of what to say if she answers the door cross my mind. The rational side of me wants to engage her in a civilized conversation and work something out that is best for the children. The other part of me, the part that worries me, wants to hit her over the head with a shovel!

Mama Pearl's block is especially dark tonight. There are no lights on in anybody's house, making it that much darker when I turn my headlights off and slowly creep up her block. Just when I think I am the only one stupid enough to be out, another car rolls up and parks right smack in front of Mama Pearl's house. Just my luck!

"I knew it!" I say under my breath. "That bitch is cheatin' on me after all!"

Janelle gets out first, followed by none other than the guy that gave me this diminishing welt on my forehead – JOE BANGER! He is profilin' in a spankin' new 2004 Escalade, something Downtown Records probably gave him as part of his signing bonus. My first reaction is to get out and start swinging, but instead do the sensible thing: I wait it out.

Entering her mother's house, Janelle and her accomplice momentarily leave my sight. I contemplate flattening his tires, but quickly realize I would be taking the punk way out. After all, only jealous women run around messing with another man's car or keying it

125

David L.

up. My motive for sitting in my car waiting to see what happens next is still unclear. Before I have a chance to formulate a plan, Joe Banger exits the house and gets into his ride. Janelle is standing at the front door waiting for him to pull off.
    "It's time for some action!"
    I stay at least a half block behind Joe Banger to avoid any unnecessary attention to myself. Every now and then, I put on my turn signal to make like I don't know where I am going. Turning onto a block with a dead end sign, I quickly realize my time to strike back is now. The roads are deserted, and with the exception of a couple lighted gas stations on either side of me, my immediate surroundings are completely barren. Before making my move, I take a deep breath. I haven't had an all out brawl since middle school, and I know my skills are probably rusty. Although Joe Banger is about my size, my best chance at retaliation is to catch him off guard, especially if he is packing a weapon. Hunched over and apparently looking for something in the back seat of his ride, my luck couldn't get any better.
    "Remember me?!"
    I daze him momentarily as he turns around. With a swift barrage of left hooks and uppercuts, I got him bent over like a bitch about to get back shots in the ass.
    "You thought you and your faggot ass boys could walk up into my spot and punk me, huh?"
    "Yo, man, your wife put me up to it! She paid me a thousand bucks to walk up into y'all house that night!"

Over Your Dead Body

Joe Banger's plea for redemption is futile. No wonder Janelle was in such a hurry to run over to the bank and withdraw my money. If what Joe Banger said is even partially true, she is going to have to reap the consequences after I am done with him.

Joe's mouth is busted wide open, and I think I cracked a few ribs because he looks like he is having problems breathing. My adrenalin rush is at an all-time high, whereas Joe Banger is moments from passing out on the side of the road.

"I ain't got no beef wit' you, but the money called my name! You can take the money back, man! Let me go, and you and I can call it even!"

Joe's pleas for forgiveness fuel my indifference. After all, not only did he disrespect me in my own crib, but he is probably bangin' my wife, too! My standing in the community is important to me, and I can't be placed behind bars again. I can still feel those handcuffs tightening around my wrist.

"Where's the money, Joe? And my gun?"

"They're both in the back seat of my truck…in a blue duffel bag."

"Tell me the truth, man…you bangin' my wife?"

"Nah man, nothing like that! She came to me with some money and I took the bait! Nothing more…nothing less!"

Pausing briefly to get my emotions under control, I grab Joe's bag from out of his truck.

"Go 'head and take it!" Joe Banger declares. "I ain't even gonna say nothin', man! You and I are considered even!"

127

David L.

"Nah man...you and I can never be even, muthafucka!" I say with an unexpected rage in my voice that surprises even me.

What happens next is incomprehensible and totally out of my character. Checking the contents of the duffel bag, I grab the one thousand cash and my .380 pistol. My gun is cold to the touch, just like my feelings for Joe Banger and Janelle. It hasn't occurred to me that I should find out his connection with my wife, but right now, I am reacting by pure emotion and logic has undoubtedly taken a back seat. An old song from rapper Nas called "I Gave You Power," in which he raps from the perspective of his gun's point of view, enters my mind. Probably sensing my hesitation, Joe Banger does his best at reverse psychology.

"You ain't gonna shoot me, man! You ain't even built for that!" Joe Banger heckles.

Either this fool is brave or not the brightest guy in the world. I guess he has never had a gun waved in his direction before, because he doesn't even flinch when he makes his ill-timed remark. Either way, he is playing games with the wrong man. Something no one should ever do when you have involved yourself with a man and his family.

"What did you say to me, you faggot ass bitch?"

"I said you won this battle. Now go on back home before you do something you'll regret later! Trust me, you don't want none of me! I can have you killed without even blinking an eye!"

My response is immediate. I aim my gun right at Joe Banger's face until I can see the white of his eyes. He is still not showing any fear.

"Let's be honest, Preston. When was the last time you banged your wife? I was tryin' to do you a favor by telling you that I wasn't hittin' your wife on the regular. To tell you the truth, every time I ran up in her, I had her cummin' in like sixty seconds!"

Joe Banger knows the rules of the game, and one thing a man never does to another man is talk about his sexual indiscretions with his woman. This time, Joe Banger's mouth wasn't going to get him out of this predicament.

Closing my eyes and tightening my grip on the trigger handle of my .380 pistol, a shot is fired, followed by another. The sound of my gun causes me to lose my hearing for several seconds. I haven't used my gun in years. I used to go to the shooting range and practice with it, but the smell of gunpowder is unmistakable. My heart races and my hands shake suddenly as I realize what I have just done.

As I quickly enter my ride, lights begin to come on in people's houses. In other nearby homes, blinds are rolled up and a few people's curtains are pulled back.

"Ain't nobody seen anything," I say quietly to myself, hoping to convince myself that my identity will remain a mystery.

The drive home, although less than a few minutes, feels like over an hour. Pulling up to my driveway, I run into my house for a change of clothing and to get rid of the gun. After wisely reconsidering keeping the gun at my own house, I jump back into my ride and head over to Skip's house – after all…the perfect alibi!

David L.

* * *

If the sign of a sociopath is ambivalence to his intended victim, I would be the poster child. I haven't slept this good in weeks.

"So are you gonna tell me what happened last night or what?" Skip questions.

The smell of bacon burning on the stove has prematurely awakened me to Skip's interrogation. He is standing over me, refusing to leave until I give him an answer.

"I just needed a place to crash, that's all. Can't a man come check his boy out to make sure he is doing alright?"

"Man, who you think you foolin'? You come runnin' up in here early this morning like a damn runaway slave! What stupid thing did you do this time?"

Skip's questioning goes unanswered as I realize I overslept and am already late for work after only my second day at the job.

"I need you to hold this for me," I say to Skip, handing him my gun. Just the mere sight of it brings back in vivid detail my experience with Joe Banger several hours earlier.

"Man, I ain't touching that thing! What did you do – kill Janelle or something?"

Skip is laughing, but my facial expression alerts him to the seriousness of my demeanor.

"Don't tell me you went and really killed Janelle! Hell no, you didn't! That ain't your style!"

"Nah man, I didn't do anything to Janelle. Not this time anyway!"

Over Your Dead Body

"Then what's up with the gun? You got beef with someone? Let me know and we can go and handle it. You know how I gets down!"

"I don't have no beef. Not yet anyway! But I did put a couple of holes in that Joe Banger dude I was telling you about. He's the one that ran up in my house and caught me off guard. He said he did it because Janelle paid him a thousand dollars! Can you believe Janelle would take this so far?"

"Pres, you used your gun? What the hell were you thinking? Ain't your gun registered? Man, you going to have to turn yourself in! It's only going to take a day or so before they trace the shells back to you."

All of my vital organs feel like they have just shut down. Everything happened so fast that I never thought about what would happen if I use my gun.

"I can't turn myself in, Skip! I'm not going to jail! NO WAY!"

"You might not have to go to jail. Think about it! You followed him home because you saw him with Janelle. The two of you got into an argument, and as he pulls out his weapon, you manage to get to your gun that is in your ride, and in a heated moment of fighting, the gun goes off, shooting him. This guy probably has a record a mile long for all we know! Tell the story exactly like that and you will get over. Trust me on this one!"

Skip is a damn genius! He is right. If I hide, I'll appear like I'm guilty or something. However, if I go straight to the police and explain my side of the story, I will look like the victim. Besides, I got the gun out of

David L.

his duffel bag. His fingerprints have to be on the gun, too.

Accompanied by Skip and Uncle Cliff, I follow Skip's advice and immediately head down to the Mount Vernon police station. Inside, I see a bunch of familiar faces and attempt to walk fast to avoid a conversation.

"What up, Preston!" an old acquaintance says, holding his hand out for me to shake. He is an old neighbor of mine from well over ten years ago; however, his wife kicked him out of the house because he was eventually caught with over a pound of marijuana in his possession. Last I'd heard, he was in and out of drug treatment clinics throughout Westchester County.

"You did the right thing by turning yourself in," Detective Adams tells me.

Detective Adams and I know each other very well, as we once both worked together on a drug prevention committee to talk to the neighborhood youth about the dangers of drugs.

"One of the neighbors got your license plate number as you drove away. I was getting ready to leave here in a few minutes to go over to your house to see if you were there."

Handing the detective my gun for evidence, I am seated in an isolated room as Uncle Cliff and Skip are instructed to wait for me in the general lobby area. Walking in with another one of his partners, Detective Adams makes my experience as pleasing as possible. Hell, at one point, he even offers me some coffee and donuts and asks me how the wife and children are doing.

"So Preston, what made you follow this man back to his place and pull your gun out on him?"

"My wife and I have been separated for a while. He dropped her off at her mother's house and they appeared to be arguing. At one point, it looked as if he was about to hit her!"

"So that's why you followed him to his house?"

"I met him a couple of times before. He's actually a recording artist at my last place of employment. I didn't even know he had a place in Mount Vernon."

"Well, according to city hall records, he just bought the house about a month or so ago."

I'm in the interrogation room for about an hour. Everything that comes out of my mouth, Detective Adams stops the tape during our conversation and coaches me on wording it correctly.

"One more question, Preston. Why didn't you come straight here?"

Pausing momentarily to get my story in order, I respond, "I didn't want to turn myself in to anybody but you. Don't get me wrong, but a lot of your co-workers aren't the most honest people in the world."

Nodding his head in apparent agreement, Detective Adams instructs me to keep my mouth shut and not to talk to anyone. I'm then instructed to go home and that he would call me in a few days to follow up on his report. With an ounce of humanity still remaining in my soul, I ask about the status of my alleged assailant.

David L.

"Detective, is he going to be alright?"
"No, he is far from alright. Preliminary reports indicate that he suffered massive hemorrhaging while he laid on the concrete waiting for paramedics to arrive. He is dead."
I am partially relieved because now I have no one to go up against if this case is taken to criminal court. After all, the last time I checked, dead men tell no tales. I have the detective, my unblemished criminal record not counting my recent DUI, and the fact that Joe Banger did have an extensive criminal background on my side. I am in the clear! My thoughts shift to my scandalous wife - Janelle. When she is called in for questioning, and she will be, she is going to say I made up the whole story about her and Joe's argument in front of her mother's house.

Media reports of Joe Banger's death are minimized to a two-liner in the police blotter of the local newspaper which includes a fifteen second recap on the local news channel. More than likely, Janelle has not been notified yet, and all is good as far as I am concerned.
"How are you holdin' up, boy?" Uncle Cliff questions.
"I'm feelin' good. I mean, it's kind of too bad he's dead and all, but oh well…it was me or him! And I chose him!"
Uncle Cliff has always had my back from day one. Ever since my mother passed when I was a young boy, he always made sure I was taken care of.

"If things begin to get hectic or reporters start showing up at the house, you can come crash at my place."

"Thanks, Uncle Cliff. I'll keep that in mind."

As my Uncle Cliff heads home to get some sleep from doing an all-nighter at his bar the night before, Skip and I plan my next course of action.

"You think Janelle is going to go blabbin' to the cops?" Skip questions.

"I don't know, man, but I don't trust her for a minute. With everything that's been happening in the last several weeks, she's likely to do anything."

"Well, remember what that detective told you. Don't go runnin' your big mouth to no one."

"You don't have to worry about that. I ain't talkin' to no one about any of this."

I spend the rest of my day catching up on much-needed rest and looking at old wedding photos of Janelle and me. Thoughts of taking Janelle's life are momentarily suspended as the rush from pulling the trigger is still in my mind. Watching Joe Banger's body drop to the hard concrete is all the incentive I need to know that I handled my business. I don't know what angers me more, the fact that Janelle used him to get at me or him telling me that he has been sexing my wife behind my back! Besides, Janelle is not the only one involved in this crazy, twisted web of deceit. There is only one other person that could've introduced the two of them – Dani!

* * *

David L.

I am working after hours at Destiny Records to make up from lost time yesterday. It is six thirty at night, and besides a couple of cleaning people that speak little or no English, I am in the office by myself. With nothing to do with my time, I go on the Internet to see what is new over at the Downtown Records website.

"Oh snap! They got an album release party over at the Wet Spot for Joe Banger tonight. I bet his ass will be a no-show." I chuckle under my breath.

Trying my best to keep a low profile, I call up a local cab service to bring me home.

"Keep the change," I tell the cab man that graciously followed the various shortcuts I gave him to get me home even faster.

"Hey Preston, hold up a second!"

My nosy next-door neighbor is running down his front steps in a robe and slippers trying his best to get my attention.

"What's up, Mr. Brown? Everything alright?"

"I know it ain't my business, but…well, are you messin' around on your wife? What I mean is…you got some woman that's mad at you or something?"

"No, sir. Why you ask me that?"

Mr. Brown points over to my Range Rover that is parked in the driveway.

"Damn! What happened to my truck?"

"I heard an alarm going off, and when I came out to see what was going on, some female drove off quickly in a rental car."

"How do you know it was a rental car?"

"'Cause there was a big Hertz Rent-A-Car sticker on the rear bumper."

"Janelle is out of control!"

"Oh no, it wasn't Janelle. I know that for a fact. I know what your wife looks like, and it definitely wasn't Janelle."

"Are you able to give a description of who did it then?"

"Nope, it all happened too fast. By the time I got to my window, she drove off."

Mr. Brown gives his apologies and returns to the confines of his home, leaving me to the remains of my Range Rover. Upon closer inspection, every single window has been broken every tire flattened and my leather seats ripped to shreds with what looks to have been the work of a razorblade! I wonder aloud the amount of time it must have taken to do all of this damage and why it took so long for my alarm to go off. Mr. Brown was wrong. Janelle might not have directly done this, but she is definitely the mastermind behind it. I am willing to bet my last dollar bill on that.

I got a picture of Malcolm X in my den that accurately portrays the way I am feeling. It is the one where he is holding out his rifle, looking sideways out of a window – fighting for his life! Going to sleep is not an option tonight. I still have vivid memories of Joe Banger and his goon squad entering the sanctuary that is my home, promptly leaving with my children. Even more so, my unwarranted beating by his hands is still fresh in my mind. A visual of Janelle and one of her homegirls, probably Shontell, coming back to finish off the work done to my Range Rover is also not helping me want to close my eyes anytime soon.

David L.

Instead, I stay up all night by my bedroom window writing about my plans to take out my enemies. Wisely, I change all of their names on paper to avoid future prosecution. On my wish list of executions, I place a check mark next to the created name of "Jim Boogie."

"If this list is ever found, no one will ever know I changed everyone's names but only kept the first letter of their names," I whisper.

Second on my wish list is Dani, or "Deena." After all, she got me fired from Downtown Records and probably co-conspired my whole set-up with Janelle. And for the grand finale – Janelle, or "Jessica." I got to save the best for last! Placing an asterisk at the bottom of the list, I write "Shanice," which is my code name for Shontell. I am putting her on my list just in case I find out that bitch is the one responsible for smashing up my Range Rover. Placing my list of names in an envelope with the words "DO NOT OPEN" on it, I place a stamp and Skip's address on it and leave it on the dresser so I can mail it off tomorrow when I leave for work.

* * *

The last week and a half has been crazy over at Destiny Records. My secretary with the nasty attitude has called in sick for the last three days, two of my morning appointments have cancelled on me, and my new boss, Abe Silverstein, has me going over to some hole in the wall nightclub later on tonight to scout some unsigned acts for his urban music department. Mr. Silverstein is one of those typical rich guys with no knowledge of the urban music industry, but figures if everyone else can make money off of it, why can't he. With not much to do before it is time for me to leave to meet up with Skip, I check the messages at home. One message that stands out is from Dr. Rogers, our marriage therapist. Doing as requested, I call him back and this time, I get his voice mailbox.

"Dr. Rogers, this is Preston Price calling you back. You called the house and left me a message about possibly coming in with Janelle for some much-needed counseling. I don't think I am going to be able to make it in there anytime soon. Thanks anyway."

Too much has happened in the last month for me to think about therapy now. Besides, Janelle probably wouldn't even show up. Instead, I plan to take out my frustrations on Skip and some of our boys in a game of basketball. With no gear to play in, I have to pillage through my car garage for a pair of basketball shorts and some sneakers.

"Yo Skip, this was a good idea to get a membership here at the 'Y'."

Today is our first official day at the gym. It was Skip's brilliant plan to get back in shape for the summer and flex for the ladies. Shontell probably made some sarcastic remark about his emerging potbelly and now he wants to use the gym as an excuse to get back into shape.

"One more body up in here and we can get a full court game," Skip responds.

My two for ten at the three-point line alarms me to the fact that my once lethal jumper is taking an unplanned hiatus.

David L.

"Watch the master get busy!" Skip remarks.

Similar to my vanishing jump shot, Skip goes three for ten, doing his best to downplay his lackluster performance.

"That's still one more than you! Besides, here comes my man Clyde walking in now! Now we got enough for a full court game!"

Clyde's face looks vaguely familiar. Oh yeah! I helped get him a job about a year and a half ago working out of the Mayor's office. He is a reformed crack head that was in a drug treatment program I was sponsoring for my Stay Away From Drugs campaign several years ago.

"Hey, Preston Price. Good to see you again, brother," he says, walking towards me.

Clyde is looking as clean and healthy as probably ever in his life, and has added some weight to his once bony frame.

"Thanks again for everything, man. I recently got married and have been clean for approximately four hundred and ninety eight days and counting."

"That's a good thing, man! That means you owe me, right? You can pay me back by making me look good out here on the court today!"

Although I am somewhat serious in my remarks, Clyde ignores my sacrificial request and scores half of his team's points on me. He ends the mostly lopsided blowout by swishing a three-pointer right in my face.

"Sorry I had to do that to you, Pres. I'll see you around."

And like that, Clyde disappears into the locker room, leaving me with an aching back and four

Over Your Dead Body

teammates who are mad at me for not playing better defense. As bad as I may feel right now, I instinctively know I am going to be hurting that much more tomorrow morning.

"My boy Clyde sure bust dat ass up good!" Skip sarcastically says.

"That's alright. I'm out of shape right now, but I got something for him the next time I see him! So anyways, what's up wit' you and Shontell?"

"Everything is everything! I mean, I told you before she ain't my girl or anything like that. That's just something to hit right now for the moment. Why do you ask?"

"No reason. Well, I mean 'cause she's on my list of names, that's all."

"What list? What names? Why are you talkin' in code?"

"Nothing. Oh yeah, did you get something in the mail from me yet? A letter that says 'Do Not Open' on it?"

"Yeah, I've been meanin' to ask you about that! What's that all about?"

"Just do as the letter says, and don't open it no matter what...at least not yet anyway. Just be patient. You will have all the answers you are looking for in due time."

I can sense my unwillingness to reveal what it is I am talking about is beginning to mess with Skip's mind. Whenever Skip is annoyed about something, he changes the subject to fit his needs.

"So Pres, you going to see that stripper from the Nasty Kitty again?"

David L.

That's a low blow! But then how could he know what went down in his own house? There is no way I am telling Skip that a stripper played me like a trick and ran off with my money.

"I don't know. It was a good piece of ass and all, but she does that for a living. I ain't tryin' to be seen wit' no stripper. I might want to run for Mayor of Mount Vernon or somethin' one day."

With my ride in the body shop still waiting to be fixed, Skip drops me off at my house.

"You comin' in to get spanked in a game of Madden football?"

"Nah, man. I'm pickin' Shontell up from the hair salon. I'll hang out wit' you tonight over at that spot on Tillary Avenue in Brooklyn that your boss is sending you to."

"Alright then, pick me up around nine o'clock."

There has to be at least thirty to forty men and women inside of "The Tav" tonight. Respectable numbers since it was recently closed down about a month ago for a shooting which is still unresolved.

"How did your boss find out 'bout this place?" Skip questions.

"Man, I don't even know! For a white boy, he is on top of his game, though. I heard he started Destiny Records a few years back after paying his dues as a promoter out in Staten Island somewhere for like twenty years."

"That's what I'm talking about! I want to open up a chain of Chinese fast food spots all across the five boroughs some day."

"You are a fool, Skip! What the hell do you know about starting up a Chinese restaurant?"

"You the fool, Pres! Don't you know Black people love Chinese food more than they love any other kind of food? I would make a fortune!"

"Yeah, well, you don't want to make too much money with your Chinese restaurant scheme because 'whitey' is going to make you give half of it to your ex-wife."

"That was a low blow, man. Besides, you shouldn't be talking. You ain't too far away from dealing with that your damn self."

Point well taken! I've already gotten several reasons to off Janelle, and after what Skip just said, I now have one more reason!

The Tav has been operating as an underground gambling spot slash number running joint for many years. Even back in the days when I was a shortie, The Tav used to always be on the news for a shootout or a drug bust. Big Al, the owner, greets me with a firm hug. Him and I go back to my younger years when I used to hand out promotional flyers for him for a local promoter way out in Brownsville, Brooklyn.

"What up, Big Al! Anything happening out here tonight that I need to know about?"

"I couldn't even begin to tell you, young buck. Anything is bound to jump off at any given moment around these parts. You know that."

"Don't forget I used to get you all the young, sexy girlies from back in the day to come up in here and spend their money."

David L.

"I know that! Why you think I take care of you whenever you decide to show up and check me out for old times sakes!"

"That's nothing! I'm loyal, Big Al! I'll always have your back!"

Skip, the renowned party lover, slaps hands with the mostly male crowd. Over at the corner of the bar, two young twenty-something-year-olds eye me seductively. I am on to their game and avoid direct eye contact. I will be damned if I'm going to be set up by another female, especially one in The Tav.

"You cost me five hundred bucks the other night, man!" a voice from behind bellows.

"Are you talkin' to me?"

"Yeah, man. You and I both know I was the hottest MC out there at the contest! How you going to let that wack ass girl with her weak ass rhymes take the prize home?"

The "prize" he is talking about is from the Open Mic contest the other night.

"Hold up a minute, brother. I wanted you to win that contest. I thought you were the best out there that night. Those two other judges wanted the girl to win. They thought if she won, they could get with her after the contest was over."

"You serious?"

"I'm dead serious. You had a tight-ass flow and your rhymes went together perfectly. Y If you ask me, you had the total package."

Pleased with my response, the up-and-coming MC goes about his business, but not before I hand him one of my business cards and instruct him to stop by my office in the next few days to talk some more. Just

Over Your Dead Body

as I think my trip over to The Tav was in vain, I hear an MC who literally takes his craft to the next level. He goes by the moniker of "Almighty Divine." It is a fitting title based on his skill level and vocal delivery.

As expected, Skip and I wait as hungry fans, self-proclaimed "industry heads," and record company personnel court the coveted MC with promises of future fame and wealth. When it is my turn to approach Almighty Divine, I hit him with all the charisma I can muster with such short notice.

"That was one hell of a performance you put on out there tonight, man!"

"Thanks a lot, man. I appreciate all the love. I've been hittin' the streets for a minute now tryin' to make this rap thing happen."

Five minutes speaking with the young MC and I realize that not only is he talented as hell, but very humble, too, which is an extremely hard combination to find in this modern day rap game. He is not adorned in too much gaudy jewelry, and he talks as if he has already been coached by a publicist. I know there is no such thing as the perfect rap artist, but damn, he is close to it!

"Let me get right to the point, man. I want you to be my first marquee artist over at Destiny Records. Do you have a manager?"

"Yeah, I got a manager. If you have a card, I'll have him give you a call in the next couple of days. He was supposed to be here tonight, but he got caught up in traffic over on the FDR."

David L.

"Yeah, I can definitely relate to that! Tell your manager to call me as soon as he gets a chance. Maybe we can all do something together."

Almighty Divine signs a few more autographs for his fans and promptly exits The Tav. Skip, who always has his ear to the streets, is always a bonus when he accompanies me to these types of events. Very opinionated and direct, he is hard to please and a very tough character to sell.

"Dude was good, man. Real good! He did his thing on the mic tonight!"

"Yeah, I know. I want him. I want him bad. But I don't want him to know that."

"Well, make sure you sign him before someone else beats you to it. That dude is not going to stay a free agent for long."

"Yo Skip, trust me when I tell you this: He is mine!"

* * *

I am in New Rochelle Family Court waiting to see the judge. Sitting in an all white-walled room filled with lost souls, I quickly realize my life is officially in ruins.

"Mr. and Mrs. Price? Are you here?" a voice from the back calls out.

Both half asleep from waiting in the courtroom since nine thirty this morning, Janelle and I barely hear our names called. The time is now twelve noon, and we both take a seat in a back room of the family mediation section of the courtroom. Introductions are made and explanations as to why Janelle and I are here today are explained once again. It seems that in order to get her divorce papers finalized, mediation has to be first attempted since we have not been legally separated from each other for at least one year.

Giving my side of the story, I purposely leave out all of Janelle's attempts to destroy my life. Similarly, Janelle leaves out damaging evidence that would undoubtedly lead to further questioning and legal involvement.

"You can both have a seat back in the lobby. A judge will review your request for a divorce shortly," the female mediator announces.

Not surprisingly, the entire time we wait in the lobby, there is no conversation between Janelle and myself. No wandering eye contact, just a cold, emotionless stare on each of our faces. The once crowded lobby filled with crying babies and quarreling couples is a distant past. Left are Janelle, myself, and an aging court officer trying his best to stay awake.

"Janelle and Preston Price! Please present yourself!" a voice booms through the once closed courtroom doors.

On cue, Janelle and I enter, and what took us over four and a half hours to wait for, is over in a little under ten minutes. Surprisingly, Janelle admits to her infidelity, probably knowing if she does not, by law we would have to wait one year before the divorce can be finalized. After a few papers are stamped and testimonies are made for the court's records, Janelle and I are given the green light to depart the courtroom.

Outside, I follow Janelle over to her car and speak to her directly for the first time.

David L.

"I want to see my children, Janelle. I want to see them now!"

"Or else what? You're going to shoot me like you did Joe? I don't think you got the guts!"

My poker face is on full blast. Although we both know who was behind the shooting several weeks ago, today is the first time it has been brought out into the open for discussion.

"You runnin' around tellin' people that? While you're doin' that, are you tellin' them about how you paid Joe one thousand dollars of my own money that you took from my bank account to run up in my house to bring the children back to you? Or how you tried to destroy my Range Rover? You tell anyone that?"

Janelle is silent for the first time in years. She is either trying to formulate her next excuse or devising her next plan to get at me.

"You think you so smart, huh, Preston? You really think I would go through all of that? You ain't even worth it! And as for Joe, I'm glad you took him out! He was no good in bed anyway! Just like you!"

Janelle's unnecessary taunts about my sexual prowess do not do anything to faze me. After all, our marriage is over anyway. My only concern from this point on is being with my children. I realize at this point that a mutually agreed upon visitation schedule is nowhere near good enough. This bitch is crazy for real! I have to take Destiny and DeShaun from her, and no court is going to let me do that legally.

"What is it going to be, Janelle? You should already know by now I'm not going to just let you keep me from my children!"

"You ain't got no choice, Preston! HELP! SOMEONE HELP ME…PLEASE!" Janelle screams at the top of her lungs.

"What the hell is your problem, Janelle?"

Her screams for help continue until two overweight court officers coming off of their lunch breaks attempt to intervene.

"Miss, are you alright?" one officer questions.

"No, I'm not alright! Do I look alright? This man is trying to kill me! He is threatening to hurt me if I don't leave with him!"

"I'm not trying to kill her! She just started screaming for no reason! She is crazy!"

The other officer begins to inch closer to me, as if to say he is ready to make his move just in case Janelle is telling the truth.

"I just want to go home and not have to worry about him following me!"

"Sir, we need you to remain here while she leaves to go home," the first court officer says.

Privately admitting defeat for now, I decide to do the sensible thing and let Janelle go home. After all, I know where she is staying anyway. Standing helplessly while Janelle drives off to be with my children is beginning to become a habit! The two court officers return to their posts only after they are assured I can no longer pose a threat to my alleged victim.

* * *

"So Pres, you want me to throw you a divorce party?" Skip questions.

David L.

We are both hanging out at a local pool hall just up the block from his apartment. The last time I was here, I almost had a fight with some clown who was pissed off because I took him for about eighty dollars on the pool table.

"What the hell is a divorce party?"

"It's just what it sounds like. You have a party to celebrate your divorce! I had one. It was the best day of my life."

"That has got to be the most ghetto thing I have ever heard of in my life. I ain't havin' no damn divorce party!"

Skip begins to laugh and takes his shot at the eight ball. Another miss.

"Damn! My shot has been off all night!"

"Your shot has been off ever since I met you."

"Let's see if you can do any better."

"Double or nothing says I can."

Hitting the eight ball into the side pocket off of two bumpers, I raise my hands in victory.

"That's how you do it, baby! Go get my drink, loser!"

Doing as instructed, Skip motions for the waitress to bring another shot of Absolut for me and a rum and Coke for him. The evening shift must have just changed, because from out of the back comes the most gorgeous waitress I have ever seen in my thirty plus years of life.

"Who got the Absolut?" she asks.

"That would be me," I proudly declare.

Although I am usually the shy, introverted one, the dim lights of the pool hall and my recent divorce status has me feeling brave.

"I've never seen you in here before. You must be new, huh?"

"Yeah, I was over at Rollo's pool hall over in Co-op City before this."

"I think I'm going to have to start coming here more often. What's your name?"

"I'm Cassandra."

"If the two of you are finished flirtin' wit' each other, I would like to get another chance to redeem myself over at the pool table."

Cassandra and I both laugh, partly because we both know Skip is right. We are kind of flirting with each other, and it is not until she is called away to pick up some more drinks that we stop talking to one another – at least for the moment.

"You can't ever not be wit' a woman, huh, Pres?"

"What do you mean by that?"

"I mean, you just got out of a crazy marriage and here you are at it again!"

"Calm down, man. I ain't tryin' to marry the girl. I'm just messin' wit' her, that's all."

"I've known you for damn near all your life and you have never been the kind of guy that just messes with someone."

"You should talk…days after hooking up with Shontell and now she is like your main piece of ass all of a sudden!"

"You just hatin', that's all! Just make sure you don't leave out of here tonight without at least getting her phone number."

Sure enough, by night's end, Cassandra and I have traded phone numbers and I promise to call her

David L.

by the end of the week. With a renewed sense of hope in the opposite sex, I head out the pool hall with Skip who is still pissed off because I beat his ass again on the pool table.

Over Your Dead Body

CHAPTER SIX

June 20, 2004 ~ Father's Day
It is extra packed today at the New Hope Baptist Church. Men and women who have not visited church since Easter are all in attendance. My rationale for being here today is of a devious nature, but I am sure GOD will understand why I am doing what it is I have planned.

Today, I am in church to follow Janelle home afterwards. She is no longer living with her mother and I am dying to see my son and daughter. Today, I may not get a Father's Day gift from Destiny or DeShaun, but I will be damned if the next man gets to enjoy their company.

Today's sermon is about the importance of family and the downfall of the nuclear family. How ironic! Maybe it is my own paranoia, but I could swear at least three people seated in front of me looked over when the words "broken family" was uttered during the service.

Thirty minutes into the service and people are still walking in from the streets. Church members are lined up against the wall and standing in the hallway as I thank myself in silence for getting here early this morning for a seat. One lady in front of me who is singing a horrible rendition of "Amazing Grace" almost causes me to burst out in laughter. Surprisingly,

David L.

the church service does not run too much over, but I still have not seen Janelle anywhere inside.

"Happy Father's Day, Preston. Where is the family today?" Mrs. Gertrude questions.

She is the neighborhood "gossip queen" and I am sure she is just testing me to see how I will respond to her.

"Janelle and the children went out of town. I couldn't go with them because I had to work."

She has a doubtful look on her face like she knows the real deal, but she does not let on.

"That's too bad. I heard your little one is walking now."

"Yeah, he sure is!" I put on my best poker face, but something within me makes me think she knows I am lyin' my ass off.

I catch a glimpse of a few of the children from the church choir playing over by the church yard and walk over to say what's up. They stop whatever it is they are doing, and if I did not know any better, I would think they were up to something. Sure enough, the lingering smell of cigarette smoke is in the air.

"What are y'all doin' back here behind the church? And don't even try to lie to me."

"Nothing," one child responds. "We were just hanging out."

They are all children I know from the neighborhood: two boys and two girls who all range in age from about fourteen to sixteen.

"I smell cigarette smoke back here! Are y'all tryin' to pull a fast one on me or something?"

"Nah, nothing like that, Preston. You not going to tell my father, are you?" another child questions.

154

Over Your Dead Body

I immediately recollect a time in my younger years when I cut school one day with Skip. We were both about twelve years old and got caught smoking cigarettes in the back of my house by my next door neighbor.

"No, I'm not going to tell...THIS TIME! But don't let me catch you back here again messin' around. Is that a deal?"

"You won't. We'll wait 'til we get home next time," another child says, laughing at my concern.

"You guys listen to those gospel CDs I donated to the church?"

"Nah, not really. I use it for an ashtray personally," one child declares.

He is the smart mouth one of the group, the one the others usually end up listening to and getting into trouble with because that is all he knows how to do. Not wanting to waste my good intentions on deaf ears, I give each child a hug and go about my business.

"See ya later, Preston!" they all say to me, pulling out another cigarette in front of me, probably waiting to see what my reaction would be.

"Alright y'all. Peace out!"

* * *

I must be losing my competitive edge because it takes me a little over two weeks to snare a meeting with Almighty Divine and his manager, Louie Burns. This guy, Louie Burns, is rumored to be one of the fastest talking, slickest cats in the record business when it comes to getting his artists whatever it is they want. I am accompanied by my boss, Abe Silverstein,

David L.

in the boardroom to discuss the specifics of today's meeting. After some pleasantries are exchanged between the four of us, we get down to business.

"So Mr. Burns, what kind of time frame are you looking at in terms of your artist's record coming out?" I diplomatically question.

"I'm a practical guy, Mr. Price. I would say ten, maybe twelve months – TOPS!"

"That sounds pretty reasonable, and it sounds as if we can make that happen for him. What about advance money and publishing percentages?"

"Now Preston, don't be so impulsive," my boss Mr. Silverstein interrupts. "We got plenty of time to talk about all that stuff."

Almighty Divine is busy scribbling something a piece of paper, which he passes to his manager to review. He is staying uncharacteristically quiet, wisely allowing his manager to do all of the talking for him.

"My client wants to know if he can eventually purchase his masters in the event that the relationship does not work out for whatever reason…for the right buyout figure of course."

Sensing a downhill battle on the horizon, I immediately interject.

"Well, that's not really the conventional thing that normally happens in the record business. It really doesn't happen too often, especially for an artist who hasn't even put out his first single yet."

"Well, we got a similar offer that you're proposing over at Downtown Records, except there is a clause that states my client could conceivably purchase the rights to his masters after his fifth record release."

Over Your Dead Body

More phone numbers are exchanged and everyone shakes hands at the conclusion of today's meeting. I could not really tell if the meeting was a success or not, but only time will tell. I know Downtown Record's history, and they can be pretty persuasive when they want to be. And as far as relinquishing the rights to his masters – well, I made that mistake before! This time, I am not going to be too eager to give in so quickly if I can help it. As Almighty Divine exits the boardroom with his manager, I notice an inquisitive look on my boss' face.

"Downtown Records? Who over there offered this guy a chance at his masters? You used to work there, Preston. Who could want that contract for Almighty Divine so bad that they would offer him a chance at his masters?"

Pausing for a brief moment and looking down to the floor to gather my thoughts, only one name enters my mind: Dani!

I'm doing something after work that I swore I would never do in my life...I am sitting at a local bar in the city enjoying a drink – BY MYSELF! Not exactly drowning my sorrows, I am sipping on a weak-ass rum and Coke that has not yet offered me the slightest buzz. This bar does not exactly put me in a better mood because it is a place Dani and I used to hang out at when she first came over to Downtown Records a few years ago. Thinking about her early days at Downtown Records brings a slight smile to my face. She was the most eager, relentless worker out of the bunch of us – with the exception of me, that is! She was so eager to prove her worth that she used to come

David L.

into the office at least an hour before she was supposed to be there just to get a head start on everyone else. Habits she picked up from me are now coming back to haunt me. How was she able to even snag a meeting with Louie Burns and Almighty Divine before me? Damn, she is good! But no matter how eager and relentless she may be, I have to keep reminding myself that I am the teacher and she is just the student. There is no way I could ever live with myself knowing she was able to take an artist from under my nose – NO WAY!

"Care for another one?" the bartender asks.

I graciously decline and gather up my stack of papers in front of me to leave. As I exit, it immediately occurs to me that I never called that girl Cassandra from the pool hall. Locating her number on my speed dial, I let the phone ring and leave her a message on her voice mail. I am about halfway home and Cassandra's number comes up on my phone screen. We continue to talk for the entire ride as I pull up to the front of my house.

"So what are you doin' tonight?" I question, hoping maybe the two of us can find somewhere to get a bite to eat – or something else.

Agreeing to my request, Cassandra and I finally decide to meet over at Sammy's Diner on White Plains Road in the Bronx. While I am in the company of Cassandra, I temporarily forget about all of my family and work problems.

"So Preston, you never told me what it is you do for a living."

"I guess you can say I am kind of like a talent scout. I sign artists to my record company and help

Over Your Dead Body

them out with their albums. I kind of oversee the entire creative process."

"That sounds like a very interesting job. I used to sing when I was younger."

"Oh, you did, huh? I bet you could sing really well, too."

"I used to get down back in the day. Maybe one day I will let you hear me."

"I'm going to be looking forward to that day, too. I have to make sure I don't do anything to lose touch with you before that happens."

"I'm sure you won't do anything to make that happen. You look like a real sweetheart. Sweet and sensitive."

"You make me sound like a punk or something. You aren't comparing me to Mr. Sensitivity Ralph Tresvant, are you?"

"How about sweet and thoughtful? Does that sound better?"

"Yeah, much better. I think I like the way that sounds."

We spend the rest of the evening enjoying each other's presence, and at the same time, learning more and more about each other as the night grows longer. Who would have guessed immediately after my untimely divorce from Janelle, I would find someone I am attracted to…and so quickly! All of the signs show I have the go ahead to kiss Cassandra goodnight, but I wisely back off from my instincts. I remember Uncle Cliff telling me a long time ago that if you kiss a girl goodnight the first time you take her out, she runs out of things to look forward to the second time around. How insightful coming from a man who thinks treating

159

David L.

a woman to dinner means asking her if she would like fries with her hamburger!

"I am going to talk to you sometime again real soon, right?" I question with just a hint of suspicion in my voice.

"I sure hope so!" she gratefully responds.

Cassandra has a wide-eyed smile on her face, which minimizes my suspicion about her interest in me. Walking her to her front door like Uncle Cliff taught me, I wait patiently for her to walk inside and then go home to get ready for another day at the job.

* * *

It does not take Skip long to convince me to go with him over to the Nasty Kitty tonight. There is a small part of me that wants to slap the taste out of Mocha's mouth if I see her here tonight, but my common sense prevails for once in my life. After all, it was me that violated rule number one of the game of life – and I was promptly punished because of it!

"Yo Skip, I know you got some weed on you, right?"

"Do I have weed? Now you are talking, Pres baby! When did you start smoking weed again?"

"I haven't. For some reason, I just got this crazy impulse to get high tonight. Do you have any problems with that?"

"Hell no! You're a grown ass man. But I must say, it's about time you stop acting like a punk and live a little!"

Over Your Dead Body

"Oh, I'm a punk now 'cause I don't run the streets like you? Or is it because I went and got me an education that makes me soft?"

Skip gives me one of those looks like he has no idea what I am talking about. Maybe I am just rambling, but I just released over a decade of jokes at my expense because I didn't hang out on the block and smoke my life away like most of our friends from the old neighborhood. Either way, I got my point across pretty explicitly! With one hand on the steering wheel, Skip reaches into a tiny compartment just above his vanity mirror and hands me a small plastic bag.

"You got any cigars?" I question.

"Damn, that's what I forgot to pick up!"

Making a wild U-turn, Skip heads to the nearest corner bodega so we can light up. Although I have not smoked in a little over a decade, I can tell right away this is not any regular weed. My high from the questionable contents are immediate.

"What the hell is in this stuff, Skip? It's got me feeling real crazy!"

"That right there is the good stuff, man...the real deal...stuff that will make you want to walk up to someone and slap the taste out of their mouth...just for living!"

"Muthafucka, just tell me what's in it!"

"It's weed mixed with angel dust."

Skip's mouth is moving in slow motion as the words are uttered.

"Man, are you fucking insane or something? You gave me angel dust to smoke? I ain't no damn dust head! I knew I shouldn't have fucked with you tonight!"

161

David L.

"Chill out, Pres. It ain't gonna kill you. I've been lacing my stuff with it for a few months now. I get it from one of my boys out in Canarsie. Why do you think I'm always making trips out to Brooklyn like every other week?"

My high is now in overdrive and I swear Skip's car is not touching the ground! I got my head out of the window and the night breeze is hitting me in the face. I'm hoping it will lessen my high, but it has no effect.

"Slow down, Skip! You're driving too fast! You're going to get us killed!"

"Damn, Pres, you must be high as hell! I'm only moving like ten miles an hour!"

Every after school special and "Just Say No" campaign I have ever seen flashes in and out of my mind. I think of all the people who are in drug rehabs across the country. Is this how they got their start, too? Am I going to turn out to be like one of them after this is all over?

"What are you sitting there daydreaming for, Pres? Get out of the car! We're here!"

The Nasty Kitty looks different tonight, but I know it is only the angel dust making me think like that. The first thing I want to do after I get through security is go and choke Mocha if she happens to be working. Luckily for her, a big three hundred plus security guard informs me that she is not working again until next week.

"Check out that one over there!" I blurt out, pointing to a big-breasted Asian hottie working the pole directly in front of us.

"You ever bang a Chinese girl before?" Skip questions.

162

Over Your Dead Body

"Nope, not yet, but before tonight ends, I might be telling you something different."

"You must think you are the man or something! You really think you going to bang another stripper from up in here? You ain't me! Your skills ain't that on point!"

"Whatever. Just give me until the end of the night, and you're going to be saying something entirely different! The last thing you want to do is sleep on my skills!"

Not even five minutes inside the club and I am breaking the most important rule: Never spend all your time or money with just one girl. The Asian hottie I eyed while walking in has now made out with at least fifty of my hard-earned dollars. To make matters worse, she is acting all stuck up and will not even let me get in any cheap feels for all the money I just spent on her.

"Let me get four shots of Absolut," I say, handing the sexy bartender my money.

My angel dust high is at its peak as I slam down all four shots, one after the other. Skip has left me to get himself a lap dance from a big-ass chick with nipple rings and a large tattoo of a dragon on her lower back. With each passing moment, the strobe lights spinning on the ceiling cause my head to spin. Two female patrons that look to be lesbians are sitting in a corner watching my every move. Either they want to get involved in some type of unholy threesome, or they are looking for their next naïve victim to set up.

I have been back and forth twice so far to the bathroom and there is no sign of Skip. As loud as he can be when he is having fun, he should not be too

David L.

hard to find. Knocking down my last shot of Absolut for the night, I hit the bartender off with a generous tip. Just as I reach for my car keys, I realize I did not drive tonight. As I flag down a cab to take me home, a thought enters my mind...thoughts of revenge against my trifling ex-coworker Dani.

"You need a ride or what pal?" the cab driver yells out.

Waving him off, I immediately realize I am only a few blocks from where Dani lives and begin to walk in the direction of her house.

I have no idea why I am sitting on Dani's steps trying to count all the stars that are out tonight. Skip's sorry ass has not even called to see if I am alright. Hell, he is probably still in the middle of a lap dance. Either that or he ran out of the joint to meet up with Shontell. I should be worried my high has not worn off yet, but I am too focused on Dani's house. Her lights are all off and her car is not even in the driveway...a sure sign that she is not home yet. Just as I begin my walk to the nearest lighted corner to catch me a cab home, I see from a distance headlights moving closer towards me. Headlights that look to belong to Dani's car, and sure enough, my intuition is correct. I get a flashback to my high jumping days back when I was in junior high and leap into her bushes to avoid detection.

"Good, she's by herself," I whisper under my breath as she pulls into her driveway.

While I am spitting dirt out of my mouth from my lunge into her bushes, she is busy looking at a section of her newspaper.

"Get out of the car, bitch. I'm beginning to cramp up," I whisper.

Just as my words are uttered, Dani exits her jet black BMW convertible and heads towards me. I inch myself deeper into her bushes to prevent her from seeing me. Dani stops at her top step, reaches into her mailbox to gather her mail, and then proceeds to unlock her door. My next move has to be exact and precise.

"WHAT THE HELL…?" Dani blurts out as I pounce on her, tackling her to the ground right inside her doorway.

Before she has the opportunity to scream for help, I place my hand over her mouth to muffle her voice. I watch in glee as her face turns a light shade of blue from either lack of oxygen or fright.

"GODDAMN!" I squeal out loud as Dani manages to catch me off guard with a well-timed kick right smack in my ribs.

I hit her with everything I got as she tries to stand up, and she falls right back to the ground. She is a feisty woman and pretty strong in her own right, but she does not stand a chance – and I think she knows that!

"Why are you doin' this?" she pleas helplessly.

"Why am I doin' this? You can't really be asking me that now, can you?"

"Don't do this, Preston…PLEASE! Your wife is relentless when she wants to be! She paid me money from your bank account to get you fired so you wouldn't stand a chance against her when she filed for divorce!"

David L.

"But why? If she wanted a divorce that bad, I would've given it to her!"

"She needed insurance in case you tried to take the kids from her. That's why she had Joe Banger catch you off guard in your house."

So now it is finally beginning to make some sense! I knew Janelle was the mastermind behind this whole thing, but now I have all the proof I need. With each attempt to stand on her two feet, I drop Dani back down to the ground with either a right hook or an uppercut. She must be trying to inch her way to the kitchen for some type of weapon because she is giving it all she has to get somewhere in a hurry.

"And just where do you think you are going?" I question as I connect with another mighty blow to the side of her head.

"Preston, don't do this! I'm begging you! You're going to kill me!"

"That's the idea, bitch! You really think I can leave here tonight knowing you will go straight to the cops? You think I'm that stupid?"

Dani is now silent, and her once beautiful face is a pale remnant of what once was. Each blow I throw in Dani's direction becomes more aggressive in force. At one point, I cock back and unleash a blow that draws blood, causing droplets to land aimlessly on her living room curtain. Dani is beginning to bleed from her nose and mouth, and within seconds, her once all-white shirt is blood-stained. She is becoming visibly desperate in her attempt to thwart my hostile advances because she reaches onto her living room counter and flings her remote control in my direction.

Over Your Dead Body

    Dani's helplessness continues to fuel my already-inflated rage, and I am smiling from ear to ear. With one last gasp of will and determination, Dani finally gets to her feet; however, her quest for redemption is denied as I again connect with everything I can muster. She immediately falls backwards onto her television with a force which causes the screen to crack. I draw a blank stare as Dani remains motionless. A few more minutes go by and still no movement from Dani. I check for a pulse, and as I suspect, there is none. Dani's eyes are wide open, but she is as dead to the world as Elvis. Even Dani's death does not diminish my angel dust high, and instead of fleeing the scene of my heinous crime, I lay down in a fit of exhaustion and fall asleep on Dani's sofa.

    I wash my hands and face in Dani's kitchen sink as if nothing happened hours earlier. I must have been asleep for at least five or six hours. Her bloody corpse remains next to her broken television set, and the sight of her carcass strangely brings a smile to my face...almost a type of renewed sense of hope in my own cry for justice and redemption to the ones that have wronged me. Finally down from my high, I return to my senses and plan my escape route out of Dani's house. The morning sun radiates brightly, and one neighbor across the street is taking out his trash. Placing a towel over the doorknob to cover my fingerprints and exiting out of Dani's house through the back door, I spot an alleyway a few houses down and make my move to safety.

David L.

"Yo Skip, I need you to pick me up in front of the Nasty Kitty in about five minutes," I say, leaving a message on his phone.

I am standing in front of the nudie bar for over thirty minutes before I come to the realization that Skip is a no-show. With even more time to gather my thoughts, I conclude Dani's death will be discovered in probably less than twenty-four hours. After all, not only was her front door left wide open during our all-out scuffle, but the smell of her deceased frame will begin to spread outside soon on this warm, spring day.

* * *

Three days pass before Dani's name shows up in the Daily News police blotter section. Luckily for me, Skip only reads the sports section, so I don't need to do any unwanted explaining. Besides, he doesn't know her last name anyway.

"When was the last time you saw your children?" Skip questions, stuffing what is left of a Subway sandwich into his mouth.

"It's been a couple of weeks at least. I have a court date tomorrow for joint custody."

"Good luck, man. You know the legal system is out to bring down Black men anyway."

"C'mon now, it ain't even like that. They're going to have to give me at least joint custody. I make more money than Janelle, and I probably know at least half of the people at that damn courthouse."

"You can't be that stupid, Pres! The man don't care how much money you got. He just wants to destroy the Black man. And how do you do that? You take away his Black family, that's how. Wait 'til tomorrow…you'll see what I'm talkin' about."

Skip's ongoing ranting and raving of "the man" has me visibly worried about tomorrow's court date. Uncle Cliff promised to accompany me, but even his presence is not going to be enough to guarantee my parental and GOD-given right to be with my children.

"So where did you end up going the other night?" Skip asks, interrupting my present train of thought.

"I hooked up wit' that girl from the pool hall at the last minute. I called you the next morning, but you never called me back."

"I didn't call you back because I was getting my groove on! I think I must have spent over five hundred dollars in that joint."

I desperately want to tell Skip about what I did the other night to my ex co-worker Dani, but I cannot take the chance that he might run his mouth to someone else mistakenly…or even worse, Shontell!

I promptly leave Skip's apartment and go across town to the pool hall where Cassandra works. Looking over at my radio, the clock reads ten minutes before nine o'clock, which means she is getting ready to end her shift for the night. If I can maneuver through this damn congested traffic and beat most of the lights, I can catch her before she jumps into a cab and heads home. Weaving in and out of traffic, I arrive at the pool hall just in time. Cassandra is outside and just as a cab pulls up to take her away, I wave her down to get her attention.

"What are you doin' here?"

David L.

She looks just as good as when I first saw her – maybe even better! She has a surprised look on her face, and I privately hope it is because she is glad to see me.

"I'm your personal chauffeur for the night, baby. So what do you want to do first?"

"How 'bout we go and get somethin' to eat?"

"That's a great idea. I know the perfect spot."

We immediately head over to an IHOP located on Boston Road in the Bronx. After several minutes of waiting to be seated, I order a hamburger deluxe and Cassandra tries to play the shy role and orders herself a Caesar salad.

"I don't know why you are frontin', girl! You know you're hungry. You said it yourself!"

"I know, but I got to watch my figure. I can't hold it all down like you can!"

"Let me worry about watching your figure. Go 'head and order yourself a real meal."

We both laugh at my comments and finish up our meals. It is unseasonably chilly tonight and I hand Cassandra a jacket that I keep in the trunk of my truck for such an occasion. It is my same Downtown Records jacket I used to give Janelle to wear whenever she used to complain of being cold. The jacket I would use right now to suffocate her ass if only I had the opportunity! My house is located about a mile and a half from IHOP, and Cassandra and I return there after spending time in the IHOP parking lot tongue-kissing for about twenty minutes. With no earlier plans of expecting company, I apologize for my messy place and attempt to clean up around the living room area as fast as I can to the best of my ability.

Over Your Dead Body

"Would you like something to drink?"

I privately hope she says yes so I can offer her some wine, or preferably, something a little stronger. It would make going for mines that much easier when the time is right!

"That depends. What do you got?"

We both enter my dining room and an impressive bar on wheels is on display. Everything from Jamaican Rum to exotic-flavored wine coolers is on the showcase for her to choose from.

"Let me try one of those."

I am thinking how ironic it is she picks an old liquor bottle of Cisco that I have had sitting around for when my boys from my college days come through. I make sure I wipe the dust off of it before handing it to her.

"You don't want any of this stuff. It will mess you up!"

"Don't worry about me. I'm a big girl."

"Okay, don't say I didn't warn you."

Doing as requested, I pour some Cisco into a glass with ice for Cassandra and fix myself one of my favorites, a rum and Coke. I can tell the intoxicating affect of the Cisco is beginning to take effect on her already. She is busy talking to me a mile a minute and very loudly. Not too loud where she is becoming obnoxious or unruly, though.

"So how does it taste?"

"It's kind of fruity. It kind of tastes like a wine cooler."

"Yeah, that's kind of what it is…a wine cooler."

David L.

I know I am lying my ass off, but hey, she asked for it! Shy by nature, liquor has always unleashed my hidden self and allowed me to go for mine when my verbal game wasn't on point. It does not take long before Cassandra and I are kissing passionately on my living room couch. No longer watching the movie I put in earlier, we fondle each other until I lift her from off the couch and carry her upstairs to the bedroom. In a matter of minutes, Cassandra's pants and shirt are spread across my bedroom carpet. She is under my covers wearing nothing but a pair of panties and a bra that I am slowly working on getting off.

"Hold on a sec. Let me help you with that," she replies, referring to my inability to get her bra unsnapped.

Damn! What a marvelous pair of breasts she is endowed with! A pair of breasts that would make any Jet centerfold green with envy! I got an old Al B. Sure song playing on my clock radio and the television set is on mute. The room is completely dark except for the slight glare emanating from the television screen.

"Do you have protection?"

Damn! My first instinct is to run to the store and get me some, but I don't want to look desperate. My lack of response and the dumbfounded look on my face is answer enough for her.

"Well, I know I am safe. I was just checked a month ago," Cassandra announces.

"I'm clean, too," I quickly respond. "The last time I had unprotected sex with anyone besides my ex-wife was over ten years ago," I proudly add.

Over Your Dead Body

    My fondling and groping continue, and once again, I prepare to enter Cassandra before she changes her mind. She is wet with anticipation and moaning with passion. I count at least four tattoos on both of her arms, and a fifth one right below her belly button.
    "You have to take it slow. I haven't had sex in months." Cassandra gasps, bracing herself underneath my rigid body.
    Doing as requested, I slow down my rhythm. Not because I really want to slow down, but mostly because I don't want to finish too quickly.
    "How is that? Better?"
    Cassandra doesn't respond, but the sweat beads forming on her forehead and the slight grimace on her face makes me suspect that I am working it tonight. Her once stiff body is now beginning to convulse under the weight of my own body. Either she is an excellent actress or she is cummin'. Either way, my ego is fulfilled. Feeling her hips and lower torso shiver with each thrust excites me to the point where I cannot prevent my own inevitable release. We both moan in unison as the room becomes hotter with each passing minute that I remain inside her.
    "Oh my GOD! Oh my GOD!" she screams out loud.
    With each "Oh my GOD" that resonates from her mouth, a slight smile forms on my face. Now that I have her where I want her, she will probably never look at another man the same way again. I have ruined it for every other brother that attempts to hit it after me. My mind wanders momentarily to Janelle. She once told me that she had never cum before, and I thought I was going to roll over and die. I used to feel

David L.

like half a man from that moment on, but not any more. Tonight, I reclaim my manhood!

The sheets are soaked from our bodily fluids, and I cannot even reach down and grab my boxer shorts to wipe myself off with them. Inching a little closer to Cassandra to avoid the "wet spot" in the center of the bed, I embrace her tightly, and for the first time in weeks, I fall into a deep, relaxing sleep.

* * *

I'm at least twenty minutes early for court, and there still looks to be over fifty people in front of me waiting to get inside. I'm damn near asked to get naked before they allow me through the metal detector. I'm accompanied by Uncle Cliff, and seated across from me in the waiting room area is Janelle and her mother. Neither me nor Janelle make eye contact with the other, and just as I begin to doze off in my chair, some Hispanic dude is escorted out of the waiting area by armed security for threatening to kill his baby's mama.

"Whatever you do, don't let that be you being carried out like that," Uncle Cliff whispers.

He's smiling, but at the same time, I can tell he's serious about me not going over the deep end if things don't go my way. Uncle Cliff knows I have always had a quick temper.

"Today, I am in total control, Uncle Cliff. Besides, what can go wrong? Janelle is keeping the children from me against my will, and I am a positive person in the community. Everyone loves me!"

"The legal system don't care who you are, boy. Or how much money you may have in your pockets. You will always be just another nigga to dem."

"Not you, too, Uncle Cliff. Skip was talkin' that same mess yesterday. Watch when I go up in there...I'm going to represent for all Black men today."

My demeanor gives off a cocky overtone, but it is just probably masking a slight fear...most likely a fear of the unknown nature of the court system. I want to believe in my heart the justice system is color blind, but is it really? Am I just another nigga to them? Janelle sits in her chair emotionless, looking over a stack of papers that are perched on top of her lap. Mama Pearl is asleep in her chair, waking up on occasion to adjust her girdle, and Uncle Cliff is busy checking out some poor white trash over in the corner of the waiting area whose breasts are partially exposed.

I have a look of satisfaction on my face as our case is called – after only three plus hours of waiting patiently! My mannerisms in the courtroom do not give away how I really feel, which is nervous and afraid. After all, the next few minutes could possibly affect the rest of my life. What if for some strange reason, I actually did get custody of my children? Could I provide for them, spend quality time with them, and maintain a hectic work schedule? Would DeShaun's constant whining, fussing, and using the bathroom on himself make me want to choke him in the middle of the night? What about Destiny? In a few years, she will begin to look at boys in a different perspective. Will I be ready for that, or am I going to

David L.

want to beat down the first boy that comes knocking on the door to take her out? I present my reasons for wanting custody of the children first, followed by the judge's rebuttal. Then, it will be Janelle's turn to give her reasons for sole custody. Just as I expect, Janelle pulls out her stack of papers and what looks to be a journal of some sort.

"Your honor, my ex-husband does not even visit with his children. The last time he saw them was over a month ago."

"That is a lie, your honor! She would not let me see them!" I respond defiantly.

After a few errant threats from the judge to hold me in contempt of court, I wisely silence myself to avoid prosecution.

"Furthermore, your honor, he cannot even keep a job. Here are his termination papers from his last place of employment. If you look very closely on the last page, you will see exactly why he was fired."

Janelle is pulling out all of her tricks, and it appears to be working to perfection. The judge looks at me with suspicion as I give my reasons behind my termination from Downtown Records. For her grand finale, Janelle plays her trump card and forwards a copy of my DUI – a copy I didn't even know existed until today! I never checked the police blotter or the arrest reports at the police station to see if they were available to the general public. How did she know I was even arrested? My chances of reuniting with my children grow more far-fetched with each syllable that exits Janelle's mouth. Even the court stenographer is looking over at me and shaking her head in disgust. The room grows silent as the judge reads over various papers that were put in front of him by one of the court officers. I'm burning a hole in the side of Janelle's head, but she wisely declines to look in my direction.

"We are going to break for lunch and continue this matter in approximately one hour. You may both leave and return at one thirty."

Just as the judge announces recess, I quickly exit the courtroom to plan my retaliation.

"I'm getting destroyed in that courtroom, Uncle Cliff!" I moan.

Asking for further clarification, Uncle Cliff listens attentively as I give him a play-by-play of what just went down. He does his best to offer support, but my mind is already set. I can feel the decision going in Janelle's direction, and the thought of losing is angering me even further.

"There is no way I am going to win this case! She has the entire courtroom on her side, and they are all probably in there right now making up their minds against me!"

"Now, boy, just have faith. You are a good father. You know that and I know that. Everything will eventually work itself out in the end."

I am so tense, I don't even eat lunch. Instead, I proceed to pace through the court hallway waiting for my case to be called again. Reentering the courthouse, Mama Pearl slips me a fake smile as if to say there is no way she is going to part with her grandbabies.

"With all the fathers missing in action, Janelle, you would think it would be important for me to be in their lives!" I say, looking over in Janelle's direction.

David L.

"They already got a man in their life, and it ain't you!"

I'm smart enough to keep my cool, but holding back my emotions is hard work. Some random chickenhead who appears to be pregnant is seated next to her and giggles discreetly under her breath. Joe Banger and Dani's murders linger in my subconscious. Not because I feel guilty, but because I am unsure of how it will play out in the courtroom. It is ironic that after everything Janelle pulled earlier in the courtroom, Joe Banger's name never once came up. And does she even know about what happened to Dani? They were definitely keeping in touch with each other. But just how close were they?

Janelle and I are both called into the courtroom, and her verbal assassination of my good-natured character continues as if there was never an intermission.

"Mr. Preston, are you aware that you have been late on multiple occasions picking up your son from daycare?" the judge questions.

Janelle is good! She has obviously been planning this for quite some time now. She must have gone back to DeShaun's daycare and asked for his attendance records.

"Your honor," I interject, "that is absolutely not true! My ex-wife and I used to take turns picking up my son. On one or two occasions, I was late. I admit that. But she used to always be late! And then I would have to hear it from the daycare staff!"

More head shaking and looks of disgust are thrown my way as I attempt to gain momentum by

Over Your Dead Body

mentioning my status in the community, the four-bedroom house we share in Mount Vernon, friends and family, and my current status of employment making almost six figures at Destiny Records. There is further silence as the judge vacates his chair and exits through a back door to make his decision.

It feels like hours as I sit patiently waiting for him to return with his verdict. Janelle has an expressionless look on her face while I sit fidgeting with my belt buckle. The judge returns and proceeds with a five-minute recap of the events which recently transpired. Moments later, he gives his decision...a decision which will affect my very being from this moment forward.

"This is an unusual case, and at the same time, an unfortunate one. Not once did I hear any mention of any loss for those two children. Just two disgruntled ex-lovers who can no longer even look at each other. My decision is a difficult one, but one I feel will most benefit the two children to the fullest. I give full custody to the mother – Janelle Gwendolyn Price!"

My heart stops and my fists are clenched.

"Full custody? What about my visitation?" I yell in obvious anger. "You call this justice? You are a GODDAMN joke! You ain't no judge in my eyes! You are a devil!"

Just as if it was scripted on an episode of *Law and Order*, the judge looks over at the two court officers standing to each side of him and orders my immediate removal from the courtroom. Facing arrest for a second time this year and thoughts of being handcuffed yet again cause my further escalation towards my antagonists. Not giving in easily, I

179

David L.

promptly resist arrest and end up being carried out and detained in a holding cell nearby. Once inside, my handcuffs are removed, allowing me to clear my thoughts to plot my eventual revenge against Janelle, and once and for all, reclaim my children.

Over Your Dead Body

CHAPTER SEVEN

July 10, 2004

It is hard to believe I was born thirty-three years ago on this day. As far as I am concerned, it is just another Saturday afternoon. I have not spoken to Skip since I found out he ran his big mouth to Shontell, but I should have known better. Besides, he is throwing me a birthday party tonight at The Tav and has promised me it is going to be a night I am never going to forget. I am a last minute person by nature, but I am already dressed for my night out. My cell phone has been ringing non-stop from friends and family wishing me a happy birthday.

"Let me get twenty dollars on regular," I say to the gas station attendant.

I'm already on my second pack of cigarettes today, the most cigarettes I've smoked in my entire lifetime.

"You might want to change that tire, pal. You got a big bubble sticking out on the side," the gas station attendant informs me.

I thank him for his concern and proceed towards my destination: Skip's house. While at a red light, I think about getting my tire changed, but reconsider after the urge of liquor and takeout pizza at Skip's house becomes too tempting to pass up.

David L.

"Slow down on the drinking, Pres. You're going to be passed out before we make it to the club tonight!" Skip warns.

As expected, he has the usual line-up of knuckleheads at his apartment to share in my born day. Sitting on the couch drinking a forty ounce of Old English beer is Benny, otherwise known as Benny "Backdraft." He got his nickname because of his nasty ass habit of running up in women raw dog and getting burnt because of it. Instead of learning his lesson and wearing a Jimmy hat, he jokes about it all the way to the free clinic and tells everyone that he is "keeping it real." Lonnie a.k.a. Lonnie "Love" has half of his body in Skip's refrigerator, looking for something to snack on while we wait for the pizza to be delivered. He got his name because he can't live without being with a woman. As soon as he ends a relationship with one woman, he is in love with the next. Last, but definitely not least, is Sammy B. otherwise known as "Showtime" Sammy. He is the life of the party…the one that stands out in the crowd and always has to be heard.

Sure enough, Skip's warning was valid, because just as I finish my last can of beer, I get the feeling I am going to regurgitate all over myself. Showtime Sammy, sensing my inability to maintain whatever is in my stomach, hands me two slices of bread from out of Skip's refrigerator to chew on.

"I think we got him on the ropes!" Lonnie Love exclaims. "One more drink and he's a goner!"

I prove everyone wrong and gather my senses. A couple more slices of bread and three glasses of cold

Over Your Dead Body

water later, I am on my feet and ready to head out to The Tav to celebrate my birthday.

There is the usual assortment of regulars sprinkled in with a bunch of college dudes trying to hang with us older cats. Surprisingly, there is a line of about forty people; however, I give "Big Red" the security guard a head nod and he pulls open the rope to let me and the rest of the crew in.
"Showtime is in the house, everyone!" Sammy B. yells out, alerting all of The Tav patrons of who he is.
Benny heads straight to the bar to order the drinks. We all privately huddled up together minutes earlier and decided he would get the first round of shots because otherwise, he would not come out of his pockets for the rest of the night.
"Look at the honey sitting in the corner!" Lonnie Love blurts out. "I think I just found my wife tonight up in here!"
Everyone but Lonnie laughs privately at his comment. Probably because he just broke off an engagement about a week ago. Something about my laughter towards Lonnie makes me feel like a hypocrite. It was just days after my divorce from Janelle that I met Cassandra at the pool hall. Then again, my situation is very different. Lonnie falls in love with the first woman that gives him some attention. I don't love Cassandra. Hell, she is not even my girl!
"That girl over there wants to buy you a drink," Skip says, pointing to a light-skinned honey sitting at the bar.

183

I look over towards her, and sure enough, Skip is not bullshitting me. Before she has a chance to reconsider her proposal, I walk over and introduce myself.

"I'm Gazelle – you know…kind of like the animal that runs real fast. I saw you come in with your boys and something about you stood out from the rest of them."

Just my luck! Of all the first names in the universe, I have to meet someone whose name rhymes with Janelle! I decline Gazelle's offer for a drink, and instead, offer to buy her one. After I subtly hint that today is my birthday, she insists on paying for it.

"So do you have a girl? I don't see a ring on your finger, unless you take it off whenever you go out to the club."

Not only does Gazelle have a sense of humor, but she is pretty damn fine, as well. We share some small talk for a few more minutes until she reminds me that I never responded to her question if I was seeing anyone.

"Yeah, uh, I guess. I recently met someone, and I've been talking on and off with her for a couple of days…nothing serious or anything."

Even in the darkened lights, Gazelle cannot hide her look of disappointment. Although the words just came out of my mouth, I can't believe I said that I was seeing someone to a woman who is so fine. Either the alcohol I consumed tonight is acting like a truth serum, or I like Cassandra more than I want to let on! Either way, I can safely bet I lost my chance at scoring tonight.

Over Your Dead Body

Back over with the crew, I am waiting patiently to see what Skip has lined up. He promised me a "night to remember" and I am holding him to it.

"So did you get that girl's digits or what?" Sammy B. questions. He has a wide grin on his face like he's hiding something.

"Nah man, I didn't get the digits. I told her I was already seeing someone."

Everyone in the crew turns up their face. Even Lonnie Love, who has managed to return with a couple phone numbers of his own, gives me a look of disapproval.

"Is you crazy?" Sammy B. responds. "Dat fine ass chick at the bar was feelin' you and you didn't get the digits? You gettin' soft on us or something?"

I decline to further bury myself with the crew and inquire about the special surprise for me instead. After all, it is my birthday, and so far, I have not really celebrated like a man turning thirty-three ought to do!

"Relax, brother. You gonna get yours real soon!" Skip announces.

Sure enough, Big Al, the owner, comes out from the back and greets me with a hug.

"Happy birthday, young boy! I got something waiting for you in the back. Follow me."

"Now you know how I am about surprises. What do you have in the back?"

Big Al wraps his arm around me and escorts me into a back room.

"It's not WHAT I got for you, boy; it's WHO I got for you!"

Skip, Benny, Sammy B., and Lonnie Love follow closely behind to make sure they don't miss any

185

David L.

of the upcoming action. I have a feeling I know what the surprise is, but I do not let on. It doesn't make any sense to spoil all the hard work it probably took to set this up.

"Go have a seat over in that chair right there," Big Al instructs.

With a handkerchief over my eyes, I'm led into a pitch black room and almost fall and bust my ass over some cable wire that is resting on the ground. One of two things is going on right now I theorize: either, I'm going to get the blowjob of my life, or Big Al and the rest of my crew is about to whip my Black ass and leave me for dead!

My eyes are still covered by the handkerchief to enhance the experience. I am now seated alone in a dark room, and every sound and smell is magnified to compensate for my lack of vision. A little over a minute goes by before I hear tiny footsteps coming towards the door. I am tempted to remove the handkerchief and open my eyes, but just as I reach for the handkerchief, the mystery person enters the room and I immediately detect the strong smell of perfume...a smell that is vaguely familiar.

"Hey, baby!" she says in a whispered voice. "I'm your birthday present for the evening. Is that alright with you?"

I crack one eyelid open, but no luck. The room is completely dark and I can barely see her silhouette. She immediately reaches for my belt buckle and proceeds to remove my pants from around my waist. There is no need to manipulate my manhood, as it is already standing at attention from all the mystery and suspense that has been provided so far.

"Lay down on the floor," she instructs with a soft whisper. "I like my men on their backs when I do this."

Doing as I am told, I am lying on my back and getting possibly the best blowjob in my entire life. In a matter of seconds, I am near climax and several thoughts enter my head. I finally unleash my load, and to my surprise, she consumes every last drop. I envision every woman in my life that refused to go down or spit instead of swallow. I privately want to contact each of them and tell them what pathetic creatures they really are!

"How was that, baby?" she whispers. "Did I give you a birthday gift you will always remember?"

As if she really didn't know the answer to that question! My "present" for the night is inching her way towards my face. Hopefully, she doesn't want to kiss me after she just swallowed half of my midsection. Always the breast man, they are the first things I grab onto as she begins kissing on my neck. And what beautiful, well-sculptured breasts they are! The scent of her body is eerily familiar. Finally, I remove the blindfold and open my eyes to get a better sample of what I am working with here. Hell, maybe I can get her to host a party or something one day. Better yet, I can get her to go down on that free agent rapper that I am after, Almighty Divine. That would surely seal the deal!

"CASSANDRA?" I blurt out, pushing her from off of me to get a better look.

David L.

"OH MY GOD! PRESTON? What the hell are you doin' here?"

I quickly pull up my pants and head to the door.

"What the hell am I doin' here? I don't want to hear any stories, excuses, nothing!"

"Now wait a minute! It isn't like you are totally innocent yourself! You were just with me, and here you are getting your thing sucked on like I didn't mean anything to you!"

Damn, she does have a point! I *was* just with her, but after all, this was a birthday gift. I didn't even know about any of this. The rational part of me wants to hang around and fix things with Cassandra, but I allow my emotions to once again dictate my course of action.

"Whatever you say, bitch! Just don't ever call me again! From this moment on, I don't know you!"

And like that, I walk out to return to the crew.

* * *

Since hearing about the recent death of Dani, his dissatisfaction with her replacement at Downtown Records, and my generous counter-offer to split the master's sixty-forty the company's way, Almighty Divine and his manager, Louie Burns, arrive at the office to sign on the dotted line.

I look at my watch and wonder in amazement how ironic life is. Exactly eight hours ago, I was gettin' blown by a girl I thought I could claim as my own one day. I never did tell the fellas what went on in that dark-ass room. I guess they figured they would just believe whatever their active imaginations thought happened. Even after careful consideration about what transpired with Cassandra, there is no way I could try to make it work with her. After all, how many other times has this happened? Just the thought of me kissing all over her with the combination of her swallowing semen makes me want to vomit!

"So what do you guys do around here when it's time to celebrate?" Louie Burns questions.

My boss and I both smile as Sandy, the secretary, walks in with a bottle of Cristal to celebrate the moment. She has the same nasty look on her face while shaking her head in disapproval as we all get to celebrate the big signing.

I have big plans for Almighty Divine as soon as I can get him booked at our featured studio about a block and a half from our main office. First, I am going to get him major spins on all the local and regional radio stations. Secondly, I am going to propose a budget to have billboards plastered across Times Square, 125th Street in Harlem, and of course, Flatbush Avenue in Brooklyn. Finally, his videos are going to be six-figure videos with lots of half-naked woman so that he can get major rotation on all the video programming channels. Because of my big signing, I foresee a major cash bonus in my mailbox within the next week or so. Money I can desperately use since Janelle has a chokehold on my personal and business accounts. Money I could have used weeks ago to hire the best lawyer money could buy to help me get custody of my children.

"We are all going to go out and finish this celebration over at the Marriott. Are you coming?" my boss asks, looking over at me.

David L.

"Nah, I got something I have to take care of. Maybe I'll catch up with you guys later."

Janelle works about twenty minutes from here if I jump on the Harlem River Drive to avoid the incoming Bronx traffic. She used to always come home for lunch to catch her soap opera stories, so if I plan it right, I can follow her as she leaves work. Just as expected, she is leaving her building and searching for her car keys in her pocketbook. I am parked behind a moving truck to avoid detection. I am dodging around frenzied taxicab drivers in order to keep up with her. She appears to be headed through some back roads, so either she finally got a place of her own or she is about to meet up with some fool for a "nooner." After a routine stop at a corner bodega, my luck continues to be on the money because she pulls up to a non-descript apartment building and walks inside. Pulling out a piece of paper and a pen, I write down the street address in the unlikely event I forget where I am.

"Make sure you enjoy your victory while you can, bitch!" I say to myself while driving off in the opposite direction. "My children will be coming home with me very soon, whether you like it or not!"

"I'm not getting involved, Pres. Leave me out of you and Janelle's mess!"

The voice belongs to Skip. I am trying to get him to find out from Shontell where Destiny and DeShaun go in the morning when Janelle leaves for work, but he is not budging.

"What do you mean you're not getting involved? You're the one that opened your big mouth to Shontell in the first place! You're the one that told her about my DUI, and Janelle used that against me when we had to go to court!"

"How you think that is going to make me look, me asking Shontell where your children go in the morning? See, that's your problem, Pres…you don't ever think out your plans!"

Unfortunately for me, Skip is right this time. If he were to ask Shontell anything about the children, it would kill any chance I had to get them from Janelle's clutches. I've become fixated on reclaiming my children, and it has been messing with my ability to produce logical thoughts. I should be out right now celebrating the signing of Almighty Divine, and instead, I'm plotting my next move against my ex-wife.

"Yo Skip, I'm out. I'll get up wit' you later in the day."

"Don't go and do anything crazy, man. Stay cool!"

"I can't be anything but cool…you know that!"

Skip flashes me with his signature smile as I head out through his apartment door. Although my motives are unclear, I know now what I must do.

Mama Pearl's car is missing from her driveway, but I got a hunch if I wait around for a few minutes, she will eventually show up. Besides, waiting for people outside their house has become some sort of sick theme for me. I am halfway through my *Best of Biggie* mix CD before the sound of Mama Pearl's old, beat up Buick Skylark enters the driveway. I laugh to myself as it cuts off right before she makes it

David L.

completely up her driveway. Destiny is waving at me from the back seat and I can see the back of DeShaun's car seat.

"Hey, Mrs. Pearl! I was just about to leave you a note. I spoke to Janelle today. She knows I'm here to pick up the children."

"You spoke to her? Janelle changed her phone number over two weeks ago!"

"I know. She told me. I ran into her around the corner from her new apartment out in the Bronx earlier."

"I don't know, Preston. Janelle didn't tell me no such thing."

"C'mon, Mrs. Pearl, how long have you known me? You think I am going to take off and leave town with my own children?"

"I just don't want to get in the middle of whatever is going on between you and my daughter. I know she can be stubborn when she wants to be, but she is still my child."

"And that's my point. You would do anything for your child, right? That is all I am trying to do for my children."

By this time, Destiny is jumping all over me and DeShaun is out of his car seat and pulling on my leg. He is getting bigger every day and finally walking around without a walker.

"I miss you, Daddy! When are you coming back to be with Mommy and us?" Destiny asks.

"I don't know, sweetheart. Maybe one day soon."

By this time, Mama Pearl has a look of guilt on her face, and I can tell she is starting to weaken.

"Janelle will be here shortly, Preston. Go on and take your children. I just hope you're not pulling a fast one on me."

I am already halfway getting DeShaun's car seat into my own car before Mama Pearl calls out to me.

"WAIT, PRESTON!"

"Yes, Mrs. Pearl?"

"Remember a while back when I told Janelle to make sure she takes her medication?"

"Yeah, I remember. What about it?"

"Preston – Janelle is Bi-polar. She was diagnosed at the hospital after she had taken those sleeping pills!.

"Is she gonna die?"

"No, silly! I've done some reading up on it. Bi-polar is a chemical imbalance of the brain. A mood disorder that causes the individual to suffer extreme mood swings, and anything stressful can set them off. She will be alright, BUT it is important she takes her medication every day."

"Don't worry about anything. Janelle said she was going to call me later to tell me how to get to DeShaun's new daycare. I will talk to her and work everything out. The children are in good hands."

It won't be long before Janelle alerts the local police. I look at the clock on my dashboard and realize Janelle leaves work somewhere around this time. That means I got just enough time to get back to the house and load my truck up with my most valuable possessions. Everything Mrs. Pearl told me about Janelle is irrelevant at this time in my life. Too many

David L.

things have happened. Janelle has finally crossed the line, and her psychiatric status means nothing to me.

"Turn right here, Daddy!" Destiny commands, motioning for me to turn the corner that leads to our house. A wide turn almost causes DeShaun to fall out of his car seat.

"Look at the children growing up so big and strong! I haven't seen those darling little faces in such a long time!" Mrs. Darcy, one of my next door neighbors, says.

After she agrees to watch Destiny and DeShaun while I run into the house, I do my best to get everything I own into the back of my truck. The first things I instinctively grab are my stereo system and X-Box game system. Afterwards, I grab as many clothes and Timberland boots as I can to last me for at least the next couple of weeks. I figure since Janelle doesn't know I am working at a new record label, I should be alright...at least temporarily.

"Are you going on vacation or something?" Mrs. Darcy questions.

"Vacation? Yeah, we're going to Florida for a few days."

"And you take a stereo system with you to Florida?"

I kindly remind Mrs. Darcy that I am in a rush and return to getting the rest of my belongings. Moments later, my truck is packed to capacity, and I have a bag full of pretzels and potato chips for Destiny and DeShaun to snack on until I can figure out my next plan of action.

"If I didn't know better, Preston, I would think you were in some trouble and you were making a

194

getaway or something," Mrs. Darcy says with a smile on her face.

"Oh no, nothing like that. It's just that I had to plan this Florida trip at the last minute, that's all."

Before Mrs. Darcy has a chance to prolong the conversation, the children and I wave goodbye and proceed to our next destination...wherever that may be.

* * *

An unusually long night was made even longer with all of DeShaun's fussing and crying. It seems he has some type of ear infection, and I had to run out in the middle of the night to the emergency room to have him checked. Luckily, I still had copies of the children's insurance cards in my wallet and the hospital has not yet been alerted to anything unusual.

I am staying at a Comfort Inn off of the New Jersey Turnpike until I can come up with a better plan. I have food and clothes for at least a week, and better yet, Janelle nor the police have no way of reaching me. I am lying on the side of the bed with a flashlight, writing Mama Pearl an apology letter for my disappearance act with the children. I know in my heart she will never forgive me for my indiscretion, but oh well! If I weaken and go back now, I will never be able to visit with my children again. Still asleep, DeShaun and Destiny look like the innocent angels they are. Too bad they have become unwilling pawns in this game called life.

"Pres, where the hell are you? Janelle and Shontell have been calling me non-stop. Janelle even

David L.

said she was on her way over to my place with the police to make sure you're not here with the children!"

Skip is frantic, trying to get me to return with Destiny and DeShaun, but that is not an option. Hell, I may never return!

"Tell them I left the country. Tell them anything! I ain't comin' back no time soon! I can definitely promise you that!"

"Where are you anyway?"

"I can't tell you that, Skip. You're my boy and everything, but with enough interrogation, your ass might slip up and dime me out to someone."

"Well, are you still in Mount Vernon at least?"

"I'll talk to you later, Skip!"

I end my phone conversation with Skip abruptly. One, because I feel paranoid and fear his phone is being tapped. Two, I don't want DeShaun waking up again and preventing me from getting a few more hours of much-needed rest.

"Wait here with your little brother while I run downstairs to get us some ice," I say, looking over at Destiny.

Her big eyes light up the room, and she is too eager to do my bidding. After all, we haven't spent quality time like this in a minute. The ice is for DeShaun. Moments earlier, he was trying to get down from the bed and scraped his knee on the side of the dresser. He has been crying non-stop, and it is either because his ear infection has him cranky or because he is not used to the strange surroundings.

"Daddy, is this going to be our new home? And when is Mommy going to come and be with us?"

Destiny questions, still wide-eyed and bursting with enthusiasm from being "put in charge."

"I don't know, baby. Maybe in a few days. For now, let us just enjoy our time together."

My first instinct is to load everything and everyone into my car and continue driving south. I got a couple of uncles and aunts that I can crash with for a couple of weeks in South Carolina. Although I am in New Jersey, I am still close enough to be spotted by someone and have my cover exposed. Who am I fooling anyway? No matter how much I tell myself I can do this, eventually, my mind is going to begin playing tricks on me. DeShaun is crying every five minutes because of his ear infection and Destiny is going to keep asking me questions about her mother. I don't have the heart to tell her that she may never see her again.

"Daddy, I need a bow for my hair. Can we go to the store and buy one?"

I shoot her a mean look and she gets my answer. We can't be seen outdoors just for any reason, and going outside right now so her hair can look right is not a good enough reason. My cell phone is turned off, and I am down to one bar because I forgot the phone charger back at the house. Skip was right about me. I don't think things through. I could stop by Uncle Cliff's place, but that would be the second place the cops would look for me…if they have not gone there already. Fear of the unknown and my growing impatience from DeShaun's crying is replaced by paranoia. Would Skip give me away or be tricked into giving me away? Can I even trust him? After all, everyone has their price!

David L.

After a late night run to the pharmacy for DeShaun's medication and to a local diner for some food, Destiny and DeShaun are finally content. DeShaun has ketchup all over his face from picking at my burger and Destiny's hands have grease all over them from the taco she was nibbling on in the car.

"Daddy, it's your turn to play a card," Destiny says.

We are on our fifth game of War, and I am beginning to nod off. She is wide awake and full of energy, probably from the package of Big League chewing gum she devoured that she conned me into getting for her from the pharmacy.

"Maybe we should finish this game tomorrow, Destiny."

"One more game, Daddy! PLEASE!"

She knows she has me wrapped around her little finger and I give in to her endless pleading. I am down to three cards in my hand when I hear a sudden knock at the door. My guard is up and my eyes widen with suspicion as I inch over to the door.

"Shhh, baby. Don't say anything."

Over twenty scenarios play out in my thoughts until I muster the courage to ask who is on the other side of the door.

"Who is it?" I question in my best "tough guy" voice.

"It's housekeeping. Sorry to be coming by so late, but we forgot to bring you new towels earlier today."

Relieved, I allow the diminutive cleaning lady to enter and drop off the towels and washcloths. I am so relieved it is not Janelle with the cops, I give the cleaning lady a ten-dollar bill for her hospitality.

"Go 'head, Daddy. It's your turn to play a card."

* * *

Three weeks have gone by and I can't front...I am ready to go home and deal with whatever is coming to me. DeShaun cries himself to sleep every night and Destiny is asking for her mother almost every hour. Today, I figure a change of scenery will do everyone justice. Today, it's time to have some fun. And what better way to have some fun than to go to an amusement park. Being that we are in New Jersey, we might as well take a ride over to Great Adventure.

Thoughts of Janelle and the cops searching the tri-state area occupy my thoughts the entire ride there. It is not until I am stuck in line for over an hour in the blistering heat that I momentarily forget my own problems. DeShaun is still cranky from his ear infection and Destiny is damn near in tears since half the rides she can't go on because she is too short. Every time a passing pedestrian looks my way, I wonder if they know I am hiding from my children's mother and have no intention on returning them to her.

"Daddy, I'm hot. Can we leave now and go back to the hotel?" Destiny whines.

"You want to leave already? We just got here!"

"I know, but...well, it's not the same without Mommy. I miss her! Can we go, PLEASE?"

I don't know if I want to slap Destiny's whiney ass or fall out on the ground in tears. Just the fact that I

David L.

am thinking about slapping her for asking about her mother is making me think I made the wrong decision taking them out of Mount Vernon. I am also beginning to think I am fighting a battle I can no longer win. The longer we remain missing, the more my daughter will grow to resent me and everything I stand for.

"So you want to see Mommy? I think I can make that happen, baby."

"Really, Daddy? Thank you! Let's go now!"

"Well, it's not that easy, baby. I've got to call a few people first and work out the details. But don't you worry. I am going to fix everything...I promise!"

The ride back to our new hotel is about a twenty-minute drive from off the New Jersey Turnpike. Although I got permission from my boss to handle my business with my children, there is no way I am going to be able to keep my job for as long as I have been gone. And right after I managed to sign that Almighty Divine dude! I can't even be there to enjoy what could possibly be my biggest act EVER!

Sounds of DeShaun's crying continue to drive me up a wall.

"Destiny, why is he crying now?"

"I think he is hungry, Daddy. He needs his bottle."

"DAMN!"

I forgot to stop at a local convenience store and pick up some milk for his bottle. That means he is going to cry all the way back to the damn hotel. What would Janelle do if she was here right now?

"Can't you do anything to shut him up? Play with him or something!"

Over Your Dead Body

"I am playing with him, Daddy, but he's upset. Why are you yelling at me?"

Destiny's hurtful stare brings me back down to earth and I am immediately apologetic for yelling at her. While I am driving in the slow lane, the loud sound of a tire blowing out can be heard.

"What was that, Daddy?"

My car almost goes into a tailspin, as I am barely able to maintain control of the steering wheel and steer the car into the shoulder of the highway. The stern warnings from the gas station attendant from weeks ago enter my mind as I notice the tire debris from my car race past us on the highway.

"Damn, why did this have to happen? Why now?" I question to no one in particular.

I am only one exit away from the hotel, but on the turnpike, one exit is the equivalent of at least five miles of walking. I can't even believe I would allow myself to be driving around all of this time without a spare tire! I don't dare call Triple A or the cops for the fear of being captured, so the children and I begin our trek back to the hotel in the midday heat.

There are over twenty messages on my cell phone when I awaken from my much-needed slumber. Destiny and DeShaun are preoccupied with watching *Rugrats* on television, and I am beginning to grow tired from the senseless hiding out routine. No matter how much I want to be with my children, even I know I cannot continue to live this life of watching my back and hiding from everyone.

"Good morning, may I speak with Detective Adams?"

201

David L.

Moments later, I am engaged in a phone conversation with Mount Vernon's finest and he is trying his best to get me to come down to the station and turn myself in.

"I'm thinkin' about comin' home, but I can't afford to give up my children...not again! If I do, you and I both know I will never get to be with them again!"

"That's not true, Preston. You just have to go about it the right way. You can get visitation...joint custody...anything."

"Fuck visitation! And see my kids when, Detective Adams? Once a month? Twice a month? That's not good enough!"

"You're putting a lot of pressure on yourself, Preston. Janelle has contacted every radio station and newspaper, and the media is beginning to eat it up. Haven't you been watching the news recently?"

My heart is racing, and for a moment, I become lightheaded. My reputation ain't worth shit now, and I may never be able to fix the mess I put myself in. Janelle is looking like the poor, innocent victim. She is definitely winning this battle so far, but I will be damned if she wins the war!

"I don't want to come down to the station...not yet anyway, detective. There are going to be cameras everywhere! What if you meet me around the corner from my house in about an hour?"

"House? What house? You didn't hear?"

"What are you getting at? What happened to my house?"

"We got a call from a neighbor right after you were spotted leaving with the children...an

Over Your Dead Body

unidentified woman poured lighter fluid into the mailbox slot, and well...the fire department was able to save fifty percent of your home."

"Unidentified woman? That was Janelle! She did it! Can't you see that?"

"You're wrong, Preston. Janelle was at her mother's house. We can prove it, because at the exact time the arson took place, she was calling us to report her missing children."

"She is going to pay for this!"

"Don't get yourself into more trouble, Preston. You've got enough on your plate right now without getting yourself into a bigger mess."

If not Janelle, then who? Of course! Shontell! Who else could it be? It is at this exact moment that I realize she must die – BY ANY MEANS NECESSARY! Detective Adams tried his best to get me to turn myself in, but Destiny and DeShaun are my "wild cards" right now. If I return them to Janelle, I have nothing! Maybe I will return tomorrow after I call the job to tell my boss that I need to take another leave of absence. For now, I need to find out from Skip where his "girl" is hanging out at.

* * *

I have been bouncing from hotel to hotel for the past three nights, unable to contain my rage. I am burning up inside because of the news of my house, but I dare not take a ride over there to see the damage. My cell phone battery is completely dead now, and I cannot remember any of the phone numbers I had

David L.

stored. With only one choice left, I dress DeShaun and instruct Destiny to go wash up.

"Where are we goin' now, Daddy?" she asks.

"We are going to take a ride over to Uncle Cliff's house. I'm going to drop you guys off for a few hours to handle some business."

As soon as we get onto the congested highway, DeShaun is asleep in his car seat. The ride to Uncle Cliff's apartment building is long, and the air conditioning in my truck has been acting up since I got my truck back from the repair shop a few weeks ago. Every police officer either behind me or to the side of me makes me nervous and causes me to sweat even more than I already am.

"Daddy, are we almost there?"

"Yes, Destiny, we will be there in a little while. Don't you worry...everything is going to work itself out, okay?"

My insatiable desire to snuff out Shontell's life is beginning to cause me to question my own morality. Six months ago, I was laid up in my bed with my beloved wife and everything was all good. It remains a mystery to me how things could change so fast. Even Joe Banger's death came unexpected. Yeah, now that I look back at what happened, I realize he was just a pawn in Janelle's plan to get back at me. But so what? He knew the rules to the game! And Dani...we used to be co-workers and good friends on top of that. And I killed her, too! What am I becoming? I privately tell myself after my dealings with Shontell and Janelle, I am going to change my ways and live life as I used to. I need to become the man I used to be before Janelle fucked up my life!

Over Your Dead Body

Uncle Cliff is standing outside his building in some type of silly looking Hawaiian suit with hard bottom shoes and a straw hat. He is smoking on a half-lit cigarette and throws it to the side when he sees me roll up with the children.

"What up, favorite uncle!"

"Favorite uncle my ass! I hope you ain't expectin' to stay here, boy! You not gettin' me caught up in yo' crazy mess!"

"Chill, Uncle Cliff! I'm not tryin' to stay up in here. But I need you to contact this guy right here. This is his number. He will come by and take the children to Janelle. Just don't call him until at least eight o'clock tonight."

I hand Uncle Cliff a business card with Detective Adams' name on it. Of course, my uncle has to interrogate me like he is some slick talking New York City lawyer or something.

"Why eight o'clock? What are you up to now, boy?"

"Just do this one thing for me, Uncle Cliff…PLEASE! I won't ask you for anything else. I PROMISE!"

Reluctantly, he grabs DeShaun's car seat out of my back seat and instructs Destiny to get her little brother out of the ninety-degree plus heat. Free from my children for the first time in several weeks, I feel rejuvenated and alive. It is ironic I feel this way. After all, I went through all of this for them to be in my life, and now I am dropping them off with my uncle. Just before Destiny walks into Uncle Cliff's apartment, I kiss her tenderly on her forehead. I then proceed to lift

David L.

up DeShaun and squeeze him affectionately until his little round eyes widen with glee.

"You're going to be back soon, right, Daddy?"

"Of course, baby – of course."

"Don't forget, Uncle Cliff – don't call that number until eight o'clock tonight."

"Yeah, yeah, boy. I heard you the first time...eight o'clock!"

Too bad DeShaun and Destiny were not just a little bit older. I probably would have never returned to New York. I am not built to last in jail, and the thought of possible incarceration almost makes me want to grab the kids and take off again. Before I get the temptation to reconsider and leave with my children again, I drive off to my next destination: Skip's place.

CHAPTER EIGHT

September 11, 2004

    I cannot help but think that the nightmare going on in my life is all because of Shontell and her meddling ways. She always has been envious of me and Janelle's relationship, and at the same time, bitter because she could not keep a man. At least she never had any children. It would be a shame for her children to have to be split up and placed in foster care after I soon snap her neck like a twig!

    "Open the door, Skip! It's me!"

    No answer. His ride is parked outside his apartment, so I know he is somewhere close by. After several more knocks, Skip finally answers the door.

    "Where she at, Skip?"

    "Where is who at, Pres? What the hell are you talkin' 'bout now? And where are your children?"

    "You sure are askin' me a lot of questions! Why do you want to know where the children are?"

    "'Cause you actin' real crazy, that's why! You ain't the same person I remember. Janelle has really got you actin' a fool!"

    "Just tell me where Shontell is, that's all! I got some unfinished business to handle with her!"

David L.

"I haven't talked to her all day. That's my word! For all I know, she could be anywhere. Matter of fact, she is probably with Janelle."

Skip is lying. I know he is. He never was a good liar, and whenever he tries to embellish the truth, he always says "That's My Word" at the end of every sentence.

"Why don't you come inside and chill for a minute? You're sweatin' like a pig."

He is right, but I can't let on that I am on a one-man mission to eradicate his girl like she did my home. Speaking of homes, I need to check out what happened to my house and just how bad the damage really is.

"Yo, I heard about your house! I really feel for you, man."

"Don't feel for me! Feel for your little girlfriend!"

"C'mon now, Pres…you don't really think Shontell would go out like that, do you? I mean, she's got her moments and all, but she ain't no arsonist."

"And exactly how do you know that for sure? You've barely been talkin' to her but for so long your damn self!"

"That might be true and all, but I can tell you it wasn't Shontell. She was with me for most of the day when your house caught on fire."

"Listen to yourself, Skip! MOST of the day? That girl got you so pussy-whipped you can't even see what is going on here!"

"So tell me, what *is* going on?"

"Janelle knows I iced Joe Banger and probably Dani, too, so now she is trying to catch me on my third strike!"

Over Your Dead Body

I can tell by the look on Skip's face that I accidentally gave up way too much information. I never told him about my encounter with Dani after I left him at the Nasty Kitty a couple of months ago. I end my time with Skip as abruptly as it began – with him asking questions better left unanswered and me ignoring his pleas to continue.

At the first sight of what is left of my house, I want to scream out loud, but the bitterness in my soul won't let me. Even though I probably stand to make out from the insurance settlement, my home is in complete ruins. Upon further inspection, I realize Detective Adams was trying to prevent me from going off the deep end when he gave me the news about my house. Fifty percent my ass! My entire house was destroyed in that fire! Even the garden in the back where I began growing my tomatoes has been completely wiped out!

If I had any tears left, I would probably use them right now. With each passing glimpse of what was once my house, my desire to end Shontell and Janelle's life grows to epic proportions. Even my turncoat best friend is probably right now dialing Shontell's cell phone, trying to warn her of my wrath that has yet to come. It is about five minutes to eight, which means I do not have much time to act. If I plan my next series of steps out perfectly, I will have the perfect alibi for when Shontell bites the dust.

"Did you call him yet, Uncle Cliff?" I ask, referring to his promise to call Detective Adams.

"Yeah, and he is on his way to pick up the children right now. Just remember what I said, boy."

David L.

"And what's that, Uncle Cliff?"
"Don't go and do anything…"
CLICK! I hang up my phone in disgust. I am not trying to hear any of his lecturing. I am also relieved because earlier, I was able to pick up a new cell phone charger from my service provider, so now I got a full charge.

Shontell lives nearby in the projects, so getting into her place should be pretty easy. I patrolled her block a couple of times and didn't see her car, so chances are she hasn't arrived home yet. A familiar-looking homeless man eyes me suspiciously as I enter Shontell's housing project. I am already halfway to the third floor before I remember who the homeless dude is. He was on the train earlier in the year when I was still working at Downtown Records. I could have taken the elevator, but the stench of urine was too unbearable, so I decided to walk. Shontell lives on the tenth floor, and I am barely halfway there. Up on the ninth floor corridor, a group of boys are rolling dice. One boy, who looks to be about twelve or thirteen, is beat boxing and a fourteen-year-old looking boy is rapping to the beat.

"You don't live up in deez projects! Who the hell are you?" one of the boys questions.

Sensing a no-win situation, I think fast to avoid any potential problems.

"I'm lookin' for some new talent for my record label," I respond, pulling a business card from out of my pants pocket.

Two of the boys eye me with caution in case I am reaching for a gun or I am Five-O. I tell the boy that was rapping to give me a call in a few days so I

Over Your Dead Body

can keep it moving to the next floor. I remember how to get around to Shontell's side of the building because Janelle and I helped her move into her apartment a couple of years ago. Just as I expected, there is no response when I knock on her door. The elevator is around the corner and I don't expect Shontell's lazy ass to take the stairs. Every time I hear the elevator door open, I sneak a peek around the corner to see if it is her coming.

Thirty minutes pass and I am growing tired of the wait. Every time I think about leaving, the thought of my burned down house keeps me grounded. Looking around the hallway, I don't see any cameras posted and the hallways are still deserted. An hour passes by and there is still no sign of Shontell.

I am now leaned up against the wall and the realization begins to set in. Skip must have instructed her to stay away from her apartment! Just as I let out a hearty yawn and head for the stairs, the sound of an elevator door opening causes me to look once more around the corner. JACKPOT! Shontell is walking off the elevator with about three bags of groceries in each hand and fumbling for her apartment keys. I quickly run over to the far side of the hallway to avoid her seeing me. Each step has to be precise so she does not notice me and begin to scream. The thought of becoming an expert on sneaking up on people and taking out their life doesn't once enter my mind. I rationalize to myself that this is something I must do…I *have* to do.

Shontell has her keys positioned to unlock her door, and just as she bends over to grab her groceries, I

211

David L.

make my move. Previous thoughts of déjà vu are replaced with revenge as I lunge towards her while she enters her apartment.

"WHAT THE…!"

My hands wrap around her mouth like a vise grip, preventing her from yelling for help. Now inside, I quickly slam her door with my foot and wrestle her onto the living room floor.

"You think I don't know it was you that torched my house?" I say, while at the same time wrapping my hands around her throat. "You think I don't know Janelle put you up to doing that?"

Even a well-placed kick to the side of my ribs does not cause me to relinquish my chokehold on Shontell. Her face is now bloodshot red and her eyes are popping out of her skull. If I were a betting man, I would guess she is within seconds from passing out. Similar to Dani, Shontell's struggling and erratic motions of her body cause me to smile in anticipation to my eventual triumph. Seconds go past and Shontell's face changes colors like fireworks on the Fourth of July – from red, to blue, to pale white. The erratic flailing of her arms and legs and unsuccessful attempts to kick her way out of my grasp turn to defeat as her eyes close shut and her limbs finally go limp.

"That will teach you to mess with a crazy man with nothing left to lose!" I say, looking down at her with pride over what I had just done.

With nothing left here to accomplish, I reach into one of Shontell's grocery bags and pull out a half-melted Ben and Jerry's ice cream bar. After all, it doesn't make sense for it to go to waste. Besides, I haven't eaten in hours!

Over Your Dead Body

* * *

"I am a full-fledged murderer!" I grumble under my breath.

Less than sixty minutes ago, I had both of my hands around Shontell's throat. I can still envision her body sprawled across her apartment floor. Not long from now, Shontell's body will be discovered, and I will be getting a call from Detective Adams. After all, I blamed her for my house going up in flames, and both Skip and the detective know I have it in for her. And what about when Janelle is notified of Shontell's murder? She knows what I am capable of, and after all, that was her best friend. She will sell me out for sure!

With a limited number of options and no place to rest my head, I begin to head towards the George Washington Bridge. I have enough sense to know I am a sitting duck if I stay here in Mount Vernon. After what just happened over in the projects, I will never be allowed to see my children again! Several phone calls to Skip go unanswered. Several more phone calls to Uncle Cliff also go unanswered. Before I leave Mount Vernon, I need to place one last phone call to Detective Adams.

"Who is this?"

"This is Preston Price. Were my children picked up?"

"I need you to turn yourself in, Preston. C'mon down to the precinct and I will try to make this as painless as possible."

David L.

"Why do I need to come down to the station? I kept my end of the bargain. I returned the children just like you told me to do."

"Don't insult my intelligence, Preston! You're wanted for the murder of Shontell Rivers! You remember her, right? She was your ex-wife's best friend, and you blamed her for burning down your house. That is why you murdered her in cold blood!"

If Detective Adams could see my face, he would see my jaw drop in shock and bewilderment. How did he find out about Shontell's death so fast? It hasn't even been a full hour since I left her place, and now I am being hit with a murder rap!

"Shontell was murdered? And you think I had something to do with it, Detective?"

"Don't play with me, Preston! You took your revenge out on her because you think she burned down your house. You told me on the phone yourself. Besides, your fingerprints are on the inside doorknob AND around her neck AND on the ice cream wrapper you ate after you took her life! Oh yeah…and I got a sworn report from a homeless guy that identified you as you entered and left the area."

"You have to help me out, Detective! I'll get eaten up in jail! I'm not built to go to jail!"

"Turn yourself in, Preston! Whatever you do, don't become a fugitive. Off the record, I can recommend a couple of great lawyers that are good in situations like this."

I immediately hang up my cell phone. There is no way in hell I am turning myself in! Detective Adams has just made my decision to leave the state that much easier. If only I could get out of this damn

Over Your Dead Body

congested traffic that is headed towards the George Washington Bridge!

There are over twenty cops parked across the George Washington Bridge and a couple of helicopters are patrolling above. I throw my cell phone out the window in anticipation that they can somehow use it as a tracking device. My choices are beginning to run thin, and I am one exit away from making a run for it. I have got to react quickly if I am going to do this right.

Pulling over to the side of the highway, I immediately grab my gym bag from out of the trunk and switch clothes in the back seat. My plan is simple: ditch my truck and jog off of the exit ramp. If highway police were given a description of what I am wearing, they won't suspect a jogger in basketball shorts, a tank top, and a pair of Nikes on his feet. I am already sweating heavily from the scorching heat as the midday sun slowly begins to make its descent from the clouds above. Located in my socks are a couple of credit cards, a little over one hundred dollars in cash, and a picture taken with my children last year on Halloween. DeShaun was dressed up as Bart Simpson and Destiny was dressed as Storm from the X-Men comic book series. Those were the days!

I begin my impersonation of a jogger and get the obligatory stares from motorists on the highway.

"You can't jog on the highway, sir! You need to exit the highway immediately!" a young, female cop announces.

I immediately apologize and proceed to remove myself from any more unnecessary attention. I begin my narrow escape through side streets in the Bronx.

215

David L.

The sun has gone down and is now being replaced by darkness. If I am going to survive out in these streets, I am going to have to find somewhere to rest my head. Secondly, I have to totally detach myself from any communication in the event that people's phones are tapped. That means no talking to Uncle Cliff, Janelle, Skip – NOBODY! The first place I go to is a nearby VIM, looking as if I just played in the Final Four basketball tournament, and walk out in a pair of denim jeans, a Rocafella hoodie, and a bookbag to throw my gym clothes in. My next destination is Rollo's pool hall located about half a mile further south.

I have a sudden craving for a cancer stick because Rollo's pool hall is completely immersed with patrons taking pulls on their cigarettes. To top it off, all the walking I have just done has me starving for some nourishment, but I got to watch my spending habits up in here. I need to seriously gather my thoughts and remain indoors, and what better place than an underground gambling spot like Rollo's pool hall.

"What up, Preston! I haven't seen you in a minute, son. You got all corporate on us and forgot where you came from?"

It is my old running partner from the block. Ramon Rios. This was the guy that was down for whatever back in the day. a real loose cannon if there ever was one. The child your mother used to warn you about!

"What up, man!" I haven't seen you in like ten years!"

We give each other a big hug and get to talking about the good 'ol days. I've known Ramon longer than I've known Skip. If memory serves me correctly, we were even in the same kindergarten class together. He was one of the few Hispanic kids that played with the Blacks, even though our school was filled with nothing but Blacks and Hispanics. My interaction, although sincere, is also riddled with uncertainty because of his crime-filled life.

"What are you getting yourself into these days?" I ask.

"Right about now, I'm keeping a real low profile, if you know what I mean. I got a couple of out-of-state warrants I'm tryin' to dodge."

"I kind of got caught up myself!"

"Not college boy Preston! What happened to the quiet boy with the thick glasses that ran off to school and left his boys to hit it rich with all the white boys out in corporate America?"

"You got me soundin' like I sold out or somethin'!"

"Nah, never that! What up wit' Skip? You still tight with that fool?"

"Yeah, him and I are still cool. Right now, he is kind of suspect, though. I don't really want to get into it right now."

Every time Ramon turns from me to greet one of his boys or to have a conversation with one of the waitresses at the bar, I take the opportunity to check him out. Although we are both about the same age, he looks about ten years older than me. He's got a teardrop tattoo directly under his left eye, about a six-inch scar across his temple, a tattoo of a tiger across his neck, and a red bandana hanging out of his back

David L.

pocket, probably signifying he is down with a local gang of some sort.

A little over three hours at Rollo's pool hall and all I have done to address my growing hunger is snack on some pretzels from the bar and a handful of nachos at the table I am sitting at with Ramon. We are busy politicking about our fucked-up situations and figuring out a plan to do something about it. I can't trust Skip, Uncle Cliff – NOBODY! To top it all off, when my boss watches the news and finds out I am on the run, I will also be out of a job. That is if he hasn't gotten the word already. Everyone at the pool hall is either a pusher or a junkie. Either way, I need to jump on the bandwagon and create some revenue for my soon-to-be empty pockets.

Ramon and I go back to our younger years, but that was a long time ago. Can he be trusted? My only ace-in-the-hole is the fact that no one besides Skip knows who Ramon is and no one knows I know where Janelle is staying. I have got to figure out a way to use that to my advantage!

"Yo, Ramon, can you get me a gun?"

"You want me to get you a gun? You talkin' to the man! Of course, I can get you one! You got beef out here or something?"

"Nah, nothing like that. I just got some unfinished business with someone, that's all."

"That's all? Whoever it is must have done something serious for you to want to off them! You catch your girl cheatin' or somethin'?"

"Something like that. How soon can you get me a piece?"

"Hell, if you got the money, we can go now and pick it up. I've got a "connect" out in Queens that sells any type of gun you want from out the trunk of his car. Besides, he owes me!"

Every time I try to get myself back on track, the temptation of the streets remind me it is too late for me to go back to how things used to be. I can't ever go back to where I came from. My house in Mount Vernon, my six-figure salary in the record business, my wife and children that once loved and adored me – it is all just a distant memory now. A memory that makes me feel even more bitter and resentful as to what my life has become. A small part of me wants to tell Ramon no thanks and keep it moving, but my inner self tells me it is too late for all of that. All my life, Ramon and everyone else from the old neighborhood thought I "sold out" and forgot where I was from. Now is my chance to prove them all wrong!

The train ride over to Ramon's "connect" brings back memories of my stick-up earlier in the year. With Ramon having my back, that wouldn't have happened like it went down when I allowed myself to get punked by some fool with a knife. It is near midnight and the train ride to Queens is almost deserted except for a couple of teenage boys rapping and banging on the seat of the train. An elderly couple is waiting by the door; probably hoping for their stop to hurry up and arrive. The rest of the twenty-minute train ride is uneventful, and finally reaching Jamaica, Queens, Ramon's connect is waiting for us promptly like a true businessman ought to be.

David L.

Ramon's connect goes by the name of "Boomer." He is wearing a Yankees cap turned around backwards, a pair of way too large denim State Property jeans, some beige Timberland boots, and a Sean John sweatshirt. He is also leaning up against probably what is his car, a well-polished, metallic silver Lincoln Navigator with chrome rims and tinted windows.

"I don't know if I want to do this, man. I don't trust this cat. He looks like he could be Five-O to me," Boomer declares, looking over at Ramon.

"He ain't Five-O! This is my man from back in the day! He's good, son!"

"That's what you say! But how can I be so sure? If he's not Five-O, he's going to have to prove it to me somehow!"

"So then how do you want him to prove it?"

Ramon's connect pauses for a moment during his thoughts. I can tell I am not going to like what he has up his sleeve, but I am already in too deep. Any hesitation on my part and I could put myself in serious jeopardy with Ramon AND Boomer!

"Very simple. Five-O can't do a police bust if they're getting high during their assignment, right?"

Just as Boomer says that, he pulls out a white envelope from his glove compartment and passes it to me.

"Try some of dis. One hit and that will prove you ain't no pig with a badge."

"Man, I ain't putting this shit in my nose!"

Boomer and Ramon laugh at my ignorance to the drug game. The stuff in the envelope isn't cocaine as I suspected, but LSD. I am supposed to place the

Over Your Dead Body

contents under my tongue for a faster high. Not wanting to look like an undercover cop, I hesitate momentarily, but then give in. As expected, my high is instantaneous and I can feel my eyes become dilated.

"That's the good stuff right there!" Boomer declares matter-of-factly.

Maybe it is my high from the LSD hit, but I could swear that Boomer and Ramon's laughing slowly turns to growling. At one point during the plateau of my high, I look into Boomer's side view mirror and my teeth look extra sharp – almost taking on the appearance of fangs.

"Now that I know you're legit, we can sit back, drink a couple of brews, and discuss what kind of gun you are lookin' to purchase."

I walk away from Boomer with a chrome-plated .22 pistol tucked away discreetly in my waist. I got a pretty good deal on it, too! Besides, I don't need anything big weighing me down and a .22 pistol is small enough to get the job done. Ramon has been gracious enough to let me crash at his place until I can eventually find a spot of my own. I haven't totally figured out the details in my head on how I am going to use Ramon to help me get close to Janelle. When I get the drop on her, I have to make sure there aren't any witnesses, especially the children. I could never forgive myself if one of them witnessed me killing their mother. I might be a murderer, but I am not heartless!

Although I am as tired as I have probably ever been in my short-lived life, I don't get a wink of sleep at Ramon's apartment. The combination of drugs and thoughts of the looks on my victims' faces just before I

David L.

took their lives begin to become overwhelming for my good-natured soul. Ramon, on the other hand, is fast asleep on a pull-out couch in the other room, and his snoring is almost unbearable.

"This year has been a fuckin' mess," I say with a soft whisper.

To think it was not too long ago Janelle and I were actually contemplating having another child. That would have meant there would be three children soon without their mother! Within arms distance is what looks to be a Philly blunt that was half smoked by someone. Snoring even louder, I conclude Ramon is not going to be waking up anytime soon and proceed to light up. Just what I need to put me to sleep! And after a few pulls, that is exactly what happens.

* * *

"Oh snap! That's you on the T.V., Preston! You are a fuckin' celebrity!" Ramon exclaims, pointing to the television screen.

It has been approximately seven days since I choked the life out of Shontell, and about six days longer than I thought I would still be at Ramon's basement apartment.

"What are you talkin' 'bout?"

Ramon has always been a joker, and I figure this is just another one of his attempts to get a good laugh at my expense.

"Get over here, quick! You on the news!"

Almost tripping over a pile of Ramon's dirty clothes, I quickly respond to see what he is rambling on about. The sight of my picture on the television

Over Your Dead Body

screen almost causes me to drop the egg sandwich I made for myself minutes earlier.

"Turn the volume up!" I command.

Doing as instructed, we both listen attentively to the late-breaking news like it is a Sunday morning sermon.

"So that's why you wanted a gun! You killed your ex-wife's best friend, and now you want to finish the job with your wife, huh?"

"Shhh! I'll explain it all to you in a minute. Let me hear what they're sayin' about me!"

Every single detail of Shontell's slaying by my hands is captured by the channel seven eyewitness news crew, and I am sure it is getting played on every other major New York news channel as well. Listening to every word coming out of the newscaster's mouth, my stomach begins to churn as they announce an all-out search for me. To make matters worse, there is a $20,000 reward on my head, and not only did they discover Shontell's body, but they concluded by fingerprint samples and deductive reasoning that I am the prime suspect for the murders of Joe Banger AND Dani!

"Oh snap! I got a straight gangsta killa up in my crib! You like some type of modern-day deranged serial killa or something!" Ramon jokes.

He can tell by the look on my face that joking is the last thing on my mind.

"I have to go in hiding, man! Every damn cop in this city is going to be looking for me! I am a goner if I stay here! I got to leave the state – IMMEDIATELY!" I conclude.

223

David L.

"How you going to leave the state? Everybody and their mama will be lookin' for you. Every bridge is going to have state troopers and helicopters patrolling the area. Every airport is going to be waiting for you to arrive to nab your ass. What you need to do is lay low here for a few days until the heat dies down. Don't go making any stupid mistakes, Preston!"
Ramon is right. I have to stop making such impulsive decisions. It is my poor impulse control that has me in all this trouble I am in now.

Staying at Ramon's crib has been a blessing and at the same time, a curse. I don't have to shell out as much money as I would have to pay at a motel and I get some pretty decent home cooking every now and then. The problem now is that he knows my true identity. Who is to stop him from going to the cops himself to collect that reward money? Although the code of the streets dictates he would never sell me out, that is a lot of money to pass up. We go back a whole lot of years, but damn, $20,000? Shit, if I was down and out on my luck, I would probably turn myself in! But Ramon is different...or so I think!
The more I think about it, the more paranoid I make myself. I have to get out of his basement apartment as soon as possible. I haven't left his place in three days, and the isolation is driving me crazy. Ramon has been gone for about three hours. A pretty long time for someone who says they're just going to the store for a few groceries. For all I know, he could be at the police precinct right now squealing like a pig!
The only way to be sure I am not a sitting duck is to bounce out of Ramon's spot to avoid capture. But

first things first...I proceed to grab his weed stash and his pack of Philly blunts. Then, I go into his money stash and grab about four hundred dollars in twenty-dollar bills. After all, he knows I need the money more than he needs it right about now. I have to time this right or else I am going to have a lot of explaining to do. I am going to look real stupid if as I am leaving, he is walking through the door!

I am showered in literally under a minute and dressed. Who knows when I will get another opportunity to take a nice, warm shower! I contemplate whether or not I should leave him a note apologizing for the stuff I took, but decline my urges. Hopefully, he will understand.

At last, I get to breathe some outside air! Luckily for me, it is going on eight o'clock and the sun has finally left the sky. That means I can travel on foot a little bit less inconspicuous and avoid detection – hopefully! My first objective is to get the hell out of this neighborhood. Ramon knows just about every single hood and street cat in this section of the Bronx, and when he finds out I took off with his stash of weed and cash reserve, I am going to have another bounty on my head. One that will cost me my life!

"Can I get a ride?" I question a cab man, who is biting into a sandwich.

"I'm off the clock, my friend. Maybe some other time."

Inside my knapsack, I got my .22 pistol, about twenty dime bags of weed, cigar blunts, four hundred dollars in cash, a change of clothes, and leftover food I grabbed out of Ramon's refrigerator as I was exiting

David L.

his apartment. My first reaction is to take the cabbie's vehicle, but that would be just plain stupid. If I am going to get me a vehicle, it is not going to be something that stands out as much as a yellow-ass cab. No, what I got to do is catch somebody slipping and take off with their ride. If only I could find someone slipping!

Seeing my face plastered all over the news has me freaking out. The first thing I am going to do tomorrow when the department stores open up is get me a fitted cap to wear over my face and some sunglasses. I might look strange wearing sunglasses near the end of September, but at least I won't be broadcasting who I am around town!

My next destination is Yonkers. There is a seedy-looking motel on Central Avenue that I can check myself into. The one I used to send my clients to when I first started over at Downtown Records and couldn't afford to send them anywhere else. It is about at least a ninety-minute walk from where I am presently, but it is not like I have anything else better to do. If only I could get me a car!

With each passing step, I get closer and closer to my destination, but at the same time, my paranoia grows to epic proportions. Everyone who drives by looking at me, I wonder if they recognize me and are calling the cops. At one point, I am walking as fast as I can, grateful that I made it this far.

"Let me get a pack of Newports and some matches," I instruct a gas station attendant working behind the counter.

He appears nervous and fidgeting with his cash register. His punk ass probably thinks I am going to rob him or something. Like I would even waste my time robbing a second-rate gas station. Everyone knows they never keep any real money in the store anyway! I need this transaction to go as swift as possible to avoid anyone seeing me and calling in their discovery. Outside, a sixty-year-old-looking woman is busy pumping her gas, and it is at that exact moment I realize this is my chance to get me some wheels. Over on the passenger side of the vehicle, what looks to be her equally old ass husband is busy playing with the radio dial.

"Get the hell out of the car!" I say to the old man, getting into the driver's side and pointing my gun directly into his face.

His face turns bright red and I could swear he is about to have a heart attack.

"Get out of the car, Harold! He has a gun!" the old lady announces.

Doing as he is told, the old geezer shuffles out of the driver's side. Looking over at the gas station attendant, he is looking down at his counter, trying his best to avoid getting shot at.

"Sorry, old people, but I need this car more than you!" I say, driving off towards my destination.

A few minutes later, I check into the Central Avenue Motel, but not before parking my newly-acquired vehicle in the back lot to avoid any cops seeing it.

David L.

CHAPTER NINE

November 10, 2004

I have never noticed this before, but a brand new day can do wonders for a man's diminished spirit! After a twenty minute hot shower and a few episodes of *A Different World* on the motel's cheap ass television, I am ready to take on the world! I need to get in touch with Skip because I have to reclaim that letter I sent him a few months ago. That letter is proof positive I committed all of those murders, and if the cops get a hold of it, they will know Janelle is next on my list.

"Are you checking out today, sir?" the hotel man questions.

"Yeah, I guess I am."

After a few more seconds of thought, I reconsider my answer. After all, I am going to need a place to rest my head tonight, and this place is right smack dab in the middle of everything, so I might as well take advantage of its location.

"Here is twenty dollars. Is this enough for you to make sure you have a room for me tonight?"

"Yeah, sure, I can hold a room for you! But you owe me another twenty-five dollars for the night when you return."

"Don't worry about it. I got you tonight."

Over Your Dead Body

After he reminds me the room deposit is non-refundable, I make my exit and head to the nearest store to pick me up a pair of sunglasses and a baseball cap. The stolen car I am driving has got at least a half tank of gas, thanks to the old couple, and it runs like it was just taken off of the lot. I guess it is true what they say about buying a car from an old person…it will last you forever! My only problem is the smell of Preparation H that I vaguely detect coming from the seat, but some air freshener will take care of that. Most of the pay phones in the hood don't work half the time, so I have to travel an extra few miles over to Riverside to use a pay phone. Finally finding one that works, I have to find someone that will place the call for me, just in case the police have already tapped Skip's phone.

"Hey, you want to make a quick five bucks?"

"What do I have to do?"

I found two white boys on bikes that look to be about sixteen or seventeen. The one with the baseball cap turned to the side approaches me first. The other one looks on cautiously, just in case it is a set-up.

"I'm going to dial a number, and all you have to do is tell the guy that answers to meet you over by the old Chinese food restaurant from back in the day. Tell him you are calling for Ramon, and you want to meet up with him at exactly six o'clock this evening."

"What if he wants to know why someone is calling for Ramon?"

"Look, boy, stop asking me so many questions! Do you want to make five bucks or not?"

I guess he does since he doesn't say another word. I proceed to dial Skip's number. As expected,

David L.

Skip answers the phone, and just as the boy predicted, Skip wants to know why Ramon is not calling for himself.

"Tell him to just make sure he show up at the old Chinese restaurant tonight and don't forget to bring the letter that says 'DO NOT OPEN' on it," I whisper into the boy's ear.

Skip might be a lot of things, but he is no dummy. He knows how paranoid I can be at times, and he knows he is the only one that knows about the letter, so it should not take him long to figure out what is going on. Just like I promise, I hand the boy his five bucks and congratulate him on a job well done. For extra precaution, I promise him another five bucks to show up tonight at the Chinese restaurant, just in case Skip turns out to be a traitor and brings the cops with him.

It is hard to try to holler at a girl when your name has been plastered all over the news channel and you are the current public enemy number one in the tri-state area. Two beautiful light-skinned females are walking down Central Avenue, and I cannot even say hi to either one of them. I cannot even drive down any busy intersections for fear of being spotted by an undercover cop or an overzealous citizen trying to win themselves some reward money. My only alternative is to get to Janelle before she ends up being placed in some type of protective custody nonsense – that is if she hasn't already been taken care of by the authorities.

"Fill my tank up," I say to the gas station attendant.

Over Your Dead Body

    I make sure I drive into full service so my time out of the car is as minimal as possible. Even better, the guy pumping my gas has to be at least seventy years of age and does not appear to speak any English. Perfect! No chance of him calling the cops!
    For once, I am thinking logically. If this manhunt ends up being a fast-paced chase like they did with O.J. back in the day, I would look like a damn fool if I run out of gas while the chase is being televised! To top it off, I drive a block down the street to get some dark tint put on all the windows. Looking at my watch, I realize I still have several hours before Skip shows up at the Chinese restaurant. Ever since I have been on the run, it seems like the days are much longer. Maybe it is because I don't have as much to look forward to now that I am a fugitive running from the long arm of the law. I have at least a three-hour wait, and it suddenly occurs to me what I can do to kill some time: I will get a haircut over at Mr. Willy's barbershop! I don't know why I didn't think of that before. Mr. Willy is one of the few people I can trust, and to top it off, he has all types of runners, drug pushers, and lowlifes running from the law in his shop every day. How ironic it is that I now fit in with the people I detested for so long.

    It doesn't take me long to get there. It is beginning to rain slightly, and the roads are extra slick because of the half inch of snow that fell from the skies the night before.
    "What up, Mr. Willy? You think you can hook me up wit' a cut before five o'clock today?"

David L.

I get a bunch of weird-looking stares from the mostly male individuals who presently inhabit Mr. Willy's shop. One guy immediately exits as soon as I step inside. Maybe it is just me, but I could swear at least half of everyone that was either talking to the person next to them or talking into a cell phone stopped everything they were doing to get themselves a better look at me. My question to Mr. Willy goes temporarily unanswered.

"So what up, Mr. Willy? You think you can hook me up?"

"Hey Leroy, take over for me for a minute. I have to talk to this boy 'bout a few things!"

Mr. Willy hands his custom clippers to the barber next to him who is sitting down reading a Jet magazinem and then pulls me into the next room. It is a room that has been recently renovated to sell bootleg CD's, DVD's and other miscellaneous products to boost revenue for his fading barbershop customers.

"What would make you want to come up in my place of business knowing that you are wanted for murder? You tryin' to get me closed down or somethin'?"

"No. Of course not, Mr. Willy. But I've been coming here practically all my life, and I figured I would be safe here for a minute. I don't have nowhere else to go!"

"Well, you can't hang out here – that's for sure! I got enough questionable characters hanging they lazy asses all up in my place of business! I don't need to be adding any more to the list!"

"If you don't give me a break, I'm done for! You wanna see me go to jail?"

Over Your Dead Body

"What about that funny looking dude you are always hanging around with? Why don't you go stay with him?"

"That's the first place the cops would look for me. You know that! Besides, I don't trust him no ways! I think he might be connected with my ex-wife somehow, and I can't take the chance of him knowing where I am!"

Sure enough, Mr. Willy hooks me up and lets me stay in the back room. He even gives me a spare key to the barbershop, but not before reminding me that I better not be caught creeping in anytime after he locks up for the night. It is a big load off of my shoulders knowing that at least I have a place to rest my head tonight. Now, all I have to do is hook up with Skip to find out where his head is at.

I haven't eaten all day, and the fried chicken wings with fried rice that I ordered a few minutes ago has just been served to me. Even though I have been coming to this same Chinese restaurant on and off again damn near my entire life, the people behind the counter still look at me as if I am going to rip them off or something.

"You think I could get the hot sauce and some ketchup for my chicken?" I say to the old Chinese woman as she drops my food onto the table.

After saying some gibberish to her partner behind the counter, she finally returns with my requested condiments. Twenty minutes after six o'clock and Skip is still a no-show. Just as I am finishing my last piece of chicken, look who comes

233

David L.

waltzing into the Chinese restaurant. The look on his face says it all!

"Something told me it was you that I was going to see here tonight/ I haven't spoken to Ramon in years. Besides, he and you were always tighter than me and him anyway. So what up, man? You takin' care of yourself out here in these mean streets?"

"Tell me straight up, Skip...you sell me out to anyone?"

"What the hell are you talkin' 'bout? Sell you out to who? Janelle?"

"To the cops, that's who! I am going to ask you one more time, and be honest with me...did you sell me out?"

"That's what you got me up in here for? That was pretty fucked up what you did to Shontell and all, but come on...she was just someone I was hitting on the side. You my boy from way back. I would never sell any one of my boys out. That's the code of the streets!"

I feel much better hearing those words from Skip's mouth. Although I never envisioned Skip selling me out, I had to make sure. I always knew when Skip was lying to me, and today, it looks as if he has my back for sure.

"Yo, my bad, man. I knew you wouldn't sell me out, but I still had to hear it for myself."

"So what have you been up to anyway?"

"I hooked up with Ramon for real, just for a quick minute, but I had to take off from out of there. Things were too hot where he was staying, and I didn't need the extra attention coming down on me."

Over Your Dead Body

I can't help but leave out all of the miscellaneous information. Skip was right about what he said earlier. There is a code to the streets, and I broke one of them when I left with Ramon's drug stash and money. I hate the man I have become, but I have already rationalized with myself that I needed the stuff way more than Ramon.

"That's Ramon for you. He always did know how to draw heat in his direction. What about now? You got yourself a place to stay?"

I am hesitant to tell Skip where I am staying, but like me, he knows me so well that he would know I was lying anyway!

"I'm staying over at the barbershop for a few days."

"Mr. Willy's shop?"

"Yeah, but it is only temporary. Before I head out of the state for good, I have to take care of some unfinished business with Janelle."

"You need to leave that revenge shit alone, man! It is beginning to consume your life! You know every single cop in Mount Vernon is going to be watching her extra close from this moment on just so they can get to you!"

"About the cops…you got that letter for me?"

Handing me the coveted letter that could quite possibly send me to jail for the rest of my life, I immediately tear it up into a thousand pieces and toss it into a nearby garbage can. I say my goodbyes to Skip, but not before giving him the phone number to the barbershop and promising to come by and see him before I leave New York.

David L.

With the extra five bucks that I have in my pocket from the boy that never returned to the Chinese restaurant, I figure now would be a good time to get me some real food. Entering a seedy-looking diner, I immediately sit down in the furthest corner to avoid any unnecessary interaction.

"May I take your order, sir?"

A rather feminine looking young man in his early twenties asks to take my order, and he has to be as gay as they come. If he twitches his hips anymore, one of them is going to fall the fuck off! Not only that, but he has the sweetest disposition I have ever seen and his entire mannerisms spells D-E-L-I-C-I-O-U-S!

"Can I get a chicken salad sandwich and a side of cole slaw? Oh yeah, let me get a Pepsi, too. Don't fill up the entire cup with ice."

"You look kind of familiar. Have I seen you before?"

"Nah, I doubt it. I just moved into town about a week ago."

"If you don't mind me saying, you are working the heck out of those glasses!"

"Oh these? They're no big deal."

"What are they? Armani?"

"I have no idea. I just picked them up because I needed a pair of glasses, that's all."

"Mind if I see them?"

Now this guy is starting to get on my nerves. Not once did I see him write down my order, and now he is asking me a whole bunch of crap I don't particularly feel like answering.

"I just want to get my food and head home, nothing personal."

Over Your Dead Body

I think he has finally got the hint because he walks off briskly in a huff. There is no telling what is going to happen to my food now, but I can't worry about it. Besides, what I don't know can't hurt me! Before I return to the barbershop to rest my tired body, I enter the diner bathroom to wash up in their sink. It is not the most conventional approach, but it beats washing up in Mr. Willy's sink. I think he purposely had the heat turned off so I wouldn't run up his ConEd bill. I am in a much better mood after I stuffed my stomach with food, and even my gay-ass waiter stopped asking me so many damn questions.

"Here are some promotional coupons for the next time you decide to visit the diner," my waiter says as I pay my bill.

It doesn't occur to me why he handed me the coupon, especially after I told him that I doubt I would be back, until I look on the reverse side. I can't help but chuckle to myself as I see what appears to be his phone number on the back of the coupon voucher.

* * *

According to the agreement I have with Mr. Willy, I got one more day to stay at his barbershop, and money is running out faster than I expected. If only I knew how to cut hair, I could make some extra money on the side working out of one of his many empty barber chairs after hours. Days of brainstorming have not helped me at all, and I am still pressed for making some extra cash. Even the dime bags of weed I stole from Ramon's apartment are almost all gone. I sold half of my stash to some of the regulars at the

David L.

barbershop, and the other half, I smoked. Ramon's weed was not the strongest stuff in the world, but it put me to sleep lying on the couch inside of Mr. Willy's cold ass barbershop.

"You know, Preston, I saw you on that there picture tube again a few hours ago," Mr. Willy whispers into my ear.

"Are you serious? What did they say this time?"

"Just that you were still at large and that you should be considered armed and dangerous."

"I have to get out of here, Mr. Willy. I can't take a chance on getting caught."

"You be careful out there in them streets, boy. Those cops don't give a damn about you and would love nothing more than to put a bullet in your brain."

"I know, Mr. Willy, I know. I know how to take care of myself."

"You do, huh? About three years ago, I seen one cop put a bullet into a kid's back. The kid wasn't doin' anything but reaching into his pocket to hand the cop his picture I.D.!"

"I will keep that in mind."

All of my senses have been working in overdrive since my face has been plastered for all of the tri-state area to see. Every move a person makes, every sound that can be possibly heard, even my instincts have been multiplied. That has been my survival instincts working to take care of my well-being. I think it is called survival of the fittest. So then, how come I do not notice the unmarked police car parked directly outside of the barbershop?

Over Your Dead Body

As soon as I take my first step outside of the barbershop, two more unmarked cop cars immediately pull out of the gas station across the street. There are two undercover cops in each car and everyone gets out as soon as I detect their presence.

"Stop where you are!" one cop announces.

He has not drawn his weapon yet, but his hand is on his hip, ready to make his move towards me. Mr. Willy had recommended I keep the stolen car I have been driving parked away from the barbershop so the license plate would not be traced. With the car parked about three blocks away in a deserted alleyway, I will have to make my escape on foot. I count a total of six cops, and as soon as the lead cop motions to the rest of them, I take off like a runaway slave. The only way I am going to be able to dodge these guys is to put some distance between us. I have enough sense to know they are not the only ones and that soon, more cops will arrive.

I am unable to run at full speed because of the slippery conditions from the weather. My only shot at avoiding capture is to make it into the Vincent Moyston projects, which are about five blocks away. Even housing authority police is scared to run up in there by themselves. I know I can lose these guys as long as I can maintain at least fifty feet of distance between us. My adrenalin fuels my endurance, and luckily for me, fear of capture is my only motivation. I have momentary thoughts of stopping in my tracks and grabbing an unsuspecting pedestrian to use as leverage. My only concern is the unwanted media attention that it would bring, and not to mention, the helicopters that could probably pick me off with a bullet from up

239

David L.

above. I am now around the corner from the Vincent Moyston projects, and as expected, I have been able to further the distance between the cops and me by at least another fifty feet. The projects have about twenty floors, so even if all of the officers separate; my chances of escape are greatly increased.

"Stop where you are right now!" one officer yells.

He is leading the pack, and I can tell they are getting tired because they are slowing down. An old lady almost gets knocked over as I quickly run inside before the door slams shut, preventing me from getting in. The six cops are not so lucky. Those poor fools are going to have to have someone buzz them in, and from the looks of things; the inhabitants around these parts don't take too kindly to "the boys in blue."

"How many floors up before I get to the roof?" I ask one teenage boy walking down the stairs.

He holds up both hands, so I already know I am in for some serious cardiovascular conditioning. I can hear a commotion going on about two floors down, and instinctively know it is probably the cops who managed to get inside. So far, no shots have been fired, so I am making out good.

"Is there another way out of here besides the elevator?" I ask another boy coming out of his apartment.

"Yeah, that way. You can get out of here on the fire escape, but I heard it is mad loose. It's been that way for months!"

I graciously thank the boy for his timely tip and make my way towards the fire escape. The first place those cops will probably look is on the roof, but they

Over Your Dead Body

probably won't expect me to climb down the fire escape. I am about halfway down from landing into a nearby alleyway when one of the bolts on the fire escape ladder breaks off, causing me to land face first onto the cold, cement floor. There is momentary silence until I hear footsteps coming towards me from the rear of the project building. Without much thought, I jump head first into a nearby dumpster to avoid detection. Sure enough, three cops run by just as I leap in and continue around to the other side of the project. It looks like I got away this time...but what about next time? I know in my heart that I cannot keep this up for too much longer.

    My heart is racing a mile a minute and I am out of breath. I feel like I felt after I committed my first murder against Joe Banger many months ago. His death was easy compared to what I did to Dani! After all, Joe Banger was a sworn enemy and I promised myself I would end his life. At least I once had feelings for Dani. And what about Shontell? I mean I always had a general dislike for her, but she was Janelle's best friend and I often put up with her numerous shortcomings in the past.
    Look at me...I am hiding inside of a dumpster and the smell of garbage almost makes me want to throw up whatever food is left in my stomach. In another dumpster right across from me, a huge rat is sniffing the empty contents of an empty soda can. I have been scared of rodents my entire life, but today, I just look on in anticipation to see if the six officers come back over this way. I might be scared of a rat in a

David L.

dumpster, but I am much more fearful of getting apprehended by Five-O!

"What are you doin' over in this area? This here is my resting spot! Get out of here!" the booming voice says from behind.

I immediately jump up and wave my gun towards the direction of the mysterious voice. Whoever it is, it must be their lucky day, because my first instinct is to start shooting and ask questions later.

"Don't shoot...PLEASE! I don't want to die!" the man says with genuine sorrow in his voice.

He is a homeless man, probably just looking for somewhere to rest his head and maybe fill his stomach with some of the discarded food from out of the dumpster. What a miserable and lonely life to have, wondering where your next meal is coming from. What am I thinking? I am not too far away from being hungry and homeless my damn self. Hell, I am already homeless!

I officially have no more friends from this point forward in my life. Skip sold me out to the cops...I know he did! He was the only one I told about where I was staying, except for Mr. Willy. And speaking of him, I definitely can't go back there...EVER! Now the cops are going to be hanging around his place, drawing unnecessary attention to his after-hour activities. He is about to lose a whole lot of business, and it is my entire fault!

"I'm not going to hurt you, mister. I thought you were someone else looking for me, that's all."

The homeless man looks me dead in my eyes as if he just saw a ghost. I think he is just grateful I don't blast him into nothingness as he proceeds to tell me his

Over Your Dead Body

entire life story. Any other time, I would tell him to beat it, but the combination of his wit and charisma enlightens me to listen even further.

"...And it wasn't until about a year ago when I became homeless that I just gave up all hope and started doing petty crimes in the neighborhood," the man reports apologetically.

"I lost my wife to cancer many, many years ago, and from that moment on, I just began to spiral downward. What about you? You have a wife?"

"I had a wife. I'm divorced now. I dedicated my entire life to my wife and children. Now, I have nothing to show for it."

"So you have children, huh? That is a beautiful thing. I have a son myself. After my wife passed away, I could no longer feed my family the way they were accustomed, and I began to drink heavily as a result of it. Ultimately, my son was taken from me and his mother's brother ended up raising him. But enough about me...why were the cops chasing you earlier?"

"I'm wanted for murder. I made a few mistakes along the way, and now, I have to watch my back. The cops are looking to take me out – any way possible."

"Isn't it strange how we can go from love to hate...and so quickly. You have malice in your heart, my son, and you need to cleanse your spirit. Killing someone...ANYONE...is never the answer. But I am not here to judge you...only to educate you in your time of need."

Here I am talking to a man who has nothing of material substance to call his own, and to top it off, I don't even know his name. His wisdom

David L.

notwithstanding, I can't help but think I have seen him before.
"You never did tell me your name, old timer."
"My name? That is not important. What is important is that you get your life back on track and always remember what your priorities are in life. It's too late for me, son, but for you...your life has just begun. It's just that your eyes are closed to the world and you feel as if you are trapped in a corner."
Damn, he is good! That is exactly how I feel! I give the homeless man a hug, and even with the scent of stench all over him, I feel as if he is some sort of holy prophet or something.
"Take care, old timer. And thank you for lifting my spirits."
I proceed to hand the man my last ten-dollar bill, which he refuses to take.
"You need this more than I do," he says, handing the money back. "I don't need your money. I have all of this to provide for me," he says, stretching his arms out as wide as they would go. "Goodbye, my son, and GOD bless you!" he adds before walking away into the alley behind the Vincent Moyston projects.
Still shaken up, it takes me several moments to ponder the conversation between the homeless man and myself. How well he seemed to know my situation. Almost as if he was a part of me in some type of way.
"Could that old, homeless bum be my father? Nah, no way! He can't be!"

Over Your Dead Body

With only ten dollars left in my pocket, and a broken strap on my bookbag as a result of my drop from the fire escape, I plan my next course of action.

Worried about future attempts on my capture, I swear to myself that I am going to take on a much more active role of remaining low key. I have walked around the Vincent Moyston projects a few more times to see if I could run into the homeless dude, but he is nowhere to be found. I don't know anyone in these projects, so hanging around does not make too much sense. The car I am driving is not too far from here, so at least I can recline the driver's seat and get me some sleep…at least a few hours of rest anyway. Luckily for me, the walk to my car is not too eventful and it is still where I left it…untouched and out of view from the public eye.

Racing thoughts again fill my mind as I cannot believe Skip would give me up to the police. I thought I knew him, but I guess $20,000 worth of reward money would make a man do anything these days. Now I may have to exact revenge on him AND Janelle!

Unable to sleep, I figure I would take a ride over by Janelle's apartment building. I desperately miss my children and all I need is one good look at them. I just need to know they are growing up and doing all right. After everything Mrs. Pearl told me about Janelle's condition, I just need to make sure they are being taken care of.

I am parked about a half block from her apartment, and there is no detection of any other car on the block with any passengers waiting inside. I cannot

David L.

get any closer because now that Five-O knows I am still in the area, they may be watching her even closer.

"If only I had someone that could get close to Janelle and earn her trust. That would make my job that much easier," I say to myself.

An hour goes by and there is still no sign of Janelle and no apparent activity coming from any of the floors in her building. I do not know exactly what floor she is on, so my trip down here looks like it is going to be a wasted one. Just as I turn on my headlights to leave her block, a light from what may be her apartment is turned on.

"Now that is more like it!"

A silhouette can be seen from the window shade and judging from the frame, it definitely belongs to a woman. Driving a little closer to the apartment building, my assumption is correct.

"That is Janelle! It's not even six o'clock in the morning yet. She hasn't gotten up this early the whole time we were married. I wonder what she is getting up so early for."

After thirty minutes of patiently waiting in the car for her to step outside, all of my questions are finally answered.

"So that's why she had to get up so early. She must have left her old job, and her new job requires her to bring Destiny and DeShaun to her mother's house so she can make it to work on time."

Destiny exits her mother's apartment first, followed by Janelle holding DeShaun's hand. He is walking so much better now! I cannot believe how big he has gotten! And Destiny…how beautiful she looks in her little school outfit! She looks just like the

Over Your Dead Body

pictures I have of my mother when she was her age. Janelle is turned around and talking to someone, but I can't yet tell who it is. A rather large dude walks out behind Janelle and kisses her on the cheek. He is heading up the block in the opposite direction. From the looks of things, he must be her new boyfriend because he obviously spent the night. He is probably a regular, too, because he did not leave her apartment with any bags of clothes.

A cab pulls up right in front of me, blocking my view as Janelle, the children, and her "boyfriend" gets into the cab. I know I cannot do anything right now in front of my children, but mark my words...Janelle is living on borrowed time!

I have to be extra careful on how fast I drive so I do not bring any unwanted attention my way. It would be real stupid of me to get into a high-speed chase with the cops for something as reckless as driving over the speed limit. I finally have a plan to make some extra money, and if I do it right, I can bring in anywhere from five hundred to seven hundred dollars a week. I just have to make sure I keep my sunglasses on at all times and my hat down. My first opportunity to put a few dollars in my pocket is walking towards me.

"Where do you want to go?" I say to my passenger getting into the back seat with about five bags.

"Midland Avenue. Over by Cross County Mall."

Yep, that is right. I am a cab driver for the moment. It might not be much, but it puts food in my

David L.

mouth and clothes on my back. With enough tips, I can score a few more nights at the motel for a good night's rest. The lady in my back seat is sexy as hell and knows it. She keeps giving me these seductive looks, as if to say if I wasn't driving this car, I could get out with her when we reach her destination. Or maybe it's just wishful thinking. What classy, good-looking woman in her right mind would want someone that drives a cab as her man?

"So you're going over to the mall to get some more shopping done, huh?"

"No, not exactly. I'm meeting a friend over there in about ten minutes. We're going out to get something to eat."

"Well, I hope he is taking you to a place that deserves your presence."

"And what makes you think the person is a he?"

"Just a feeling, that's all. Am I wrong?"

She doesn't say anything else for the entire ride, just a smile to symbolize that she heard what I said, but does not feel like answering the question. She probably feels like I felt when I was up in the diner and the gay waiter was hitting on me. Damn, I have to step my game up if I'm going to survive at this cabbie job!

* * *

A little over two weeks of driving a cab and I still hardly have much money to show for it. Yeah, I got some money to rest my head at night and eat a decent meal every now and then, but for the most part, I am as broke as when I first started. To make matters

Over Your Dead Body

worse, I cannot even file a claim on my house in Mount Vernon because I am a known fugitive. I have enough sense to know that as soon as I pick up the phone to file a claim and provide an address to where I am staying, I am as good as captured.

During my free time from driving people around all day, I have had numerous opportunities to stake out in front of Janelle's apartment, and I think I almost have her entire routine down to perfection. She leaves for work at the same time every morning with the children, and it looks as if the guy that has been coming out of her apartment is now living there. She gets home from work somewhere between five and six o'clock every night with DeShaun and Destiny, and her bedroom lights usually go out somewhere around eleven o'clock at night.

Today is just another day of the week, but somehow; I have a feeling things are going to start looking up for me. Hell, it is not like things could get any worse!

"Can you take me over to the Woodlawn station? I got to catch my train," a woman says to me, literally jumping into the back seat.

Without waiting for me to respond, she immediately puts on her seatbelt. I guess she figures she would rather be safe than sorry. I cannot say that I blame her. I have seen my share of car accidents in my life, and there is no way I am going to lose my life over some idiot behind the wheel that cannot drive. Just as I pull off from being double-parked in front of a Kennedy Fried Chicken spot around the corner from Webster Avenue, another woman reaches for the back car door and lets herself in on the other side.

David L.

"Make sure she doesn't eat too much candy!" she says to the woman that walked with her over to my car.

"Bye bye, Mommy. I love you!"

"I love you, too, baby. Behave yourself!"

I am not even mad that she is holding up my other passenger. It is good to see the bond between a parent and their child. From the looks of things, the other woman is probably babysitting or something, while my newly acquired passenger is on her way to work.

"I need to get to Lincoln Avenue in Mount Vernon immediately. You can drop me off about a block away from the Nasty Kitty. You know where that is, right?"

I don't say a word. I just nod my head to acknowledge her request. The woman's face is covered by a dark pair of shades similar to mine, but that voice is unmistakable. My first priority is to drop off my first passenger to the Woodlawn station, and then find out who my mystery passenger is. All signs reveal that it is Mocha, but I have to know for sure.

I was right about today being my lucky day. The first lady that gets out hands me fifteen dollars in cash and tells me to keep the change. Damn! Her fare was only five dollars! Now it is just me and what looks to be Mocha in my ride.

"You said Mount Vernon, right?"

"Yeah, is that going to be a problem?"

I am busy checking out Mocha from my rearview mirror, and with the exception of the sunglasses, she looks exactly the same. Manicured fingernails, hair done up just like I saw her last, and an

Over Your Dead Body

amazing smile that a man would kill to wake up to every morning!

"Nah, not at all. I used to live out in Mount Vernon back in the day. You on your way to work or something?"

"Yeah, something like that. I'm in the entertainment business."

"That sounds real exciting. I used to be in the music business myself."

I don't expect her to recognize my voice, and by the look of her facial expression, she has no idea who it is she is talking to. I, on the other hand, definitely know who I have in my back seat! My instincts tell me to drive to a side road somewhere and smash her skull in, but I promised myself that I would put more thought into my actions for now on. Besides, I may be able to use her to my advantage. This is going to be my first time headed back to Mount Vernon in about a month, and the thought of seeing someone I know has got me feeling kind of queasy.

The streets of Mount Vernon remain the same, not that I would expect them to change in such little time. To think I was actually contemplating running for mayor one day. Now, the only thing I am running from is the cops! I am kind of known around these parts, so I have to really keep a low profile while I am cruising down my old stomping grounds. I pass the church I was baptized in, the liquor store I purchased my first forty-ounce of beer at, and around the corner from the liquor store, where I received my first kiss from Brenda Patterson, the first true love of my life.

David L.

"You can let me off right here, sir. I want to stop at the store."

"That won't be necessary. I'll bring you right in front of the Nasty Kitty. That's where you go to make your money – and steal men's wallets, right?"

"What the hell are you talking about? Unlock the door, fool!"

For a brief second, I wonder what the hell she is talking about. Then I realize the childproof locks are activated from her side of the vehicle and she cannot get out. Before she starts screaming and making a scene, I figure now is the perfect time to reveal my true identity.

"I look familiar to you now?"

I immediately take off my dark shades for her to get a better look at my face. At first, she just shakes her head in bewilderment. Moments later, she has a real frightened look on her face.

"Please don't hurt me! I remember you now! You're wanted for murder! I saw you on T.V. and that's where I remembered you from when I was at your apartment!"

"Correction…my homeboy's apartment, not mine. I just used his place because I didn't want no skank-ass stripper at my house!"

Mocha again tries to fumble with the door handle, albeit unsuccessfully. I can sense she is getting frantic, and I don't want her to blow up my spot in any way possible. I have to think fast.

"I'm not going to hurt you. Hell, I want you to help me actually. And as for the money you got me for…let's just say that is for you to keep. That is, as

Over Your Dead Body

long as you're willing to help me get closer to my ex-wife who lives not too far from here in the Bronx?"

"I'll help you with whatever you want. Just don't go doing anything crazy!"

"First things first...let me see a picture of your daughter. And before you tell me you don't have one, I saw a picture of her on your house keys when you placed them in your purse earlier."

"What the hell you need a picture of my daughter for? Don't bring my family into this! She got nothing to do with any of this!"

"And that's the way we are going to keep it! But I need insurance, just in case you try to sell me out to the cops...or my ex-wife!"

Doing as instructed, Mocha hands me a picture of her daughter and assures me that she will not say a word to anyone about our conversation today. The funny thing is – I kind of believe her! She may be a conniving thief, but something about her aura gives me the impression she is not a liar. I finally let Mocha out of the car, and for extra measure, walk her to the front of the Nasty Kitty. Whoever said that I wasn't a gentleman!

Right before we part ways, Mocha hands me one of her business cards so that I can reach her in order to devise my plan for her to get in good with Janelle. As I drive off to find my next passenger, I realize I never did get my cab fare from her. Damn, that is the second time she got over on me!

David L.

CHAPTER TEN

December 24, 2004 ~ Christmas Eve
    December has been a much better month for me. I guess you can say I got my Christmas present early. Mocha and I have been hitting it off – Bonnie and Clyde style! Driving around during the holiday season has put some extra money in my pocket since I changed my route and started picking up the white people over by the east side of Manhattan. I think Mocha has started taking a liking to me, too, because whenever her daughter's father comes by to pick up his child, she lets me spend the night on her couch. It may not be as good as being up in the bed with her, but I will take what little I got for now. After all, I am not exactly in the best predicament to be choosy.
    "So when do you want me to make my move on your ex-wife?"
    "Soon...real soon. I'm shootin' for New Year's Eve."
    "What is so special about New Year's Eve?"
    "Don't worry 'bout all that. It's kind of symbolic for me. You wouldn't understand even if I explained it to you."
    Hanging with Mocha has definitely got its fringe benefits. Not only have I been getting up into the Nasty Kitty free of charge on their busiest nights, but I have a renewed sense of purpose. Almost as if I

Over Your Dead Body

have something to look forward to. I may have to live my life undercover and keep myself isolated from the usual partygoers, but at least I am able to get out and have some fun every now and then. Even the cops appear to have slowed down on their search. I haven't heard anything on the news recently, and from what I hear on the streets, the authorities suspect I have already left town. I have never been in a relationship with a stripper, but the perks must be out of this world. Not only does Mocha walk around all day in the skimpiest of clothing inside the apartment, but also, she has to be one of the most beautiful women in the world I have ever laid my eyes on.

"Hey Mocha, you think if I wasn't in all the trouble I was in, I would have a chance with you?"

"First of all, when I'm not at the Nasty Kitty, call me by my birth name...Maritza!"

Maybe she is getting tired of me hanging around or maybe she is just resentful that I threatened to use her daughter against her when I first saw her a couple of weeks ago. Either way, I have to get out of here and handle my business. My gun is in my bookbag, and I just recently got a tune-up for the car. I cannot begin to slack off just because Mocha, I mean Maritza, is letting me stay at her place while her daughter is gone for the holiday weekend.

"Hey Maritza, I'm going to go make some money while the stores are still open. I'll be back in a few hours."

Everyone is running around like a chicken with its head cut off trying to pick up last minute gifts for their respective family members. Every store is packed

David L.

to capacity and you cannot find a toy store in the vicinity in which the line is not at least a thirty-minute wait. Although I have some spending money in my pocket, it just is not enough. Maritza has not asked me to come up with any money yet for staying at her place, but I know that time will inevitably arrive. No woman in the world is going to respect or, for that matter, put up with a man who cannot at least put a little something down on the household bills. I have to devise a plan to get me some extra money in my pockets...quickly.

    Maritza has been hinting subtly to me for the past couple of weeks that she would like a Fendi bag for Christmas. She makes good money at the Nasty Kitty, but I think coming from her perspective, she would appreciate the bag more if it came from someone of the male persuasion. Her daughter's father is a worthless bum with no job, so she knows he probably is not going to spend what little money he has on a gift for her. Just as I am getting ready to fall asleep in my car waiting for a passenger, a rich-looking, middle-aged white woman hops her Macy's bag carrying ass into my back seat.

    "Can you take me over to the east side? I'll make it worth your while!" she says to me in a very condescending way.

    "Yeah, sure, ma'am. I can do that for you."

    My opportunity for some extra cash could not have come at a better time. This woman has to have some serious cash on her. I am checking her out in my rearview mirror, and she is iced out from the necklace around her neck to the ankle bracelet that can be seen from under her stockings. My only decision to make is

Over Your Dead Body

do I rob her for her bags and money now, or at least have some class and make sure she gets home before I stick her up? I turn around immediately and wave my .22 revolver in her face. Decision made!

"Toss all of your bags up to the front and give me all of your jewelry! Oh yeah, I'm going to need that pocketbook, too!"

"Oh my GOD! I've never been robbed before! Please don't shoot me! I will give you whatever you want! I swear!"

"I know you will! Now make it quick! I have places to go and stores to shop in!"

"You're not going to take me somewhere and have your way with me, are you? I'm a married woman! Please don't violate my body! You can have everything I have! Just don't hurt me…PLEASE!"

"Bitch, ain't nobody thinkin' 'bout touching your wrinkled up ass! I got a woman waiting at the apartment that looks a hundred times better than you!"

I think I must have struck a nerve, because her face turns bright red. I don't know if it is from embarrassment that I don't want her sexually, or if she is just plain frightened for her life.

"Oh yeah, and speaking of married, I'm going to need that wedding ring, too!"

"Not my wedding ring! This is my most prized possession! You can have everything else, just not my wedding ring!"

I wave my gun closer to her face to emphasize my request. The close range of my pistol makes her re-evaluate her last statement.

257

David L.

"Bitch, I don't give a GODDAMN fuck 'bout your ring or your punk-ass husband! Marriage ain't even sacred anyway! Now take it off!"
Doing as she is told, the woman reluctantly takes off her wedding band and places it onto the front seat. She is mumbling something under her breath, but wisely shuts her mouth after I ask her to repeat herself.
"Now get out of the car slowly, and if you start screaming like you are crazy, I'm going to shoot your ass and drive off like nothing happened!"
The lady was telling the truth about never being robbed before. It is not even dark yet and there is a crowd of people walking around all over the place. Even a little commotion and I would have a hard time driving off in all of this traffic. She does as she is told and walks off in frenzy, looking for the nearest pay phone because I also have her cell phone that was left in her pocketbook. Because of me, that poor white woman will probably never step foot in another cab ever again.

I somehow managed to purchase the last Fendi bag over at a little spot in the heart of Greenwich Village. For extra measure, I am also sitting on about seven hundred dollars in cash, courtesy of the lady I robbed. A few more well-timed holdups and I will be able to give up the cab business altogether! Just as I again begin to drift off to sleep from what I promise is going to be my last cab ride for the evening, a yuppie couple climb into my ride. The couple is decked out in matching suit jackets, tennis sneakers, and wool caps. Between the two of them, I can hardly tell which one is the male or the female.

Over Your Dead Body

"Where am I taking you two on this lovely, winter night?" I ask sarcastically.

The weather is hardly warm, and I could care less where they are traveling to...as long as they have my cab fare.

"Take us to Harlem. Over by 125th Street and Lenox Avenue," the feminine-looking guy says.

He is seated directly behind me. Right next to him, his apparent girlfriend's head is resting on his shoulder. Neither of them are carrying any bags, so they must have a little spot of their own out in Harlem. Figures! Even the yuppies are taking over Harlem now!

"Harlem, huh? I was thinking about moving out there a while back, but the prices are too steep out there," I state matter-of-factly.

I am trying my best to ease their worries because I notice they both keep looking over at me, probably wondering why I am wearing dark shades during the last week of December.

"Here you are. 125th and Lenox! You two have a lovely evening, but before you get out of my cab, I'm going to have to relieve you of your money!"

Pulling out my gun for the second straight time this evening, I make my comment become a reality as they both look at each other simultaneously in stunned belief. No more words are exchanged as they both enter their respective pockets and pull out whatever money they have.

"Eighty-six dollars? Eighty-six GODDAMN dollars! Between the two of you, that is all you can come up with?" I say in obvious fury.

259

David L.

I was hoping this would be my last stickup for the evening, but it is obvious I am going to have to get up in some more pockets before the night is over.

"Get the hell out of my ride! You both make me sick to my damn stomach! As a matter of fact, take off your sneakers! You can both walk home barefoot for all I care!"

It is amazing what people do for you when you are waving a gun in their faces! They both proceed to take their sneakers off, and as they do, I throw them in the middle of the street and watch in amusement as their footwear gets run over by an oncoming truck. Just as I drive off with their money, I cannot help but add some more verbal jabs to their already deflated egos.

"That will be a lesson to the two of you! Stay the hell out of Harlem and go back to whatever yuppie hole you came out of!"

Now that I think about it, I got a drop-dead gorgeous woman waiting for me back at her apartment. The hell with driving around town sticking people up! Sometimes, one has to know when it is time to call it a night.

* * *

Christmas morning and I am the first one up from off the couch. Maritza is still asleep and I am tempted to inch my way over to her bedroom and lay my body down next to hers. It's not like we haven't shared the same bed before, and some sex from Maritza to bring in the upcoming new year would make the perfect gift for the holidays.

Over Your Dead Body

"What do you think you are doing?" she responds, lifting her head up from off the pillow.

"Nothing. I was just coming in to see if you were ready to open up your gifts."

I open mine first, and as I sit in front of the Christmas tree playing with the knot on the ribbon that Maritza made to seal the box, I envision what my own children are doing across town. Destiny is probably sitting on her future step-daddy's lap, hugging him tightly and thanking him for all the gifts he purchased. DeShaun is probably running around the house, bouncing off the walls in excitement over his presents.

"Is this the first Christmas without you being with your children and wife?" Maritza questions.

"Yeah, but that is alright. I could be in worse places right now, so I definitely have a lot to be thankful for."

Hearing myself say those words actually helps me to feel a little better. Right now, I could be somewhere in general population upstate somewhere, lying on a cot and listening to my cellmate tell me about all of his exaggerated war stories.

Finally getting the knot out of the ribbon, my eyes widen at what my first present is: a gold-plated money clip with the money that Maritza stole from me attached! She smiles seductively when I take it out in plain view. Her eyes widen as well as she opens up her box and views the contents of what is inside: a brand new Fendi bag. She reaches over to me and plants a warm, passionate kiss on my cheek. Normally, that would not do anything for me, but a girl as sensual and sexy as Maritza can do wonders for a man's third leg! It is at that exact moment I realize not all women are

261

David L.

bad. I am beginning to see her for what she truly is: the "Bonnie" to my "Clyde!"

"So when do you want me to make my move?" Maritza questions.

We are both sitting outside of Janelle's apartment at four o'clock in the afternoon, and from the looks of things, she is at home by herself. The time to strike is getting close, but I have not yet worked out the kinks in my well-oiled master plan to end her life. She probably does not have to work today because it is Christmas.

A couple of days ago, Maritza called up the landlord to see if she can stop by and check out any of the vacant apartments that are advertised for rent. After several minutes of pleading and promising to pay the first two months of security up front with the landlord over the phone, he has reluctantly promised to show the apartment to Maritza today.

"Now remember...after you meet with the landlord, tell him that you can move in anytime after January. Janelle lives up on the next floor, so after he leaves, you can take care of business."

"I got it. I'll take care of everything."

A smile develops on my face as Maritza exits the vehicle and enters the apartment building to meet with the landlord. My plan is perfect! Not only will she win Janelle's trust because they live in the same building, but now I can track Janelle's every move without being too close to her.

I am sitting in the car for at least forty-five minutes without functioning heat before Maritza returns. She has a blank stare on her face so I am unable to figure out whether or not she was able to handle her business as promised.

"So what happened?" I ask as soon as she steps foot into the car.

"What do you mean what happened? I handled my business like I told you I would!"

"So what did you say?"

"After I finished speaking to the landlord, I asked him if I could walk around to make myself familiar with the apartment building. I still can't believe that fat old man was flirting with me! After that, I found her name on the lobby mailbox, went up to her floor, and knocked."

"And then what?"

"Well, you were right…she was home by herself! I introduced myself and asked if I could borrow a can opener because I had just moved in right below her and that my moving truck wasn't delivering on Christmas."

"Brilliant! So are you in good with her?"

"C'mon now. You can't expect miracles. A few more days of hanging around and I should be in her good graces by sometime next week."

Maritza knows all about my plans to leave New York, and although she isn't showing it, I can tell she is not happy with the idea of me leaving. We have only been hanging out with each other for a little while now, but it seems like we have known each other for years.

It is Christmas night and she has been extra nice to me: fluffing my pillows on the couch, fixing me extra helpings of Christmas dinner, and dropping hints about settling down and "me finding a woman that will

David L.

always have my back." Maybe she knows that after everything I have gone through, I am still passionate about my children. Or maybe she finds that to be a turn-on because of her own daughter and the broken relationship she has had on and off with her daughter's father.

"So do you want me to take a drive out tomorrow morning and check to see if your ex-wife is going to work?"

She has to repeat herself a few more times because I am taking a steaming-hot shower and am listening to the Hot 97 countdown on her portable shower radio.

"No, I don't think so. Besides, you don't want to be all up in her face every day. Let a day or two go by and then knock on her door again...ask to borrow some milk or something."

"Whatever you say. I'm going to bed now."

It just occurred to me that Maritza has not been working as much as before. Usually, she tries to work at the Nasty Kitty every chance she gets.

"Is everything alright? You haven't been to work in a minute. You didn't get fired, did you?"

"No, I didn't get fired. I just don't know if that is me anymore. I have some money saved up, and I think in a few days I'm going to make up my mind if that is what I want to do for the next few years of my life."

"Damn, you're serious, ain't you?"

"I am as serious as a heart attack! Maybe I'll find a man who lives life dangerously and wants himself a woman that can hold him down whenever necessary. Or maybe I will really take that apartment over by your ex-wife and start from scratch."

I swear she is talking about me when she uses words like "new man" and "new life", but I cannot be completely sure. I am not about to embarrass myself and ask if it is me that she is talking about. Just as I enter the living room to get ready for another day of plotting and schemin', who else but Maritza is standing behind me, motioning for me to come back into the bedroom. At least now I know what man and what life she is talking about!

"You know, Preston, with the right woman by your side, you could still leave New York, but you would have someone to travel with and keep you out of trouble."

"And who would that person be?"

"Don't play with me, boy! You know exactly who I'm talking about! I've held you down since I walked back into your life over a month ago. Who is the one that put you up and gave you a place to rest your nappy head? Who is the one helping you to get back at your ex-wife?"

"True, true, you did do all of that, but what about your daughter?"

"She is with her father. Besides, it's about time he step up and be there for her for a while!"

My first night sleeping in the same room with Maritza and it is a special experience. No longer Mocha, she is now officially Maritza – for good! If sex with her is even half of what it turned out to be the first time we laid down next to each other, I am in for one hell of a night. And this time, I don't have to worry

David L.

about waking up the next morning with my money missing!

* * *

I am totally exhausted from the night before, but a straight week of incredible sex with Maritza would do that to just about anyone. I know I have said it before, but I honestly feel today is going to go down in history. It is New Year's Eve and my time to get at Janelle has arrived! First things first, I still have some unfinished business to take care of with Skip. I still cannot believe he sold me out like he did. Maritza wants desperately to come for the ride, and only after several minutes of pleading and promises of what she is going to do to me sexually later, do I allow her to accompany me.

"When I pull up to his apartment, keep the engine running. If I'm not out in exactly five minutes, drive off without me," I command.

Maritza is only too eager to do my bidding, and I find that to be the ultimate turn-on. Unlike me, she was raised by a single parent and taught at an early age that if you want something out of life, you need to grab it by the horns and take it.

"Maybe I should come inside with you. He's probably not going to expect anything if you have a witness with you."

"Nah, it's not even like that. Him and I go way back. He's not even going to suspect anything. If anything, I'll be greeted by a hug or something."

My arrival to Skip's apartment has me feeling like I have never felt before in my entire life. I am feeling a combination of guilt, fear, and hesitancy. Feelings anyone would have if they knew they were here to take the life of their best friend!

Opening up the contents of my bookbag, I place my .22 pistol inside of my jacket pocket. I suddenly realize I still have the remaining contents of Banger's LSD envelope in the front pouch of my bookbag.

"Don't take that stuff, Preston! Too much of it and you don't know what could happen to you! Give it here!"

Ignoring Maritza's pleas, I grab a handful of powder and place it under my tongue. Like before, the high is immediate.

"Now I can take care of business! The way I feel right now, I can do just about anything!"

I allow a few more minutes to pass before I get out of the car to approach Skip. I can tell he is home because his car is parked outside of his studio apartment.

"Alright, baby. Remember what I said. Five minutes and you drive off…got it?"

"Yeah, I got it. Just be careful, okay?"

I am halfway out of the car before I realize I called her "baby." Damn, maybe everyone does get a second chance at love!

"Skip, open up, man! It's me…Preston!"

Five more knocks on his apartment door and Skip finally moves his curtains to see what all the noise is about. I can definitely tell he is startled by my arrival because of the strange look on his face – a look not of fear, but of uncertainty of what my motives are for arriving at his apartment.

David L.

"What up, man! I thought you would've left town by now."

"Yeah, I was going to, but I had some things I had to take care of first."

"Yeah, like what? Don't tell me you still trying to take care of Janelle. I told you to leave that shit alone! Get outta here while you still can!"

"It's not just Janelle that I hung around for. You know why I'm here, muthafucka!"

"What the fuck are you talkin' about? You look high as hell, man!"

I can tell Skip is becoming antsy because he keeps inching his way over to his kitchen…probably to ready himself to grab for a knife or something. He never did care for guns, so I know I don't have to worry about him pulling one out.

"Where you think you goin', Skip? You're not keepin' anything from me, are you?"

"Man, you are buggin! Just relax for a minute and think rationally. I've been your boy from day one! DAY ONE! That don't count for nothing no more?"

"I had the past month to think about this, Skip! You were the only one to know that I was at the barbershop! Not even twenty-four hours later and the cops are there to bust me! You must think I'm a fuckin' moron or something!"

Like a predator getting ready to pounce on its prey, I can see the fear in Skip's eyes. Not because he does not think he can take me in a physical altercation – because he probably could, but because he knows what I am capable of doing!

"You sold me out, Skip! You broke the rules! Now you have to pay!"

Over Your Dead Body

Just as I say that, Skip readies himself for a sneak attack and puts his hands up in anticipation of a fight. In my high state of functioning, I can barely pinpoint Skip's movements, and he catches me with a flurry of blows to my face. I don't feel anything, but I know that tomorrow will be a different story. Finally catching him off guard, I connect with a dirty shot below his belt that causes him to collapse to his knees. Looking up at me, Skip shows no sign of emotion. Instead, he is making direct eye contact with me. His eyes are slowly piercing into the very fabric of my soul.

"You ready to visit GOD, you fuckin' traitor?" I question, pulling out my .22 pistol.

Skip doesn't say anything. He just watches to see if I actually pull the trigger. I am immediately reminded of Joe Banger and his quest to go out "keeping it real." The only difference between Skip and Joe Banger is my loyalty and almost life-long friendship with Skip, a difference that may possibly spare Skip's life today. With a mighty swing of the butt of my gun, Skip goes crashing to the floor. He has a huge gash with blood coming out of the side of his head, but he will live – for now anyway! He is only knocked out, and eventually, he will awaken and may even alert the authorities to my presence. I am still standing ominously over him, not yet certain if I should send him to the hereafter or not, when my cell phone goes off.

"Preston, let's get outta here! We only got about fifteen minutes before Janelle leaves her apartment to pick up the kids!"

269

David L.

I am racing towards Janelle's house. Within the last week, Maritza has gotten closer to her than expected, and she remembers Janelle telling her that she had to pick up Destiny and DeShaun over at her mother's house by eight o'clock tonight because Mama Pearl was going to some kind of church service with a few of her girlfriends. As for Janelle's new boyfriend, Maritza has not seen him or heard anything about him since she first stopped by Janelle's apartment for a can opener back on Christmas day.

"Hand me that knife under your seat," I say to Maritza, pulling over to the side of Janelle's car.

I immediately get out and jab my pocketknife into Janelle's front tire. By now, she is running late to get to her mother's house and is not going to have time to call anyone to help her repair it. Maritza and I have planned this day several times now, and we each take our respective positions.

"It's about twenty minutes to eight. She should be coming out any minute," I inform Maritza.

I immediately walk across the street and wait for my cue. The night is bitterly cold and not too many people are hanging around to witness what is getting ready to transpire.

"Here she comes," Maritza whispers.

"Hey girl, what are you doin' out here in this cold weather? You not locked out or anything, are you?" Janelle asks.

"Nah, nothing like that. I'm waiting for my boyfriend to pick me up. I swear he is late for everything!"

"DAMN!"

"What's the matter, girl?"

Over Your Dead Body

"I got a flat tire! That's what! And I am late picking up my kids!"

"You got a cell phone on you? Maybe you can call somebody."

"I left my cell phone in the apartment. The battery was dead, so I left it inside to charge until I get back."

"Well, maybe I can call someone for you. Go around to the passenger side and get in out of the cold. My boyfriend should be here any minute."

As scripted, I race across to the other side of the car and drop Janelle to the ground with one swift blow to her temple. Groggy, but still conscious, I follow through with another well-aimed haymaker to Janelle's jaw and quickly place her limp body into the trunk of the car. What follows next is as equally scripted, and Maritza and I applaud each other for not deviating from the previously discussed arrangement.

"Now what are you going to do with her?"

"With Janelle? I'm going to take a ride. Don't worry. As soon as I take care of the body, I'll call you and we can meet up somewhere."

"Well, before you take off, you might want to hold on to this!"

"What is this? Why are you giving me a scratched-off game ticket?"

"Just check it out when you get a free minute. Trust me – if you didn't know how I felt about you before, you will now."

The last thing I need to worry about now is one of Maritza's riddles about the two of us and the direction we are going in. She has been instructed to return to her apartment and wait for me to call her in

271

David L.

exactly one hour. The ride to Connecticut should only take me about forty-five minutes because the streets and highways are deserted from everyone being indoors drinking laced egg nog and spending time with their loved ones. I can hear the motion of Janelle's body shifting back and forth in the trunk with each passing pothole and bump I go over. I heard her say she left her cell phone in the house, so she has no way of contacting anyone.

"How is it back there, sweetheart! Do you have enough room?" I question sarcastically.

Getting to my destination in record time, I immediately pull over near the water that is completely frozen to get a better view of my surroundings. Just as I thought, there is not another person in sight. I immediately turn the engine off and walk around to the trunk to open it for Janelle. My gun is drawn just in case she comes out swinging.

"WHAT THE FUCK, PRESTON! ARE YOU CRAZY? TRUST ME – YOU ARE NOT GOING TO GET AWAY WITH THIS!"

"I already did, bitch! There is no one here to save you, so make as much noise as you want!"

As I recommended, Janelle begins to scream at the top of her lungs.

"Go 'head, bitch! Scream some more! Here, I'll help you!"

I begin to start screaming along with Janelle, which only makes her scream even louder. Her screams turn into tears as she begins to come to the realization that there is no one out here to save her from me tonight.

Over Your Dead Body

"Just tell me one thing, Janelle...WHY? What was your connection to Joe Banger? And why did you have him come after me and take the kids away?"

"Because I knew once you found out, you would seek revenge! Your deceased co-worker introduced me to him the same day you were fired! He wasn't supposed to do what he did to you...just return the kids to me! He thought he was doing me a favor by having his boys beat up on you because he had a liking for me!"

"Did you sleep with him?"

"NO! Hell no! I'm not that easy! You of all people should know that about me!"

"Why didn't you tell me that you were sick? That you had – what is it called...bi-polar something?"

"Because I didn't want that used against me when it was time for the judge to decide who should have custody! Besides, is that something you would want the world to know about?"

"I still don't get it! Why did Dani sell me out the way she did? All I ever did was look out for her! Not only did she have me fired, but she did everything in her power to turn you against me!"

"I can't answer that one, Preston! All I know is that Dani approached me first! She stepped to us one day after Shontell and I were entering the nail salon. Shontell noticed her right away from the time she saw the two of you up in some bar all hugged up on one another."

"Her and I were never hugged up! That was a gross exaggeration on Shontell's part!"

"It doesn't matter now, Preston! She is dead and so is my best friend! And what about Skip? Are

273

David L.

you gonna kill him, too? He's been nothing but a friend to you this whole time! He would always tell Shontell and me how much of a good father you were and for me to take you back! Did you do something to him, too?"

"Nah, Skip may wake up with a headache, but he is alive."

"Preston, did it ever occur to you that a lot happened so quickly? I know I didn't believe you when you said you weren't fooling around, but I was scared! As for that "Dani girl" – did it ever occur to you that she did what she did because she wanted your top spot at the record company? Didn't you used to say the only other person as hungry and determined as you was "some chick at the job" that wanted to be "THE MAN?"

"That was a nice explanation and all, Janelle, but too much has happened. Too many senseless killings and too many hurt feelings. THERE IS NO TURNING BACK!"

"Don't do this to me, Preston! PLEASE! What about Destiny and DeShaun? Do you want them to grow up without a mother?"

"The two of them will be alright without you in their lives! Look at me. I didn't have my mother in my life growing up, and I turned out alright, wouldn't you say?"

I have a devious look on my face which causes Janelle to grow even more concerned for her life. She knows of my previous murder spree, and with no one out here to hear her screams, she knows she is living on borrowed time.

Over Your Dead Body

"Preston, wait…let's talk about this! We can make this work! I SWEAR!"

"You're real funny, Janelle. How are we gonna make this work? With me letting you leave here and me being locked up for the rest of my life? I suppose you will come visit me, right?"

"Preston, what about DeShaun and Destiny? Think about how you felt when you lost your mother to cancer all those years ago! You have a chance to give them what you never had in your life!"

The children are the last things on my mind as I grab Janelle's throat and begin to tighten my grip. She has a surprised look on her face as if to think I could never actually hurt the woman that conceived my children. How wrong she is! She is kicking and swinging wildly for her life; however, she does not stand a chance. Not only do I outweigh her by at least fifty pounds, her will to live is only overshadowed by my desire to end her life tonight. And as it has happened so many times in the past, the enraged look on my face is the last thing Janelle will ever see…again!

I continue to tighten my grip, and as I do, her limbs continue to weaken from lack of oxygen. She is fighting me with all she has, but my grip continues to drain her life force. Similar to her best friend Shontell, her face turns a variety of colors before she gives up in despair. Moments later, Janelle stops moving altogether. Then and only then, do I know it is truly over.

David L.

ACKNOWLEDGEMENTS

First and foremost, peace to the 7th letter (the all-knowing and almighty GOD) for once again allowing me to see my vision put to print; Allene Henry for the ongoing inspiration and words of encouragement; Baldwin and Violet Henry for the emotional and financial support whenever I needed it the most; my children who keep me grounded and focused for the bigger and better things in life.

Special thanks to the following people: Deneen G. Robinson for the superb job on my front cover and bringing my vision to life; Carla Dean for a superb editing job; my number one draft pick models – Darryl and Candy; Cathy from Mount Vernon Library; Kim from Westchester Botanica Bookstore in White Plains; "G-Man" Mitchell for taking care of all my shipping/handling needs; all my street team promoters.

Special shout out to friends, family members, casual acquaintances, and everyone else that purchased my first book, *It's Like Butter, Baby*, out of either loyalty to me or just curiosity to see if it was any good. Either way, good lookin' out! If you didn't support me the first time around, don't bother looking for your name here!

David L.

An even extra special shout out to all the doubters and haters who thought I was going to be a "one-hit wonder" and never come back with another classic. You continue to fuel my determination. **SAY WHAT YOU WANT, JUST SPELL MY NAME RIGHT!**

If you feel you were forgotten in any way, please feel free to add your name here: _____.

WORDS FROM THE AUTHOR

I would greatly appreciate any feedback (positive or negative) regarding what you have just read. Please email me with your interpretation of any of the following: character narration, plot synopsis, overall theme/content, exterior/interior book design, and any other aspect of this book. My primary objective was (and still is) to give readers my viewpoint on the potentially delicate fabric of an institution, such as marriage…and the unfortunate consequences and repercussions of what can happen if one allows things to go too far.

A word of caution – don't let this happen to you!

David L.

DISCUSSION QUESTIONS

What was unique about the setting of the book and how did it enhance or take away from the story?

What specific themes did the author emphasize throughout the novel? What do you think he or she is trying to get across to the reader?

Do the characters seem real and believable? Can you relate to their predicaments? To what extent do they remind you of yourself or someone you know?

How do characters change or evolve throughout the course of the story? What events trigger such changes?

Did certain parts of the book make you uncomfortable? If so, why did you feel that way? Did this lead to a new understanding or awareness of some aspect of your life you might not have thought about before?

What is this book's message?

What did you think of the ending?

In a movie version, who would play what parts?

What did you think of the plot development? How credible did the author make it?

David L.

What moral/ethical choices did the characters make? What did you think of those choices? How would you have chosen?

How do you think the main character's point of view is similar or different from the author's point of view or background?

Why do you think the author wrote this book? What is the overall message?

Over Your Dead Body

ORDER FORM

Mail to: TOTAL PACKAGE PUBLICATIONS, LLC
C/O DAVID L.
P.O. BOX 3237
MOUNT VERNON, NY 10553
www.totalpackagepublications.com

Name:_____

Address:_____

_____

City/State/Zip:_____

_____

Email:_____

TITLE	PRICE	QUANTITY
Over Your Dead Body	$15.00	

**SHIPPING/HANDLING: ADD $3.95 per Book
(Shipped via U.S. Media Mail)**

TOTAL: $_____

FORMS OF ACCEPTED PAYMENTS:
Personal checks (additional delays may incur pending bank clearance), institutional checks & money orders are preferred methods of payment. Total Package Publications, LLC does NOT recommend sending cash through the postal system. All mail-in orders take 5-7 business days to be delivered.

Contact Publisher directly about discounting availability for special bulk orders (ten book minimum).

David L.

Over Your Dead Body

David L.

Over Your Dead Body

David L.